The Mask
of Ra

Also by P. C. Doherty

The Mask *of* Ra

P. C. Doherty

ST. MARTIN'S PRESS

NEW YORK

THE MASK OF RA. Copyright © 1998 by P. C. Doherty. All rights reserved. Printed in the United States of America. No part of this book may be used or reproduced in any manner whatsoever without written permission except in the case of brief quotations embodied in critical articles or reviews. For information, address St. Martin's Press, 175 Fifth Avenue, New York, N.Y. 10010.

Library of Congress Cataloging-in-Publication Data

Doherty, P. C.
   The mask of Ra / Paul Doherty. – 1st U.S. ed.
    p. cm.
   ISBN 0-312-20560-0
   1. Egypt—History—To 332 B.C.—Fiction.   I. Title.
PR6054.O37M35   1999
823'.914—dc21
                                         99-19151
                                            CIP

First published in Great Britain by Headline Book Publishing, a division of Hodder Headline PLC

First U.S. Edition: May 1999

10 9 8 7 6 5 4 3 2 1

In memory of a good little scholar,
Charlotte Anne Spencer of Chingford,
(1/23/86 – 10/16/97) who also loved writing.

HISTORICAL NOTE

The first dynasty of Ancient Egypt was established about 3100 BC. Between that date and the rise of the New Kingdom (1550 BC) Egypt went through a number of radical transformations which witnessed the building of the pyramids, the creation of cities along the Nile, the union of Upper and Lower Egypt and the development of their religion around Ra, the Sun God, and the cult of Osiris and Isis. Egypt had to resist foreign invasion, particularly the Hyksos, Asiatic raiders, who cruelly devastated the kingdom. By 1479 BC, when this novel begins, Egypt, pacified and united under Pharaoh Tuthmosis II, was on the verge of a new and glorious ascendancy. The Pharaohs had moved their capital to Thebes; burial in the pyramids was replaced by the development of the Necropolis on the west bank of the Nile as well as the exploitation of the Valley of the Kings as a royal mausoleum.

I have, to clarify matters, used Greek names for cities, etc., e.g. Thebes and Memphis, rather than their archaic Egyptian names. The place name, Sakkara, has been used to describe the entire pyramid complex around Memphis and Giza. I have also employed the shorter version for the Queen-Pharaoh: i.e. Hatusu rather than Hatshepsut. Tuthmosis II died in 1479 BC and, after a period of confusion, Hatusu held power for the next twenty-two years. During this period Egypt became an imperial power and the richest state in the world.

Egyptian religion was also being developed, principally the cult of Osiris, killed by his brother Seth, but resurrected by his loving wife Isis who gave birth to their son Horus. These rites must be placed against the background of Egyptian worship of the sun god and their desire to create a unity in their religious practices. The Egyptians had a deep sense of awe for all living things: animals and plants, streams and rivers were all regarded as holy while Pharaoh, their ruler, was worshipped as the incarnation of the divine will.

By 1479 BC the Egyptian civilisation expressed its richness in religion, ritual, architecture, dress, education and the pursuit of the good life. Soldiers, priests and scribes dominated this civilisation and their sophistication is expressed in the terms they used to describe both themselves and their culture. For example, Pharaoh was the 'Golden Hawk'; the treasury was the 'House of Silver'; a time of war was the 'season of the hyena'; a royal palace was the 'House of a Million Years'. Despite its breath-taking, dazzling civilisation, however, Egyptian politics, both at home and abroad, could be violent and bloody. The royal throne was always the centre of intrigue, jealousy and bitter rivalry. It was on to this political platform, in 1479 BC, that the young Hatusu emerged.

Finally, I would like to pay tribute to the London Library in St James's Square. This is a veritable treasure house of knowledge; surely one of the world's finest and friendliest libraries! I am deeply indebted to its marvellous range of books, both ancient and modern, as well as this library's highly skilled, very supportive staff.

Paul Doherty

EGYPT *c. 1479 B.C.*

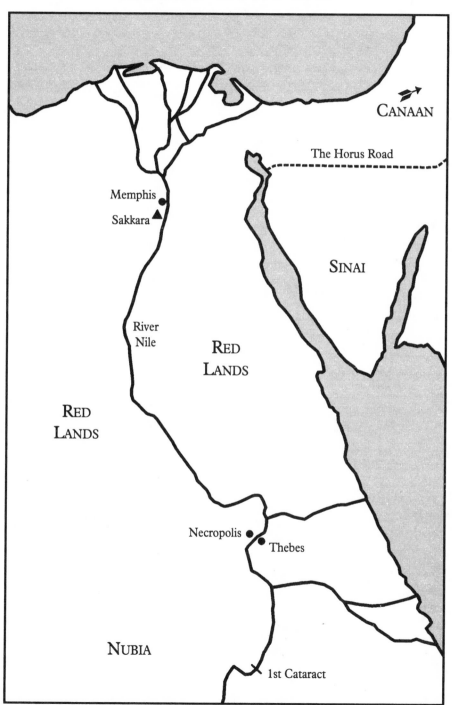

CANAAN

The Horus Road

Memphis

Sakkara

SINAI

River
Nile

RED
LANDS

RED
LANDS

Necropolis

Thebes

NUBIA

1st Cataract

Duat: the Egyptian underworld where Apep, the great snake, lurked.

PROLOGUE

In the month of Athor, the season of the water plants, the thirteenth year of Pharaoh Tuthmosis II, beloved of Ra, Hatusu, Tuthmosis' only wife and half-sister, held a great banquet in her palace at Thebes. The feasting and revelry continued long into the night. Hatusu had sat, waiting for the moment when the wine left her guests either asleep or watching, glazed-eyed, the naked dancing girls. These moved sinuously, the hollow beads around their waists, ankles and wrists creating their own languorous, attractive tempo. The dancers whirled and turned, their black wigs stiff and soaked in perfume, faces daubed in white paint, their alluring sloe eyes ringed with kohl.

Hatusu left the banquet chamber and slipped along the marble-paved corridor; the walls on either side, decorated in red, blue and green, glowed in the light from translucent alabaster lamps. The triumphant scenes depicted there sprang to life and brought back memories of her father's reign. Nubians, Libyans, the Mitanni and the raiders from the sea writhed in lifelike representation; they knelt on the ground, necks bowed, hands tied above their heads, awaiting execution at the hands of the victorious Pharaoh armed with club and mace.

Hatusu hurried on. She passed sentries standing at corners or the foot of stairs, men of the royal bodyguard in their white kilts and gold-encrusted belts, their bronze wrist-guards and torques gleaming in the torchlight. They stood like statues, spear in one hand, white and red shield in the other.

Every so often Hatusu would pause and listen to the sounds of revelry. These grew fainter as she went deeper into the bowels of the palace, towards her private chapel dedicated to the dog-headed Seth, god of the underworld. She opened the chapel door and went in. She took off her

1

gold-lined sandals, took a pinch of natron salt to cleanse her mouth and inhaled the sacred fumes from a thurible, hanging on a hook, to purify her nose and mouth before she prayed. The torches had been extinguished but lights from the alabaster vases glowed in the precious mosaic round the walls, which displayed silver melons, edged with gold, grown from the seed of Seth when he had chased a goddess and ejaculated his semen into the soil. Hatusu knelt on the cushion before the sacred cupboard which bore Seth's statue; around it pots of ivory, glass and porcelain, their handles shaped in the form of the ibis and ibex, exuded sweet-smelling incense.

Hatusu was small and lithe, delicate in her diaphanous white gown. On her head she wore a thick, black, curly wig with three plaits twirling down her neck. On her forehead rested a gold and silver headdress embroidered with red streaks; golden asps, studded with precious gems, hung from her ears; silver and gold bracelets clasped her wrists and ankles; a heavy, bejewelled necklace hung round her soft neck. Hatusu was dressed for celebration but, secretly, she was terrified. She gazed at the cupboard, closed and locked by the priests, and, lifting her arms, hands extended, she bowed her head and prayed. Seth, the god of darkness, must rescue her from these present troubles! Within days, her half-brother and husband, Tuthmosis II, would return to Thebes, victorious in his struggle against the sea-raiders along the great Nile Delta. And what would happen then? Hatusu had read the message very carefully. She was to come here in the dead of night and be instructed more clearly on what might take place. She had taken counsel of no one; the secret was too terrible to share. Nevertheless, here she was, the Pharaoh Queen, the wearer of the vulture crown, slinking like a rat through the corridors of her own palace. Hatusu trembled with rage. How would anyone be so arrogant as to summon Hatusu, beloved of the Pharaoh, into her own chapel? She stared at the black granite statues of the gods, Horus and Osiris, which stood on either side of the sacred cupboard.

All had been going so well! Tuthmosis had his concubines. True, by one he'd even had a son whom he'd recognised as his heir, but Hatusu was his Queen. She was skilled in the art of lovemaking and had drawn Tuthmosis into her net like a spider would a fly. So intense his pleasure, the Pharaoh claimed he had travelled to the far horizon and was already in the company of the gods! Hatusu had prayed that she would conceive. Costly offerings were made to Hathor the goddess of love and to Isis the mother goddess of Horus and Osiris. Perhaps it might still happen! During his campaigns Tuthmosis had sent her letters sealed under his own personal cartouche or mark. He had couched his greetings in cloying, loving terms before proceeding to tell her about his victories on land and sea. He had also informed her how he had learned a great secret during his visit to the Great Pyramid at Sakkara and, on his return, would shatter the dreams of Egypt with his revelations.

Hatusu sat back on her heels. What were these secrets? Tuthmosis had fits which the priests termed 'divine trances', when the gods, particularly Amun-Ra, spoke to him. Had this happened in the cold darkness of the pyramids? Hatusu joined her hands together and bowed her head; her eyes caught the scroll peeping out just beneath the Naos, the sacred cupboard. All dignity forgotten, Hatusu scrambled forward and picked it up. She unrolled the papyrus and, in the light of one of the lamps, studied the green and red hieroglyphics neatly etched there. It could have been written by any one of the thousands of scribes who lived in Thebes. However, the message, and the threat it contained, made the Pharaoh's Queen tremble like a child and the sweat break out on her perfumed body.

Night was falling over red-bricked Thebes. The moon rose glinting on the Nile which wound like a dark-green serpent from south of the Land of the Bow to the Great Sea. The watchers on the barge waited, staring up at the night sky. An order was given and the barge, low and squat, left the quayside, slipping through the water towards the Necropolis, the City of the Dead, which lay to the west of Thebes. One figure stood in the stern, another in the prow, each armed with a pole. They moved the barge silently and swiftly out of the cluster of reeds. Their companions in the centre, dressed in black, their faces hidden like those of the desert people, sat grouped around the witch. She had sightless eyes; straggling, grey hair framed her crazed face. This terror of the night cradled an earthenware pot, capped, sealed and filled with human blood, as tenderly as a mother would her child. The assassins, the Amemets, named after the 'devourers', the ghastly creatures which gobbled up the souls of the evil dead, listened to the sounds of the night and studied the river. They heard the bullfrogs croak, the whir of insects, but, here in the shallows, they were wary of the crocodiles which would often slide out against the unwary, before rearing up in a clash of jaws to take a man's head.

The barge moved like a leaf on a pond, and soon it was on the edge of the bird-thronged papyrus thickets on the western bank. Above them loomed the craggy outlines of the City of the Dead: the mud-bricked houses, the chapels, embalming rooms, workshops and mortuaries of the craftsmen who prepared the dead for their journey into eternity. Deeper into the papyrus the barge moved, aiming for the desolate spot where they could disembark. At last, its prow sank into the soft, dark mud. The leading Amemet, gripping his dagger, stepped on to the wet packed earth. He heard a sound and crouched, peering along the path, where he glimpsed other shapes and figures leaving the Necropolis, slinking down among the rushes to some waiting boat.

'We are not the only ones.' His whisper was tinged with humour.

The dark shapes disappeared.

'Tomb-robbers!' he muttered and snapped his fingers.

His companions, grasping the witch's arms, joined him on the river bank. They slipped through the bushes, moving as quietly and as swiftly as hunting panthers, around the City of the Dead up a steep, dusty trackway to the brow of a hill. Below them lay the Valley of the Kings, the chosen resting place of Pharaohs and their families. The leader paused; the moon was full but, now and again, clouds blotted out its light. He glimpsed the torchlight of sentries and, on the evening breeze, heard the occasional shouted order, but these did not trouble him. Pharaoh was absent, the guards were slack and why not? There was enough plunder for the robbers among the tombs and mausoleums of the fat merchants of Thebes. Only a fool would lift his hand against the royal sepulchres. The Amemet leader had laid his plans well. The tomb of Tuthmosis II was still being prepared. It contained no treasures, so why would any thief or robber meddle with it? Moreover, the tomb stood by itself, on the royal road into the Valley. The guards were only bowmen and, by now, probably drunk on the cheap beer and wine they had smuggled across from the marketplace.

The leader of the assassins led his companions on, taking advantage of the rise and dip in the land. The old witch protested.

'My limbs ache! My feet are sore!' she whined.

The Amemet leader came back. He pushed his face close to hers.

'You are being paid well, Mother. We'll soon be there. Do what you have to then it's back across the river: slivers of roast goose, the sweetest of wines and enough wealth to buy you the tenderest lover in Thebes!'

His men sniggered. The witch protested in a tongue they didn't understand, a harsh, cold sound which froze their blood and pricked their memories with stories of the power of this witch. Did she not raise the spectres and call on the evil one to send the angel of death to hover like a great hawk above her victims? The leader sensed their change of mood.

'Come on!' he urged.

The group continued. They reached the foot of the low sloping hill and gazed up at the porticoed entrance of the unfinished tomb of Tuthmosis. The leader chose two of his companions. All three crawled upwards on their bellies like snakes. They reached the top and paused. Three guards in all, lounging against the pillars, bronze helmets off, weapons laid in a pile. The men were talking, the beer jugs scattered around their feet. The assassin leader gestured back. The witch was left while the rest scrambled forward to the top of the hill. A sack was opened, horn bows and arrows distributed. Three of the assassins knelt up. One of the guards, sharper than the rest, heard the sound and, plucking a torch from the wall, ran forward. He was the first to die as the barbed, feathered arrow took him deep in the throat. His two companions jumped up and, in doing so, made themselves clear targets against the torchlight. Again the whir of arrows. Both guards died, legs kicking, coughing on their blood. The assassins raced forward. They paused at the entrance to the tomb. Men of no morals, who believed in none of the stories or the preaching of the priests, they were still fearful. After all, this was supposed to be a sacred place where Tuthmosis the Pharaoh, when his time had come, would rest in glory, his Ka be transformed as he travelled to join the gods over the edge of the far horizon.

'Go on!' their leader urged.

He thrust his way through, padding along the gloomy passageways, then turned a corner and almost crashed into the sleepy-eyed young officer. The assassin pulled his dagger and thrust it into the man's unprotected stomach; the officer fell. The assassin took a club from beneath his cloak and smashed the man's head, dashing his brains to the ground. He continued on but found no other guards so he returned to the entrance.

'Bring up the witch!'

A short while later the woman of the night, armed with her small brush and her pot of human paint, daubed the entrance with the magical words cursing the Pharaoh both now and in death. The assassin leader watched, intrigued by the signs she made, her deft movements. He marvelled that a woman with no sight could draw so expertly, summoning up the curses, the powers of the evil one.

Waiting for her to finish, he wondered at the truth behind what was happening. He and his group were often hired for this task or that, but to curse a Pharaoh's tomb? To malign his name? Perhaps even to block his journey into the west? What would cause this? What had happened to allow such hate and malice to spill out? The Amemet leader had no knowledge of the person who had hired him and the witch. The message had come in the usual way and he had replied as custom dictated, accepting the time, the place and the task to be carried out.

He went back to inspect the corpses in the porchway, and by the time he had returned, the witch was finished. She was crouched beneath the strange markings and, hands uplifted, was praying in a foreign tongue. The Amemet leader recalled the rumours among his men, how the witch was not Egyptian but came from the coastline of Phoenicia with her powers and amulets. Her prayer ended. She staggered to her feet.

'We are finished,' she whispered.

'Truly, Mother, we are!'

The Amemet leader stepped behind her and, seizing her by the hair, yanked her head back and cut her throat.

Ma'at: the Egyptian goddess of truth, depicted as a young woman with an ostrich plume in her hair.

CHAPTER 1

Tuthmosis, beloved of Amun-Ra, the Incarnation of Horus, Ruler of the Black Land, King of Upper and Lower Egypt, leaned back in his gold-encrusted throne and stared through the open-sided cabin of his royal barge. He closed his eyes and smiled. He was coming home! They would turn the bend of the river and see Thebes in all its glory. On its eastern banks, the walls, columns and pylons of the city and, on the west, the honeycombed hills of the Necropolis. Tuthmosis spread his gold-sandalled feet as the barge pitched slightly in its change of course; its prow, formed in the shape of a screaming falcon's head, still cut through the river even as the great, broad-brimmed sail billowed slightly but then subsided. Shouts rang out. The sail was lowered and the barge regained speed as the barebacked rowers bent over their oars, heaving under the orders of the steersmen standing in the stern, managing the great rudders. The leading helmsman began a chant, a muted hymn of praise to their Pharaoh:

> 'He has shattered his enemies, he is lord of the skies.
> He has swooped on his foe, great is his name!
> Health and length of years will only add to his glory!
> He is the golden hawk! He is the king of kings!
> The beloved of the gods!'

The chant was taken up by the soldiers and marines who manned the prow watching for any treacherous sand bank. The oars rose and dipped, the sun dazzling the splash of water.

Tuthmosis, his face impassive under his blue war crown, stared at his soldiers clustered in the stern: Rahimere his Vizier, Sethos, the

9

royal prosecutor, Omendap his general and Bayletos his chief scribe had gone ahead to Thebes. Now, only Meneloto, the captain of the guard, remained. He sat with his officers, discussing their impending return to Thebes, the tasks and onerous duties awaiting them. Above the Pharaoh great, feathery, perfumed ostrich plumes created a scented breeze, waves of coolness as the day was proving hot and the sunlight was strong, despite the silver-embroidered canopy above him. Tuthmosis listened to his glories being expounded but what did they really matter? What did he care? He had visited the Great Pyramid at Sakkara. He had read the secrets on the sacred stela. He had stumbled upon mysteries, yet had he? Had not the word of God simply spoken to him? Had not these mysteries been revealed because he was holy and chosen?

'Gold are your limbs, lapis lazuli your hands!' The royal poet squatting to the Pharaoh's left echoed the praises of the sailors and oarsmen. 'Beautiful of face are you, oh Pharaoh! Mighty of arm! Just and noble in peace! Terrible in war!'

The recipient of these ornate phrases blinked. What did such flattery matter? Or the treasure hoards contained in the holds of the imperial war galleys which went before and after him as he journeyed along the Nile? Such wealth was passing.

Pharaoh moved his head. He gazed through the heat haze at the banks on either side where he glimpsed the coloured standards of his squadrons of war chariots which escorted and protected him on his sacred journey to Thebes. Such power was illusory! The weapons of war, his crack regiments, named after the gods, the Horus, the Apis, the Ibis and the Anubis, these were nothing more than dust under heaven. Tuthmosis knew the secret of secrets. He had written as much to his beloved, noble wife Hatusu and, on his return, he would tell her what he had discovered. She would believe him as would his friend the high priest, Sethos, the keeper of the Pharaoh's secrets, the 'eyes and ears of the King'. Tuthmosis sighed and put down his insignia, the flail and the crook. He touched the glowing pectoral around his neck and moved his legs, the gold-encrusted kilt clinking at his every movement.

'I am thirsty!'

His cup-bearer, on the far side of the silk cabin wall, raised the ivory chalice. He sipped the sweetened wine and passed it to his master.

Tuthmosis drank and handed it back. At that moment the watcher in the prow shouted out. Tuthmosis looked to his right. They were rounding the bend, Thebes was near! The barge swung closer to the bank. In the reeds alongside the river, a hippopotamus, frightened by the noise, crashed about sending huge flocks of geese flying up above the thick papyrus marshes. The chariot squadrons on the east bank had grown indistinct. They were preparing to lead off, to join the other troops massed outside the city. Tuthmosis sighed in pleasure. He was home! Hatusu his Queen would be waiting. He would rest in Thebes!

On the portico of the temple of Amun-Ra, a group of young women stood in the shadows of the soaring pillars. Heavy black wigs of curled, shining hair hung down to their shoulders; pleated robes of fine, semi-transparent linen covered their bodies from neck to their silver-sandalled feet. Fingers and toenails were dyed deeply in henna. Their beringed hands clutched the sistra, loops of metal attached to a wooden handle. When shaken together, these instruments gave an eerie jangling sound. Now they hung silent. Soon they would ring out, welcoming the return of their god. They were the priestesses of Amun-Ra, gathered round Hatusu, the Pharaoh's Queen. She, also, was dressed in exquisite white linen. On her headdress of gold rested the vulture crown of the Queens of Egypt and in her hands the sceptre and rod of office. Hatusu heard the priestesses giggle but she did not move her kohl-rimmed eyes. She stood impassive as a statue, staring down at the sun-bright courtyard below where ranks of shaven, white-robed priests awaited the return of her husband. A breeze soothed the heat and stirred the banners and pennants which hung from the massive stone pylons around her. Looking over the heads of the priests, Hatusu glimpsed the people massed in the second courtyard, officials and administrators ranged in order of rank and marshalled by officers armed with their wands of office. Beyond this courtyard stretched the Sacred Way down into the city where its citizens lined the Avenue of Sphinxes, massed between the huge black granite statues of crouching beasts with human heads and the bodies of lions.

Faintly on the breeze Hatusu heard the sound of music, the bray of trumpets. She caught the sparkle of armour and glimpsed the lines of troops marching in from the Sacred Way. The Egyptian royal guard,

Negroes from the Sudan and the Shardana, foreign auxiliaries in their ornate horn helmets. Tuthmosis was coming home! Hatusu should be pleased but she was fearful. She had scrutinised that scroll most carefully and wondered if its mysterious writer would dare share such secrets with her half-brother and husband. Hatusu lifted her head. The massed choirs had begun their hymn of praise.

'He has stretched out his fist!
He has scattered his enemies with the power of his arm!
The earth, in all its length and breadth, is subject to him!
He tramples his enemies like grapes under his feet!
He is glorious in his majesty!'

The singing was drowned by a great roar of triumph. The Pharaoh had reached the Sacred Way. He would soon be in the temple. In the inner courtyards the great officials and masked ranks of priests ceased whispering and stood in nervous silence. Their Pharaoh was returning in triumph, Amun-Ra had glorified his majesty but there would also be a reckoning. The books would be opened, the accounts scrutinised, the judges and scribes summoned to the royal presence. In the whispered words of one of them, 'The royal cat was returning to its basket'.

Hatusu moved to the top of the steps, the priestesses fanning out behind her. All now looked towards the great bronze doors which sealed the inner courtyards of the temple. They heard the shouts, 'Life! Prosperity! Health!' A trumpet blast, harsh and braying, imposed silence. The voice of a herald rang out: 'How splendid is our lord who returns in victory!'

The great bronze doors opened, the cavalcade entered: the priests in white robes, officers of the royal bodyguard with their high-plumed headdresses, their golden torques and arm rings shimmering with light, their spear tips stretching up. Hatusu glimpsed members of her husband's council. The cortege stopped. Another blast of trumpets and the Pharaoh entered. Preceded by his standard bearers and banners, Tuthmosis was borne along in a gold and silver palanquin carried on the shoulders of twelve noblemen. The palanquin stopped and everyone prostrated themselves. Again the trumpet blast. Hatusu gracefully rose to her feet while the priestesses swirled past her down the steps, shaking their sistra and singing the hymn of welcome. The palanquin was lowered. Royal officials clustered around and Tuthmosis was helped down from his throne. The priests gathered round, shielding him as he rearranged his robes and prepared to climb the steps. Hatusu went down on both knees, hands joined before her. She watched her husband's shadow slowly climb the steps. She closed her eyes. If only she could feel the joy she should! If only she could tell her husband how the Ahket, the rising of the river Nile, had been the most fruitful for a long time! How the reports from the Nomachs, the provincial governors, had been nothing but good . . .

When she opened her eyes, the shadow was over her. Hatusu bowed her head but her husband's hand touched her under the chin and she stared up. Tuthmosis smiled; but his face, beneath the ceremonial paint, looked pale and haggard. The black kohl around his eyes only emphasised his weariness. The Queen was seized by a wild thought. Here was her husband, beloved of the gods, conqueror of his enemies, yet he looked as if he had crossed the river of death and found nothing but dust. Tuthmosis bent his head slightly, his eyes crinkled in pleasure. He quietly mouthed, 'I have missed you! I love you!', then opened his hand to reveal a golden lotus flower, studded with precious stones, on the end of a silver chain. He placed this round her neck and helped Hatusu to her feet. The Pharaoh of Egypt and his Queen turned, hands extended, to receive the acclamation and roars of the crowd.

The trumpets brayed, cymbals clashed, great gusts of incense billowed into the sky, sweetening the air and purifying all assembled. The Pharaoh would not speak: his mouth was too sacred, his words too precious. He had yet to commune with the gods. Another trumpet blast brayed. Members of the royal bodyguard hurried forward to create an avenue. Up this stumbled the Pharaoh's principal prisoners of war, dark-haired, copper-skinned captives stripped of all their finery and armour, hands bound above their heads. They were made to kneel at the foot of the steps. Hatusu closed her eyes. She knew what was about to happen. The Pharaoh made a cutting movement with his hands. The royal executioners stepped forward. The prisoners, gagged as well as bound, could make no protest as their throats were slashed. Their blood-soaked corpses were scattered in the open area before the gods of Egypt and the power of Pharaoh.

'It is over,' Tuthmosis whispered.

13

Hatusu opened her eyes. She dare not look down. The air had a different stench, of death and the iron tang of blood. She just hoped her husband would not tarry but walk on into the temple, to the great statue of Amun-Ra, and sprinkle incense. She sighed with relief as Tuthmosis turned and, with the roar of the crowd ringing in their ears, they walked into the coolness of the colonnade, along the marble floor, past the rows of painted columns. The great statue of Amun-Ra, seated in glory, loomed up before them. The Pharaoh paused, staring at the flickering flames in the great vase before the statue. A priest came forward, a golden bowl in his hand. Eyes down, he held the bowl and the silver spoon towards his Pharaoh. Tuthmosis paused. Hatusu looked expectantly at him. What was the matter? she thought. He had won great victories to the north and now, like their father, he must give thanks. Or did he know already? Had some whisperer been sent north to his camp? Tuthmosis sighed, stepped forward and sprinkled the incense. Hatusu, walking one pace behind him, waited for Tuthmosis to kneel on the scarlet, gold-tasselled cushions but he didn't. He just stood staring up at the black granite face of the god. He raised his hands, palms facing outwards as if intoning a prayer, but wearily dropped them, as if the effort was too much.

'My lord, your majesty!' Hatusu hissed. 'What is the matter?'

Tuthmosis was staring back down towards the courtyard. The cheering had stopped. It had been replaced by a low murmur of discontent, of angry protest. A priest came hurrying in. He prostrated himself.

'What is it?' Tuthmosis asked.

'An omen, your majesty. A dove flew over the courtyard.'

'And?'

'Its body was wounded, he spattered all below him with blood before falling dead from the skies!'

Tuthmosis swayed, his chin began to quiver, his jaw moved sideways, his hand went to his throat. His head went back, the great double red and white crown fell off. Hatusu screamed and caught him as he fell, trying to control the frightening convulsions as Tuthmosis writhed in her arms. She lowered him gently to the floor, his body rigid, eyes rolling back in his head. Flecks of spittle appeared on the corner of his carmine-painted lips.

'My beloved!' Hatusu whispered.

Tuthmosis went slack in her arms, then his head came up, his eyes opened.

'It's only a mask!' he gasped.

Hatusu leaned down to listen to his whispers before Tuthmosis, beloved of Ra, gave one last shudder and died.

During the month of Mechir, in the season of the planting, after the official mourning following the sudden death of Pharaoh Tuthmosis II, Amerotke, chief judge of Thebes, delivered sentence in the Hall of Two Truths at the temple of Ma'at, the lady of divine words, the divine teller of truth. Amerotke sat on a low cushioned chair made out of acacia wood. The cushion was of sacred fabric and embroidered with hieroglyphics extolling the wonders of the goddess Ma'at. On the walls around the hall were carvings of the forty-two daemons, strange creatures with the heads of snakes, hawks, vultures and rams. Each of these held a knife. Beneath them, their titles were given in brilliant red ochre: 'dyer of blood', 'eater of shadows', 'wry head', 'eye of flame', 'breaker of bones', 'breath of flame', 'leg of fire', 'white tooth'. These creatures dwelt in the halls of the gods, ready to devour souls who were weighed in the sacred scales of divine justice and found wanting. Before Amerotke stood the cedarwood tables bearing the laws of Egypt and the decrees of Pharaoh. Behind him loomed large, black granite statues of the god Osiris holding the scales of life or eternal death, and Horus, the ever-watchful.

The hall was colonnaded, the columns painted brilliant colours, and, through them on one side, Amerotke if he so wished could glimpse the gardens of Ma'at: fresh green lawns where the flocks of the goddess grazed near shady trees and gaily coloured birds whirled round fountains which splashed into ornamental pools. Amerotke, however, sat cross-legged, studying the papyrus parchments on the floor before him. The rest of the court waited in hushed silence. Down one side squatted the scribes dressed in white robes, their shaven heads bent over small desks. These bore their writing instruments: pallets of red and black ink, water pots, and a cluster of styli, hollow reeds sharpened at one end, brushes, pumice stones, jars of glue and little sharp knives for cutting the papyrus.

Prenhoe, the youngest scribe, looked expectantly across at the judge.

Amerotke was his kinsman and Prenhoe both admired and envied him. In his thirty-fifth year, Amerotke had risen to be chief judge in the Hall of Two Truths. A shrewd man, a courtier born and bred, Amerotke had won a reputation for justice and integrity. He looked younger than his years. His head was shaven, apart from one lock of gleaming black hair which, plaited with gold and red, hung down over his right ear. His body was sinewy and lithe as an athlete's and his white, red-bordered robe fitted him elegantly. Prenhoe, on the other hand, felt uncomfortable. He wanted to take his gown off, go out and bathe in the sacred pool, wash away the sweat. Thankfully, the case before them was reaching its climax. Amerotke had warned Prenhoe that this would be a dark day. Judgement of death would have to be pronounced, both here and elsewhere.

Amerotke moved on the cushions. The light caught the gold pectoral of Ma'at which hung on a gold chain round his neck. Amerotke fingered this and stared angrily at the prisoner kneeling bound before him. He looked to the right where a middle-aged man and woman stood together, arms round each other, the tears streaming down their faces. Further along stood the group of witnesses, huddled between two pillars. Amerotke breathed in. He looked to the top of the pillars as if to scrutinise the dark-red paste of the capitals carved in the shape of a lotus. All was ready. At the end of the hall, just inside the door of truth, the police waited, dressed in leather kilts and bronze helmets, armed with club and shield. Their commander, the chief of the temple police, stood with them – a stubby, thickset, balding man, a distant cousin of the chief judge.

'Is there anything else left to be said?' Amerotke raised his hand.

'There is nothing, my lord,' the chief scribe replied, bending low over his table. 'The case has been heard. The witnesses examined. The oaths sworn.'

'Is there any one of you,' Amerotke studied the line of scribes, 'who, in the presence of the lady Ma'at, can say anything as to why sentence of death should not be passed?'

The scribes remained tight-lipped. Some shook their heads, Prenhoe most vigorously. His kinsman caught his eye and smiled faintly. Amerotke placed his hands on the canopied boxes which stood on either side of him.

These, built out of sycamore and acacia, and veneered with strips of silver, contained small shrines to Ma'at. Prenhoe breathed in. Judgement was to be delivered.

'Bathret!' Amerotke leaned forward and stared directly at the prisoner. 'Lift your head!'

The prisoner did.

'I will now deliver my judgement. Here, in the presence of the gods of Egypt. May the lord Thoth and the lady Ma'at be my witnesses. You are a wicked, evil man! What you did was an abomination in the eyes of all. A terrible stench in the nostrils of the gods! You worked in the Necropolis, the City of the Dead. Your task was to prepare the corpses of those who died for burial, to assist in the rites of purification so the Ka of the dead might travel on into the divine halls of judgement. Great trust was placed in you. You abused that trust.' Amerotke pointed to the man and woman on his right, now weeping loudly. 'Their only daughter died of a fever. Her corpse was given to you. You abused it, using her poor body for your own pleasures. Members of your own guild caught you in the act of sex with the corpse of this young woman. A vile and blasphemous act! Only by handing you over to the Pharaoh's justice,' Amerotke stared down at the huddle of purifiers and embalmers, 'have they escaped the full judgement of the law!' Amerotke clapped his hands, the rings flashing in the light. 'Now this is my sentence. You are to be taken to the Red Lands south of the city. No one will accompany you except the guardians of this court. A grave will be dug. You will be lowered in and imprisoned. You are to be buried alive!' Amerotke clapped his hands again. 'Let the judgement be recorded and carried out immediately!'

The prisoner writhed and screamed, shouting obscenities at Amerotke even as the police seized him and thrust him out of the Hall of Two Truths. Amerotke waved forward the group of embalmers as well as the grieving parents. The men were frightened, pale-faced and wary-eyed in the presence of this judge and his terrible sentence. They fell to their knees, hands outstretched.

'Mercy, lord!' their shaven-headed leader begged, fleshy jowls quivering. 'Mercy and forgiveness!'

'He was one of yours,' Amerotke declared tonelessly. 'Compensation has to be paid.'

'It will be, lord. In gold and silver, finely cut,' he wheedled. 'With the assay mark clear and distinct.'

Amerotke gazed hard at him. The judge's large, dark eyes seemed to bore into the man's soul.

'There is more?' the leader of the embalmers wailed.

Amerotke just stared, his hand on the pectoral of Ma'at.

'What more can we do?' Another embalmer spoke up.

Amerotke's eyes shifted.

'There is a lot more,' the leader hastily intervened. He was sharp enough to see the look of distaste in the chief judge's eyes. 'We will build a tomb. With galleries, chapels, chambers and storerooms for this delightful family who have suffered so much.'

Amerotke looked at the victim's parents; he heard a grumble of dissent among the embalmers.

'Is there any objection?' Amerotke asked. 'Is there any of you who wishes to join your companion out in the Red Lands?'

'No, my lord,' one of the embalmers declared. He spoke honestly, his gaze never wavered. 'What he did was an abomination. I do not ask for compassion for ourselves, but to be imprisoned in the hot earth? To let the soil fill your mouth and eyes? To die a rotting death with only the howls of the hyenas as a hymn to your soul which is about to go out across the desert of death?'

'You ask for compassion?' Amerotke said.

'I do, my lord. I humble myself in the dust before you, that man was my cousin.'

Amerotke looked at the grieving parents. 'Nothing can avenge the insult to your daughter,' he declared. 'But you accept the compensation offered?'

The parents nodded, the husband putting his arm around his wife's shoulders.

'And you want compassion to be shown?'

'For the sake of our daughter's soul,' the man replied, 'my lord, death will be sufficient.'

'So it will be recorded,' Amerotke said, beckoning one of the couriers who stood behind the scribes. 'Tell those who take the prisoner how it is the judgement of the court that the miscreant be allowed poison before he is buried.'

The courier hastened out. Amerotke got to his feet, a sign that the session was finished.

'The judgement of the court is known,' he pronounced. 'These matters are finished.'

The embalmers backed out, bowing and scraping, grateful that they themselves had not been included in any punishment. Amerotke clasped the hands of the parents, saying they were to return and inform him immediately if the compensation was not paid in full. He then walked into the small antechamber which served as his private chapel to the lady Ma'at. He knelt before the sacred cupboard, sprinkled incense on the flickering flame and composed his thoughts. He was glad the matter was finished. He was satisfied that the embalmer had acted on his own and that justice had been done. The case had scandalised Thebes, and had also done great damage to the guild of embalmers, so his judgement might restore the balance. He closed his eyes and prayed for wisdom. Other matters awaited him. He heard footsteps behind him.

'My lord, we should go!'

Amerotke sighed and got to his feet. The chief of the temple police stood in the doorway, staff of office in one hand, the other on the hilt of his sword. Amerotke hid a smile. Whatever the weather, however hot and humid it became in the law courts, Asural always insisted on wearing his bronze corselet, leather kilt and plumed helmet now held under his arm. Nevertheless, although fussy and sometimes argumentative, the chief was a man who could not be bought or bribed.

Asural spoke. 'It will soon be time.' He grinned, the creases of fat almost hiding his eyes. 'I welcome your judgement. It will teach those rogues across the river a lesson they'll never forget.'

He stood aside to let the chief judge back into the hall but then gripped him by the elbow. Amerotke smiled. Asural loved to do that, to show everyone present how the chief judge and himself were not only colleagues but firm friends.

'I wish I could make headway on the other matter,' Asural grumbled.

'More robberies?' Amerotke asked.

The chief of police nodded. 'So clever, so cunning,' he declared. 'The tombs are always sealed. Yet, whenever they are opened to receive another dead body, something is always found missing. They say it's demons. For how can flesh and blood pass through thick, mud-brick walls?'

'And what do these demons take?' Amerotke asked.

'Necklaces, statuettes, rings, small boxes, bowls and vases.'

'But nothing large?'

'No.' The chief of police shook his head.

'So, we have demons who are only interested in small, precious items? Nothing large or cumbersome?'

The chief of police studied Amerotke's face for any hint of a smile.

'I don't think it's demons,' the judge observed. 'But some very cunning thief. Prenhoe!' he called across.

The scribe, clustered with his colleagues, chattering now the case was finished, sprang to his feet. He waddled across, trying to hide the ink stain on his gown.

'Yes, Amerotke . . . I mean, my lord.'

'Find out the name of that embalmer who spoke and asked for mercy, he may be of help. The answer to this grave robbing,' Amerotke continued, 'lies in precise knowledge of which tombs contain what. Someone in the Necropolis will have to help us.'

'Yes, my lord, and the other case . . . ?' Prenhoe looked expectant.

'All is ready,' Amerotke replied. 'I just wish I didn't have to sit in judgement.'

He stared across at a statue of Ma'at. Three months ago, he thought, Pharaoh Tuthmosis had returned from his victories only to die suddenly before the statue of Amun-Ra. His death had caused consternation both in the court and the city. People whispered and rumour ran thick and rife. His son, who bore the same name, was only a child of seven, while his widowed Queen, Hatusu, was unskilled in government. There was talk of a regency, of power being vested in the Grand Vizier Rahimere. Of course, the Pharaoh's sudden death had had to be investigated. A royal physician had been summoned. On the heels of the royal corpse he had found the bite of a viper. Everyone then recalled how weak and frail the Pharaoh had looked as he had been borne on his palanquin along the Sacred Way. The only time his sacred foot had ever touched the ground was when he left his throne on board the royal barge. A search had been made and a viper found, curled up beneath the royal dais. No foul play had been suspected but the finger of accusation had been pointed at Meneloto, the captain of the Pharaoh's guard. He had been accused of negligence, of failing in his duties, and been committed to trial before Amerotke in the Hall of Two Truths.

'What time is it now?' Amerotke asked, breaking from his reverie.

Prenhoe went and examined the water clock above a small ornamental pool in the far corner of the hall.

'The eleventh hour!' he called out. 'We have three hours!'

'There is the other matter,' the chief of police insisted.

The murmur among the scribes grew. As Amerotke looked round two grotesque figures came striding up the hall. They wore red and gold kilts, black studded belts criss-crossed their bare chests; the jackal mask of Anubis hid their faces, and in their hands they carried the silver-tipped wands of office. Amerotke touched the pectoral of Ma'at and prayed for courage. The two emissaries of the lord executioner bowed.

'All is prepared!' The voice behind the mask was deep and hollow.

'Sentence is to be carried out!' the other echoed.

'I know, I know,' Amerotke replied. 'And I must witness it.' He gestured with his hand. 'Then let it be done!'

Horus, son of Osiris and Isis, often depicted as a hawk or as a young man with a hawk's face.

CHAPTER 2

Preceded by the masked assistants of the lord executioner, Amerotke, accompanied by Asural and Prenhoe, left the precincts of the temple. They crossed a small courtyard and went down into the House of Darkness, that labyrinth of dungeons and cells beneath the temple of Ma'at. At the bottom of the steps Amerotke raised his hands and allowed the mute servant to pour sacred water over them. The chief judge then turned the pectoral of Ma'at to face inwards on his chest, as if to hide the eyes of the goddess from what was about to happen.

They went down a long passageway, the black, obsidian stone gleaming in the light of oil lamps placed in niches in the walls. Amerotke always felt a chill of fear whenever he entered this antechamber of death. Usually, the sentence of the courts decreed that, if a prisoner had been condemned to take poison, he or she would be provided with the luxury of being accompanied back to their own house or sometimes could even swallow it in the court itself. This case was quite different.

The condemned man had killed his wife and her lover and, before he left, tipped some oil lamps over, turning the opulent house of a senior officer in the Egyptian army into a blazing inferno which had consumed other surrounding buildings, including his own servants' quarters. Beside the murder victims, seven other charred corpses had been dragged from the ruins. Amerotke had to remember that. If a body was destroyed then the funeral rites could not be carried out. The Ka of the dead people would be denied entry into the afterlife: a case of blasphemous sacrilege as well as murder.

The two assistants stopped at either side of the door, built of reinforced Lebanese wood and strengthened with copper bands. The room inside was black as night, the only light flickering from solitary torches fixed into niches in the wall. Two soldiers, mercenaries from the Shardana corps, stood in the corner, their swords drawn. At the far end of the room, a man squatted on a low reed bed. His nearly naked body gleamed in the torchlight; his only dress was a pair of papyrus sandals and a soiled loin cloth. Beside the bed, dressed in a pleated black kilt edged with gold, stood the lord high executioner. His face, as customary, was covered by a jackal mask made out of boiled leather painted black, the ears, muzzle and mouth tipped with gold.

'I am here,' Amerotke announced.

'You are Amerotke.' The executioner's mask muffled his voice and made it sound more ominous. 'Chief judge in the Hall of Two Truths in the temple of Ma'at.' The executioner pointed his ceremonial two-headed axe. 'You are here to see sentence carried out. We only await the divine father, the high priest Sethos.'

Amerotke bowed. He knew the ritual. Sethos was a high priest of Amun, the royal prosecutor, the eyes and ears of Pharaoh. It was his duty to prosecute cases and ensure Pharaoh's justice was done. Amerotke had often crossed swords with him yet this only hid a deep bond of friendship between the two.

Sethos was a judge and a priest and like Amerotke, a child of the divine house. He had been raised and educated at the court of Tuthmosis I, that venerable but very cunning Pharaoh who had thrust Egypt's enemies beyond its borders before he took the eternal journey to the far horizons.

Amerotke tried not to look at the prisoner. If he did glimpse the compassion in Amerotke's eyes, the prisoner might, as others had, fall on his knees and beg for his life. Nevertheless, judgement was passed and the only person who could lift the sentence was Pharaoh, a mere child of seven. Indeed, according to the whispers there was no Pharaoh. The sudden death of Tuthmosis II had plunged the divine house into chaos and Thebes was full of whispers and gossip.

Amerotke heard footsteps in the passageway outside and turned slightly. Sethos arrived beside him. His head was shaven and oiled, and he was dressed in a pleated white linen robe, his palm-leafed sandals edged with gold. A necklace, brilliant in the light, its emeralds and purple amethysts catching fire, circled his neck. Draped over his shoulder and falling down his back hung the leopardskin coat of a chief priest. A silver earring dangled from the lobe of one of his ears, dancing and shimmering at his every movement.

The lord high executioner went through the usual ritual of greeting. Sethos bowed and replied.

'I have come to the House of Darkness!' Sethos' voice was rich and strong. 'To see that the sentence of Pharaoh, the beloved of Amun-Ra, the eye of Horus, King of the Two Lands, blessed by Osiris, is carried out.'

He turned and smiled sympathetically at Amerotke. The chief judge simply tightened his lips, a secret understanding, for neither of them relished such occasions.

'Let the sentence be carried out!' Sethos declared. 'In the presence of witnesses!'

The lord high executioner picked up his axe and tapped the condemned man on each shoulder.

'Do you have anything to say?'

'Yes.' The prisoner got to his feet.

Only now did Amerotke see the chains on his wrists and ankles. He shuffled forward, the masked executioners stepping with him while the mercenaries in the corner also stirred as if wary of what the prisoner might do. The condemned man's thin face broke into a lopsided smile.

'I mean no offence.' He bowed to Amerotke. 'My lord judge, the dispenser of justice.' The condemned man's eyes held Amerotke's. 'You have reviewed the evidence?'

'All that was submitted during your trial,' Amerotke replied. 'You pretended that you had joined your unit in the desert to the north of Thebes. You claimed that you had left your house to take advantage of the cool of the evening. Your own charioteer took an oath on this.' Amerotke rubbed the insignia of Ma'at on the rings of his hand. 'However, whoever broke into your house at the dead of night knew where to go, even though neighbours claimed the building was cloaked in darkness. Only you had that knowledge. Moreover, only someone who knew there was oil in the cellars and dried papyrus reeds in the storage rooms could have caused such a conflagration.'

'Your charioteer lied,' Sethos added. 'And he is now in a prison camp in the Red Lands. He will stay there for the rest of his life and reflect on his lies though, of course, he must be praised for his loyalty.'

'You are guilty,' Amerotke stated. 'Will you lie to the gods? Your soul is soon to be weighed in the scales against Ma'at's feather of truth.'

The prisoner sighed. 'I killed my wife yet I loved her,' he confessed, 'more than life itself. You know what it's like, sirs, to gaze into a woman's eyes, to hear her lips say she loves you while, in your heart of hearts, you know she is lying?'

'Sentence must be carried out!' the executioner growled.

The prisoner turned. 'Then hand me the cup.'

The executioner picked up the deep greenstone bowl, its edge rimmed with gold, and handed it to him.

'What am I to do?'

'Nothing,' the executioner replied softly, 'except drink!'

'And then?' A note of nervousness entered the condemned man's voice.

'As soon as you have drunk all the wine, walk about until you find your legs become weary, then lie down upon the bed.'

The condemned man took the bowl without any emotion, his eyes fixed on Amerotke. He raised it in silent toast and, throwing back his head, drank the poisoned wine.

Amerotke repressed a chill. It was always the same. Most condemned drank the potion as if in a trance, resigning themselves to the approaching darkness. He quietly prayed the executioner had done his job properly, that the wine was heavily tinged with poison so there'd be no clumsiness, no prolongation of the agony. Amerotke glanced down at the floor. It was said that men like this condemned officer, stripped of the cares of life, could see hidden truths. Had he glimpsed something in Amerotke's eyes? Did he know that the judge who had condemned him also had a soul tortured by suspicions that his beautiful wife had loved, perhaps still did, another man? And how, on this very day, Amerotke would sit in judgement on this former lover Meneloto, captain of the guard, accused of criminal negligence in the care of his beloved Pharaoh? Amerotke broke from his reverie as Sethos cleared his throat. The eyes and ears of Pharaoh spread his feet as if to ease his own tension. The prisoner was walking up and down, the chains clinking, like the rattle of some priest ushering him towards the darkness.

'I feel weary!' the man gasped. He lay down on the bed. 'I cannot feel my feet!'

The executioner took the man's sandals off and pressed his toes. He did the same to his legs and thighs.

'Cold and stiff,' the condemned man whispered. 'Death's water creeping up my body. Make sure my debts are paid.'

'It shall be done,' Amerotke replied.

One of the functions of the court was seizure of this man's wealth and property and the settlement of any claims before it was handed over to the House of Silver, Pharaoh's treasury.

On the bed the man convulsed, his body arched and lay still. The executioner pressed his hand against his neck.

'The life pulse has gone,' he declared.

Amerotke sighed.

'Pharaoh's justice has been done,' Sethos stated.

He bowed and, followed by Amerotke, left the death house and walked along the corridor to where Azural and Prenhoe were waiting. Only when they had climbed the steps and were back in the small forecourt did Sethos clasp Amerotke's wrist.

'And how is the lady Norfret?'

'She is well.'

'Black are her tresses, as black as the night,' Sethos quoted from a poem. 'Black as the wine grapes the clusters on her hair.'

'She's as beautiful as ever,' Amerotke laughed, hoping the keen eyes of his friend and colleague would not catch any glimpse of hurt.

'Both she and you were friends of Meneloto?'

'As always, my lord Sethos, you come abruptly to the point. Meneloto was once my house guest. Later today I sit in judgement on him.'

'You have read the evidence I have submitted?'

Sethos lifted his small hand-fan and cooled his face, his eyes scrutinising Amerotke carefully. Does he know? Amerotke wondered. Can the eyes and ears of Pharaoh even learn the secrets of the bedchamber? Or the troubles of the heart?

Sethos glanced over his shoulder at Asural and Prenhoe then gently ushered Amerotke closer to the small fountain so the sound of tinkling water might hide their conversation.

'They can be trusted!' Amerotke said.

'I am sure they can. You have no qualms about trying Meneloto? I mean, he should have taken greater care!'

'This afternoon,' Amerotke replied, 'we will sift the evidence. We shall hear the testimony of witnesses and then, my lord Sethos, I will decide.'

The chief prosecutor laughed. He joined his hands in obeisance and bowed mockingly.

'I stand reproved. My regards to the lady Norfret.'

Sethos walked away, softly humming a hymn to Amun. A cunning man, a veritable fox, Amerotke thought. Sethos had been the beloved friend of Pharaoh. A principal priest in the service of Amun-Ra, former chaplain to the Queen Mother. Did Sethos want vengeance against the man whose carelessness, he maintained, had caused his friend's death? Sethos, a member of the House of Secrets, had used all his skill in building a damning case against Meneloto. Amerotke glanced at the glittering water. But was it Sethos? Amerotke had heard rumours that the royal prosecutor was reluctant to prosecute but someone in the palace insisted.

'It went well, my lord?' Asural and Prenhoe drew closer.

'Death never goes well,' Amerotke replied. 'But sentence has been carried out and his soul is now in the antechamber of judgement. May the all-seeing eye of Horus present the full truth when his soul is weighed in the balance.'

'And now?' Asural asked.

Amerotke poked him playfully in the stomach.

'The court will not reassemble for another two hours. You, my captain of police, are hungry and thirsty.' He tapped Asural's head. 'You should visit the barber. I have never seen a man's hair grow so fast.'

'It's the heat,' Asural mumbled. 'But, yes, it will be nice to sit under a sycamore and share a jug of beer with a friend.'

The chief of police glanced sideways at Prenhoe.

'Aye and watch the girls go by,' Amerotke joked. 'Prenhoe, the evidence for today's trial? You'll make sure all is ready?'

His scribe agreed.

'Then leave me for a while.'

He watched his two companions walk away and stared up at the blue sky. Amerotke would have liked to join them. Perhaps walk through the bazaar in the marketplace, become lost in the ordinary, everyday things of life? But he felt dirty, soiled. He turned the pectoral round the proper way. Somewhere in the temple a conch horn blew, an invitation to worship. Amerotke glanced down at the goddess Ma'at, expertly carved on the pectoral, admiring the flowing tresses of her hair, sloe eyes, her graceful hands joined in supplication, the beautifully formed body shrouded in diaphanous robes. He sighed. Whenever he looked on the image of the goddess it always reminded him of his wife, yet this made him feel uncomfortable.

Amerotke stared at a drawing on the temple wall of a grotesque dwarf with a fierce face, a depiction of the god Bes, painted above the courtyard to drive away scorpions and snakes. Amerotke touched his lips in a sign of gratitude.

'I thank you,' he murmured, 'for reminding me!'

Amerotke had always wanted to do this, slip out and see how his household page, the dwarf Shufoy, whiled away his time when waiting for his master in front of the temple of Truth. Amerotke was pleased at something to do. He walked through deserted courtyards, crossed a small ornamental bridge over the canal, dug to bring Nile water into the temple precincts. He then followed the boundary wall, walking under the shade of acacia and sycamore trees, and went through a small side gate and along a beaten trackway which reeked of vegetables and cooking odours. This took him into the great open expanse which stretched before the huge soaring pylons of the temple of Ma'at. Crowds thronged about: visitors from as far south as the first cataract; Libyans; desert wanderers; peasants from the village; mercenaries from the garrisons; and the different citizens of Thebes. They all came either to shop in the nearby markets and bazaars or stream up through the great painted gateways of the temple, to perform sacrifice.

Amerotke hoped he would not be recognised as he walked to the edge of the great square. The palm and acacia trees provided welcome shade from the heat of the noonday sun; barbers, pedlars, sellers of fruit and sweet-breads paid heavy sums to the House of Silver in the temple of Ma'at for these choice locations.

'Where there's food,' Amerotke said to himself, 'Shufoy will be close by!'

Sure enough, just off the main concourse, taking full advantage of an acacia tree, sat Shufoy the dwarf, his parasol stuck in the ground beside him. Shufoy was busy. On a small carpet unrolled before him lay a mound of turquoise amulets.

'Approach and buy!' the dwarf called out in his deep, bell-like voice. 'You visitors to the holy place who throng to pay sacrifice to the goddess of truth! For a few debens of copper, an amulet of Ma'at, blessed by no less a person than my most holy master, the august lord Amerotke, chief judge in the Hall of Two Truths!'

Amerotke made sure he kept his distance. When Shufoy turned his face, Amerotke caught the terrible disfigurement where his nose had been sliced. Shufoy was one of the rhinoceri, those felons condemned in the courts to have their noses slit. They congregated in their own community, a small village to the south of Thebes. In Shufoy's case, there had been a dreadful miscarriage of justice. His appeal had been brought before Amerotke, who upheld it. Pharaoh's pardon had been issued but justice had also to be done. Shufoy, a former leather worker from Menonia, had entered Amerotke's household as a page, parasol-carrier and, whether Amerotke liked it or not, a dispenser of patronage.

Amerotke smiled and turned away. Now, at least, he knew the source of Shufoy's newfound wealth; it was harmless enough though he wondered from where Shufoy bought the amulets in the first place.

Amerotke joined the rest of the pilgrims streaming up towards the pylons. On each side of this great gateway were huge paintings of the goddess Ma'at.

'May your name be reverenced!' Amerotke whispered.

On the left of the gateway, Ma'at was dressed in a pleated linen gown, leaning back on her heels, arms crossed. From her head rose two great ostrich plumes, symbols of truth and integrity. On the right side of the gateway was a scene from the Book of the Dead: the gods Thoth and Horus were weighing the souls of the dead. In one scale lay the dead man's heart, in the other justice and truth. Ma'at looked on, ever waiting for which way the scales would go. If it was for truth, the dead would be admitted to the divine house, to the pleasures of the gods. If it was against truth, those grotesque creatures, the 'devourers', were waiting to tear the soul to pieces.

The temple of Ma'at was a favourite shrine for the citizens of Thebes and elsewhere. The air was thick with the noise of chatter, different tongues, clashing dialects. High-class ladies in their ornamental wigs and embroidered, pleated skirts, together with their husbands, merchants or persons of importance in white robes and gold-fastened sandals, rubbed shoulders with peasants, visitors from the Delta, artisans and workmen. The air held a mixture of scents. Myrrh and frankincense, unguents which the rich used to pamper their bodies, mingled with the cooking oils which permeated the scant clothing of the artisans or the rich earth which clung to the bodies of the farmers and peasants. Parasols, fans and perfume-drenched plumes were wafted to provide some coolness against the heat. Amerotke followed the pilgrims, keeping his head down. He did not wish to be recognised, particularly by the scribes from his own court.

They went along the Dromos, the pilgrim way which led up to the main doorway. On either side stood a row of sphinxes, lion bodies with human heads or those of bulls and rams. Amerotke went through the gateway where scribes clustered, their linen robes stretched across their laps to serve as makeshift desks. Ever ready with pen and scraps of papyrus, these scribblers touted for custom, to write down petitions which the poor could dictate and then hand over to the priests in the shrine.

The temple, however, was not only a place of worship. Leading off the main hall of columns were the minor courts where lesser judges and scribes heard the petty cases brought before them. Outside one of these a furious row had broken out between two neighbours. One claimed how, when she had gone swimming in the Nile, the other had pushed a wax crocodile among her clothing: a curse to summon up that truly dreadful beast of the reeds to kill her. Her opponent, a large, fat-bellied fishwife, was loudly declaiming that she didn't even know how to fashion a wax crocodile and might the goddess of truth be her witness! It would take a legion of crocodiles to kill a woman as evil as her neighbour! Next to them a scribe was taking down the plea of a copper-worker, the man declaiming his grievance in a loud voice. How he had paid good bronze rings for a physician to heal his child with the toothache. He had faithfully boiled a mouse and placed the bones in a leather bag near the child's cheek. However, her toothache hadn't gone and the child, rolling over on the bed, had gouged her cheek against the sharp bones in the sack.

Amerotke loved to listen to such business: the hearing of cases, the weighing of evidence, the handing down of decisions, no matter how petty it was. Ma'at was done, justice was implemented. He looked down at his hands. Perhaps it was the light bouncing off the brilliantly coloured pillars but his fingers seemed tinged with red. He recalled the execution he had witnessed earlier in the day. He hurried on through the hall of hypostyles, its columns covered in gold plate, their supports painted in brilliant colours and shaped in the form of the lotus flower. The beauty of the place always delighted Amerotke, with the star-studded ceiling and its floor, painted so it felt as if you were walking on water. He left by a side entrance and took the path leading down to the academy or House of Life where the temple physicians, astrologers, archivists and scholars studied. He crossed the open parkland with its different trees and shaded walks. At last he reached the divine pool which stretched before the Red Chapel, a unique small shrine dedicated to the goddess and reserved for principal judges and priestesses of the temple of Ma'at. Over the doorway, which fronted the pool, was a picture of Ra in his golden boat crossing the heavens.

Amerotke stood and waited for one of the minor priests to approach.

'My lord Amerotke?'

'I wish to purify myself.'

'Hast thou sinned?' came the formal reply.

'All men sin,' Amerotke answered according to the ritual. 'But I wish to immerse myself in the truth; to purify my mouth and cleanse my heart.'

The priest waved to the sacred pool, purified by the ibis birds which drank there.

'The goddess awaits!' the priest murmured.

Amerotke took off robes, rings and pectoral. He unfastened his loin cloth and handed everything to the priest who placed the garments on a basalt stone seat. Then Amerotke walked down the steps. The pool was lined with green tiles and the water, pouring in from a spring, danced and shimmered in the sunlight. He breathed in and closed his eyes. He caught cooking smells from the kitchens and cookshops, the faint tang of blood from the slaughter sheds behind the temple. He waited and breathed again. This time the air was pure. He put his hand out and the priest shook a few grains of natron salt from a gold cup. Amerotke wetted them with water, rubbed his palms together and washed his face. Only then did he lean forward, swimming slowly, allowing his full body to become submerged under the water. He opened his eyes, revelling in the coolness which washed away the impurities, sharpened his mind, restored that sense of harmony he would need in the difficult and dangerous case awaiting him. He turned, swimming as adroitly as a fish back to the steps. Once out of the water, he shook himself gently, accepting the great linen bands the priest handed over to dry himself. When he had finished and dressed, Amerotke sipped at a small cup of wine mixed with myrrh and walked into the Red Chapel of Ma'at.

The place was dark, lit by lights in pure alabaster vases placed on shelves along the walls. As soon as he was inside, an old priest shuffled forward, proffering an incense boat. The smoke rose thick and strong. Holding this before Amerotke, the old priest walked backwards. Amerotke followed slowly. Before the shrine, or Naos, the priest paused. He placed the incense boat down and opened the sacred cupboard. Amerotke looked upon the gold and silver statue of Ma'at and prostrated himself, then raised his head. The goddess's statue was draped in cloth of gold. He looked upon the face and caught his breath: that black, shiny hair, beautiful long face, those full lips and slanting, kohl-edged eyes. He was certain the goddess would speak. Those lips would move but it wasn't Ma'at, it was his wife Norfret. Beautiful, cool, serene. Amerotke bowed his head to the ground before sitting back on his heels.

'Are you a follower of the truth, Amerotke?' The old priest, crouching to one side, began the ritual questions.

'I have taken the oath. I have pursued justice and truth.'

'Whose justice?'

'That of the divine Pharaoh.'

'Life, health and prosperity.'

But the old priest's voice quavered. Amerotke sensed his uncertainty. Indeed, he reflected, who was Pharaoh? The boy Tuthmosis III? Hatusu the dead Pharaoh's wife? Or was real power in the hands of Rahimere, Vizier and Grand Chancellor?

'If you pursue the truth,' the priest's tone took a conversational note, 'why do you purify yourself in the ibis-kissed waters?'

'I have witnessed death,' Amerotke replied. 'My heart is heavy, my mind dulled.'

'For what you have done,' came the teasing reply, 'or what you are about to do?'

Amerotke just made a third obeisance. The old priest sighed, clambered to his feet and closed the door of the Naos. Amerotke stood in the gloom, never turning his back to the shrine while the old priest brushed the floor with feathers, removing, according to ritual, any sign of Amerotke's visit. Once outside the old priest joined his hands and bowed.

'You prayed for wisdom, Amerotke?'

The chief judge walked further away, lest they be overheard by the priests who now thronged around the sacred lake. He sheltered under the shade of a tamarisk tree; the old priest followed, his sandals pattering noisily.

'We have heard what will happen today in the Hall of Two Truths,' the old priest began. 'Don't you trust me, Amerotke?'

'Tiya!' Amerotke kissed him gently on the brow. 'You are a divine father. You kneel constantly before the goddess in her shrine of the Red Chapel.' He laughed sharply. 'But you are still a busybody, like one of those little flies which hop along the water.'

'Or a fish which hunts that fly,' the old priest slyly retorted. His rheumy eyes gazed up at the young judge. 'You are a child of the palace, Amerotke. A soldier of some repute. A judge of fearsome reputation. You have a beautiful wife and two young sons.' He touched Amerotke's chest. 'But you are never at peace, are you? Do you really believe in the gods, Amerotke? Is it true what I have heard? The market chatter, the temple whispers?'

Amerotke glanced away.

'I believe in divine Pharaoh,' he answered slowly. 'He is the personification of the god Amun-Ra and Ma'at is his daughter. She is the god's truth and justice.'

'A good reply for someone who attended the House of Life,' Tiya remarked. 'But do you live in the truth, Amerotke? Or are you still haunted by nightmares that your wife does not love you? That she once lay with a handsome captain of the guard who, later today, stands trial before you?' He drew closer, wiping a bead of sweat from his upper lip. 'The season of the clouds is upon us,' he said quietly. 'In Thebes the hand of Ra's beloved can still be felt. However, divine Pharaoh is dead. Soon the imprint he made will be covered by sand. A time of the sword! Soon, Amerotke, the season of the hyena will be upon us! Take care how you walk!'

Seth, the red-haired god of destruction: often depicted as
a man with a dog's face.

CHAPTER 3

The ram horns blew, shattering the silence of the temple courtyard as Amerotke sat in the judgement chair, inlaid with lapis lazuli. Its leather back was edged with gold, its legs fashioned in the likeness of crouched lions. Before him lay the volumes of Pharaoh's law. To his right the scribes had placed a small shrine of the goddess Ma'at. The horns stopped their wailing. The trial was about to begin.

Amerotke glanced quickly at Sethos sitting on a stool of black leather. The eyes and ears of Pharaoh was tense and watchful like a snake ready to strike. Amerotke's eyes moved. The scribes, too, had lost all sign of weariness. They squatted, cross-legged, the papyrus squares resting carefully, their pens and ink horns at the ready. Prenhoe caught his eye but Amerotke just sat and stared, ignoring his kinsman's slight smile. He must not show, by any sign or word, the tension seething around the case before him. At the back, Asural and the temple police were organising the witnesses. Another braying horn; members of the royal guard from the regiment of Horus led Meneloto, once a captain in their ranks, into the Hall of Two Truths.

The soldier was tall, slim-built, and he walked with a slight swagger. His slightly hooked nose gave his face an arrogant twist. He looked straight ahead, the only sign of nervousness being the occasional licking of his lower lip. He stopped alongside Sethos, bowed and then squatted down, crossing his legs, hands on his raised knees. He stared directly at Amerotke. The judge held his gaze, searching those eyes, that scarred soldier's face, for any hint of amusement, of sardonic mockery.

'My lord judge.'

Sethos' voice was so sharp Amerotke nearly jumped. He hid his disquiet by playing with the rings on his fingers.

'You have my attention,' Amerotke told him calmly.

'My lord judge,' Sethos continued, turning slightly in Meneloto's direction. 'The case before you is brought by the divine house and concerns the death of our beloved Pharaoh, His Majesty Tuthmosis II, darling son of Amun-Ra, the incarnation of Horus, King of the Two Lands who has now journeyed to the far horizon and is with his father in paradise.'

Amerotke and the scribes bowed their heads, murmuring a short prayer in Pharaoh's memory.

'Amun-Ra gives us life!' Sethos continued. 'And when he calls his son to him that is a matter of his divine will. We are all in the hands of the gods. We also know that they are in our hands as well.'

Amerotke blinked. He admired the cunning of Sethos' words. A true fox! Any defence would be that Tuthmosis II's sudden death was a matter of divine will but now the royal prosecutor had neatly turned it round.

'We are all charged with duties to Amun-Ra's beloved son. You have read the evidence?'

Amerotke nodded.

'Captain Meneloto was charged with the good care of the Pharaoh's person and the security of his ship the *Glory of Ra*. Now, in the month of Athor, the season of the water plants, Pharaoh, beloved of . . .'

'Thank you,' Amerotke broke in. 'The divine person of the dead Pharaoh is well known to us. Accordingly, during this trial, references to our god will be a simple "Pharaoh". It will keep matters brief and save a great deal of time. We are not here to debate theology,' Amerotke continued, raising his voice, 'but to determine the truth. The death of Tuthmosis II was a grievous blow to the Kingdom of the Two Lands. Cries of grief echo from the Delta to the Black Lands beyond the First Cataract.'

'And our enemies rejoice,' Sethos interrupted.

A hiss of disapproval rose from the scribes. Sethos bowed his head; even though he was a high priest of Amun-Ra, the friend of Pharaoh, the eyes and ears of the King, he must never interrupt the chief judge. Amerotke touched the pectoral of Ma'at and held up his right hand.

'We are here to determine the truth,' he declared flatly. 'Matters regarding the defence of our borders are the responsibility of the House of War. You will continue.'

Sethos rubbed his hands together. He stared up at the star-studded ceiling.

'In which case,' the prosecutor declared, 'these are the facts. The royal barque, the *Glory of Ra*, docked at the quayside of Thebes. Divine Pharaoh came down from his throne. He left his cabin and ascended his palanquin which was then borne into the city. Many people, fortunate enough to look upon his face, remarked that Pharaoh was ill, grievously tired, wearied by his burdens of state. In reality, when the divine foot had touched the cabin floor of the *Glory of Ra*, he'd been bitten by a viper. By the time Pharaoh had reached the temple of Amun-Ra, the poison was coursing through his body. He collapsed and died.'

'And where did the barque dock before it reached Thebes?' Amerotke asked.

'When divine Pharaoh visited the pyramid at Sakkara. On other occasions it simply moored midstream.'

Amerotke stared full at Meneloto.

'You were captain of divine Pharaoh's guard?'

'Of course.'

'And the security of the *Glory of Ra* was your concern?'

'Naturally.'

Amerotke ignored the touch of arrogance in the soldier's responses.

'And you searched Pharaoh's cabin for asps and scorpions?'

'Both human and those who crawl in the dust!' came the angry reply.

One of the scribes giggled. Amerotke glared across.

'Captain Meneloto, do you realise the seriousness of the charges brought against you?'

'I do, my lord.' The title was given reluctantly. 'I also know how dangerous it is to face a well-armed, charging enemy. I am innocent of any crime. The royal barque was searched from prow to stern at Sakkara and after leaving every other mooring place. No viper was found.'

'In which case, my lord,' Sethos broke in, 'would the captain of the guard like to tell us what was discovered after beloved Pharaoh's death?'

'Tell him yourself!' Meneloto snapped. 'You seem to know everything!'

'My lord.' Sethos addressed Amerotke. 'I call our first witness.'

The trial continued. Both sides called witnesses; Meneloto's swore that he was a faithful, conscientious soldier who had scrupulously searched the cabin on the royal barque for any danger to Pharaoh. Sethos, remaining cool and objective, summoned others to declare he had not. They all trooped forward, put their hands on the shrine of Ma'at and swore to tell the truth.

The more witnesses were called, the greater Amerotke's uncertainty grew. Something was very wrong here. He implicitly believed that Meneloto had been most conscientious in discharging his duties. However, members of the royal guard who had searched the barque had found a saw-scaled viper curled up beneath the royal dais. The viper had been killed and its mummified body was produced in court. It looked so lifeless and pathetic, yet it had brought down divine Pharaoh and caused ripples which had spread to the Delta and across the Red Lands to the east and west of Egypt.

'My lord?'

Amerotke raised his head. Sethos was looking at him strangely.

'My lord, what is the matter? Are you confused about the evidence?'

Amerotke cupped his chin between his fingers and allowed himself a smile. He glanced out towards the courtyard where the sunlight was fading; a light breeze had sprung up.

'I am truly confused, my lord Sethos,' he replied slowly.

For the first time, Amerotke glimpsed a change of expression on Meneloto's face. Was it hope? Or surprise? Did Meneloto really expect that Amerotke would use his cartouche, the divine seal of the court, to approve everything that was brought against him?

'My confusion is great,' Amerotke continued. 'Let me show you why.' He raised his left hand. 'Captain Meneloto's witnesses swear that he was a most professional and conscientious officer who searched the royal barque from prow to stern before it left Sakkara. Nothing was found.' Amerotke raised his right hand. 'On the other hand, lord Sethos has produced expert witnesses to say how, after beloved Pharaoh's death, in the presence of the captain of the royal barque, a search was made and a viper was found and killed. Are you sure? Are you so certain in your heart, my lord Sethos, that this viper was the cause of Pharaoh's death?'

Sethos stared coolly back.

'And why did it just strike Pharaoh? Why not someone else?'

'My lord.' Sethos lifted his hands. 'The royal cabin was made of the costliest linen, stretched on poles, the sides and front open so divine Pharaoh could look out.'

'And?'

'The royal throne and footstool were inside on a hollow dais which appears to have hidden the viper. The docking of the royal barque, Pharaoh's standing beside the dais ready to ascend the palanquin, could have aroused the serpent. It struck, then retreated back into the darkness where it was found.'

'So why didn't Pharaoh collapse immediately?'

Sethos bowed. 'My lord, my next witness will clarify the confusion for you: Peay, physician in the divine house.'

Amerotke nodded. 'I know Peay. Personal physician to Pharaoh, his wife and others.' He smiled. 'A man of expert knowledge.'

The ushers of the court brought forward Peay. Amerotke knew the small, swarthy man by reputation, a man who liked to dabble in gossip, a collector of fine things, who loved to show off his ostentatious wealth by the rings which covered his fingers and the heavy necklaces shimmering round his throat. So costly, so lavish, Amerotke secretly wondered how the physician could bear their weight. The physician bowed, put his hand on the shrine and gabbled the words of the oath and, taking his time, squatted on the cushions to Amerotke's right.

'Sir,' Amerotke began. 'You know why you are called?'

'I personally attended divine Pharaoh,' Peay replied, his voice harsh and guttural. Despite his wealth and education, Peay felt self-conscious about being a provincial. He glared around, ruffling back the sleeves of his linen gown, as if challenging anyone to laugh or mock him.

'On the evening Pharaoh died,' Amerotke asked. 'You were summoned to the temple of Amun-Ra?'

'I was, as the ritual dictates, just after sunset.'

'And you began divine Pharaoh's preparations for his journey to the far horizon?'

'I did. I also searched for the cause of his death.'

'Why?' Amerotke interrupted.

Peay sat back, eyes round in amazement.

'Pharaoh had collapsed. He suffered from the divine sickness. He was an epileptic,' Peay stuttered. 'I thought there was a possibility that he might have been in a swoon, one of the deep sleeps which this sickness brings on.'

'But this was not the case?' Amerotke asked.

Peay shook his head. 'The Pharaoh's soul had travelled on. There was no life pulse in his neck or his hands. I was concerned because the death was so sudden,' Peay added. 'I removed the Pharaoh's sandals and there, just above the heel, I saw the viper's bite. A dark purplish colour, for the fangs had bitten very deep.'

'On which leg?' Amerotke asked.

'On the left.'

Amerotke leaned his arm against the chair.

'And such a bite would be fatal?'

'Of course. The saw-scale viper is most venomous, there is little we can do.'

'Tell me. If Pharaoh was bitten as he left the royal barque, why didn't he complain when it first occurred?'

'Ah!' Peay rocked himself backwards and forwards. If he hadn't remembered where he was, he would have wagged a finger at the chief judge as if addressing scholars in the House of Life. 'My lord, you must remember two matters. Beloved Pharaoh was about to enter the city. He was a soldier, a warrior, victorious over his enemies. If he felt any discomfort he would hide it.'

'I agree,' Amerotke replied.

'Secondly,' Peay continued, 'the bite itself may not be so painful. I have known of men bitten who carried on with their business unaware of the venom racing towards their hearts.'

'And how long does such a race last?'

Peay blinked.

'I accept your first suggestion,' Amerotke explained. 'But surely Pharaoh would have collapsed much earlier? Is that not true?'

'It, it depends,' Peay stuttered.

'On what?'

'It can differ from one person to another.' Peay wiped the sweat from his face. 'On their build, their physique. You must remember, my lord, Pharaoh did not move until he reached the temple. When a man is poisoned, the more energetic he becomes, the quicker that poison acts.'

Amerotke recalled the officer executed earlier in the day. He made a sign with his hand that he accepted what the physician had said.

'And you are certain about the viper bite?' Amerotke insisted.

Peay then called, as fellow witnesses, those who had dressed the royal corpse for burial, as well as others who had taken it across the Nile to the City of the Dead. Good, trustworthy workmen, they all took the oath of what they had seen and how the viper's bite had been most apparent.

'The evidence,' Amerotke summarised, 'would indicate that this viper was on board the royal barque the *Glory of Ra*. One could argue, though I speak from little knowledge of such snakes, that the viper came aboard while the ship was making its way along the Nile, probably at Sakkara where the barge would be brought into the bank, not just moored midstream. I admit it is strange no one saw it, but such serpents can hide themselves in dark corners, and only emerge when disturbed. This apparently happened at Thebes: divine Pharaoh was most unfortunate; he was bitten, hid the discomfort but, on entering the temple of Amun-Ra, collapsed and died.' Amerotke glanced at Meneloto. 'Do you have any evidence to challenge these facts?'

The captain of Pharaoh's guard raised his head.

Amerotke glimpsed the faint smile and realised Sethos had blundered into a trap. It was like when he played the game of Senet with his wife: Norfret always kept her face impassive but, just before she struck, closed the game and won victory, her eyes would smile, her lips slightly tighten. Amerotke blinked. He must not think of her, not now.

'Do you wish to challenge my conclusion?' he asked.

'I do, my lord.'

The reply caused ripples of murmurs around the court. Amerotke raised his hand.

'I would like to call the priest Labda.'

'Who is he?' Sethos interrupted.

'I wish to call the priest Labda.' Meneloto kept to the ritual of the court.

'Bring forward this witness!' Amerotke shouted down the hall.

The crowd parted as Asural led forward a hobbling old man, his limbs like sticks, his skin yellowing with age. His head and face hadn't been properly shaven and this caused a few giggles. The chief of police eased him down on to the cushions then winked at Amerotke who stared stonily back. The chief judge could see the old man was uncomfortable. Every movement of his joints made him wince, his toothless mouth creased in pain. When he peered at the shrine of Ma'at over which he was supposed to take the oath he stretched forward one claw-like hand.

'There's no need, sir,' Amerotke said, 'to touch the shrine itself. I will take the oath as your proxy.'

'You do me great honour and show me compassion.' The old man's voice was surprisingly strong as his milky eyes gazed blearily in Amerotke's direction.

'I swear, my lord Amerotke, as your hand touches the shrine of Ma'at, that I speak the truth. I am not long for this prison of flesh and I prepare for my journey to the tents of eternity.'

'What is your name?' Amerotke asked.

'I am Labda, priest of the snake goddess Meretseger.'

Sethos started in surprise as he realised why this old priest had been called. Meretseger was venerated by the workers of the dead in the Necropolis.

'And why have you been called?' Amerotke pressed on remorselessly.

'As you know, my lord, the worship of the snake goddess means the study of the different serpents: those which inhabit the banks of the Nile as well as those which thrive in the hills and valleys around the city of Thebes.'

'And?' Sethos snapped.

The old priest didn't even bother to turn his head.

'To put it bluntly, my lord, a saw-scaled viper's bite is most deadly. True, a physician may say that poison is helped by the speed by which the victim moves; that is particularly accurate about any animals this viper attacks. They recoil in fear and they run away but they do not travel far. The more agitated they become the faster they die.'

Amerotke wanted to interrupt but he sat, hands on thighs.

'If,' the old priest continued, 'our beloved Pharaoh was bitten as he left his barque on the Nile he would never have reached the gates of the city.

The journey is too long. He would have collapsed and died long before he entered the temple of his father, the divine Amun-Ra.'

'How do you know this?' Sethos asked.

'I know it because it is the truth,' Ladba replied. 'Why should I tell a lie? I am an old man. I am on oath. There is nothing about snakes I do not know.'

Amerotke surveyed the court. The old man's voice was loud and strong. Even the scribes had stopped writing and sat staring across at Labda. If he spoke the truth, if divine Pharaoh had not been bitten as he left the *Glory of Ra*, then how had he died?

'Was the palanquin searched?' Amerotke asked. 'The royal throne on which Tuthmosis sat as he was borne through the city?'

'I made a rigorous check,' Sethos replied. 'A viper could not hide there. It would have been seen and caused consternation. Moreover, before you ask, my lord Amerotke, the same is true of the temple of Amun-Ra. Divine Pharaoh left his palanquin at the bottom of the steps and climbed them. The wife of Pharaoh, the beloved Hatusu, was there waiting along with priests and priestesses. No viper was seen or detected.'

Amerotke hated this moment. It was as if the onlookers were expecting him to perform some trick, some feat of conjuring, and reconcile two conflicting truths.

'My lord.' Meneloto spoke up, his voice harsh. 'Labda has spoken the truth. I therefore challenge, in the presence of the goddess Ma'at, those who brought these charges to prove me a liar!'

'How?' Sethos asked.

'We have condemned prisoners in the cells. Men who have been rightly found guilty and sentenced to horrific death by hanging or, in some cases, poison. Let one of them be taken down to the quayside of the river Nile. Let a viper strike his heel. Let him be carried through the city. My lord Amerotke, I swear by the goddess that if the man survives, I will plead guilty. I will contest this charge no further. But, if he dies, then I ask you, lord judge, for these charges to be dropped.' Meneloto glanced at the eyes and ears of Pharaoh. 'I know my lord Sethos is only the mouthpiece of those who wish me ill but he must accept my challenge. I appeal to Amun-Ra, to the divine Ka of our beloved Pharaoh, whose life I treasured more than my own, that I be put to the test!'

Amerotke covered his face with his hands, the formal sign that a judge was considering a verdict which would be published. Should he accept Meneloto's challenge? He has appealed to the gods, Amerotke thought, let the gods decide! He took his cupped hands away.

'My lord Sethos,' he asked softly, 'how say you?'

'There is more,' Labda added. 'Captain Meneloto has spoken too hastily.'

'In what way?' Amerotke asked.

'So far, my lord Amerotke,' the old priest waved one vein-streaked hand, 'we have talked about time and places. But I ask the court, has anyone here ever seen a man bitten by an asp or viper? Some snakes can bite and it's like a bee sting.' He pointed to the desiccated corpse of the saw-scale viper. 'But that one's bite is different. A true scourge.'

Amerotke steeled his face. He had wondered when Meneloto's defence would raise this matter. He knew little about vipers but, when he had been a member of Pharaoh's chariot squadron, Amerotke had seen a horse bitten by such a snake and the animal's convulsions had been terrible to behold.

'Continue,' he said.

'May the goddess Meretseger bear witness that I speak the truth. My lord Sethos himself will also know this but, if divine Pharaoh had been bitten by such a viper, his convulsions would have been terrible to behold.'

'But he did convulse,' Sethos retorted, rather flustered. 'In the temple of Amun-Ra, the beloved Hatusu, the god's wife, says that he convulsed.'

The old priest tried to hide his surprise.

'But that was too late,' he protested. 'It should have happened before!'

'I have appealed to the gods,' Meneloto interrupted. 'I have asked for their judgement.'

Amerotke turned to his scribes but they kept their heads bowed. He glanced towards the darkening courtyard. He needed to think, to reflect, to sift among the evidence.

'The court will adjourn,' he declared. 'It will convene at the prescribed time tomorrow morning. I will make my decision. Captain Meneloto, you are, I understand, under house arrest?'

The soldier, looking strangely relieved, nodded.

'Then you will be taken back there and brought before the court tomorrow morning for my judgement.' Amerotke turned the pectoral on his chest so the goddess no longer looked out over the court. He clapped his hands gently. 'That is my verdict!'

The court then broke up. The old priest shuffled away from the cushions and a murmur of conversation rose from the scribes and witnesses. Amerotke remained seated. Only when Meneloto had left the hall did Sethos rise and come over. He crouched down before the judge.

'What can I do for you, eyes and ears of Pharaoh?' Amerotke sardonically asked. 'You have heard my decision. The court will wait!'

Sethos pointed to the volumes of law.

'There is nothing in the procedure against divine Pharaoh's prosecutor asking the judge of what sentence or punishment you will inflict if the case is proved.'

'Surely you are not asking for this man's life? The court will not allow that. Perhaps a downgrading in rank, a fine?'

'Exile!' Sethos replied sharply. 'Exile to an oasis in the Red Lands to the west!' He glimpsed the astonishment in Amerotke's face. 'I, too, am under orders,' he explained. 'The royal circle wanted his life. I tempered their anger.'

'We shall see.'

Amerotke rose from his seat and, although he knew he was being discourteous, turned his back on Sethos and walked into the small side chapel of the Hall of Two Truths. He stretched out and touched the huge ankhet, the symbol of truth, painted just within. On the wall which held the door, an artist had depicted Pharaoh Tuthmosis dealing justice to Egypt's enemies, arm raised, his club about to descend on a Kushite captive. The artist had caught Pharaoh's features most accurately: his thin, pointed face, the perpetual frown Tuthmosis had always seemed to wear. Amerotke bowed. Did Pharaoh's Ka now visit this temple? Did he watch the proceedings?

Amerotke closed the door, turning the intricate key so the wooden tongue caught the clasp and held it. He took off the pectoral and other insignia of office and put them in the mother-of-pearl inlaid casket. Afterwards, as customary, he crouched before the statue.

Something was terribly wrong. He didn't blame Sethos; the eyes and ears of Pharaoh looked most uncomfortable with this case. There was, indeed, an inherent contradiction. If Pharaoh had been bitten by that viper on board the *Glory of Ra* he would have convulsed. He would never have lasted until he reached the temple of Amun-Ra. So why were these charges being brought against Meneloto? Was he to be a scapegoat? Or was it something else? Dark and more secretive? If divine Pharaoh had not been bitten as he left the royal barque, what had happened? Amerotke recalled the rumours. Hadn't Pharaoh's sepulchre been desecrated? Curses and maledictions daubed in human blood on his unfinished tomb? And hadn't doves, blood streaming from their bodies, fallen from the sky? Was that an accident? A mere coincidence? But the desecration of the royal tomb could not be so easily dismissed. After all, here was Pharaoh returning in victory from his battles along the Delta. Across the Nile, in the City of the Dead, a group of determined blasphemers had committed the most horrendous crime. They had killed Pharaoh's guards and desecrated his tomb. Why? Grave robbery was common but such sacrilege very rare.

Amerotke played with the ring on his finger. Why was divine Pharaoh being cursed? Was his death some sort of judgement? But, if that was the case, it was no longer a matter of incompetence but of murder. And why hadn't the desecration of the tomb been mentioned during the trial? Yes, he would raise that matter tomorrow, but he would have to be careful: he could not discuss this with anyone; even the merest hint that Pharaoh had been the object of a murderous conspiracy would throw Thebes into confusion. And, if he could not prove it, he would not be the first judge to receive a proclamation, signed with the royal cartouche, ordering his removal.

Amerotke leaned his head against the wall, relishing its coolness. He heard a knock on the door but ignored it. He would walk home this evening and, yes, he would spend his evening quietly. Let his mind go back over what he had heard and seen today. Sethos was only the tool, but who was the person pressing this case? Tuthmosis' heir was only a boy, a mere child. So, was it Hatusu, Pharaoh's wife? Or Rahimere the Grand Vizier? Or was General Omendap, Pharaoh's commander, jealous of Meneloto? Or Bayletos that cunning chief scribe of the House of Silver? Amerotke recalled playing on the sandstone cliffs above Thebes and going into a long, dark cave. He felt the same now and wondered what horrors waited in the shadows.

Hathor: the Egyptian goddess of love.

CHAPTER 4

The knocking became more insistent. Amerotke rose and unlocked the door. Asural slipped through. In the poor light his face looked ashen; his eyes, usually crinkled in pleasure, shifted about. He put his helmet down and tapped his sword belt, fingers playing with the hilt carved in the shape of a jackal's head.

'Amerotke,' he whispered as if the room were full of witnesses. He jabbed a thumb over his shoulder. 'Do you realise what was being said in there?'

'I listened to the evidence.'

'My lord, don't play tricks with me.' Asural wiped the sweat from his dome-like head, drying his hand on his kilt. 'My mind may not be as sharp as yours. I am a soldier, blunt and honest.'

'I'm always wary of people who call themselves blunt and honest,' Amerotke replied. 'And don't play the hearty soldier with me, Asural. You are cunning, sly and, although heavy in body, fleet in mind.' He patted Asural on the arm. 'You are a fox, Asural. I, for one, am not taken in by your bluff ways. But you are a good policeman. Honest, you don't take bribes. More importantly, I like and respect you.'

Asural sighed and his shoulders sagged.

'So, don't come in here,' Amerotke continued, 'trying to make me feel more agitated than I am. I know what was being said out there. I don't believe divine Pharaoh was killed by that viper and neither do you. But how and why he died is a mystery. I have to decide where the power of my court ends and the tortuous ways of the royal circle begin.'

'There's also the tomb robberies,' Asural said, scratching the side of his head. 'We've received information about another. An old noblewoman. She was married to a Hittite general who settled in Egypt. The family went to her tomb on the cliffs above the City of the Dead. The false door was undamaged, the secret entrance undiscovered. No sign of a break-in but amulets, necklaces and small cups left in the porchway of the tomb had been removed. They are going to start complaining,' Asural continued. 'They'll send in petitions to the House of a Million Years; they'll look for a scapegoat and that will be me.'

'Which reminds me of a story I intend to tell my children tonight,' Amerotke replied.

Asural groaned and looked away.

'I promise you,' Amerotke continued kindly, 'once this business is finished, we'll go searching for these tomb-robbers who can walk through rock and mud. What do you think of the evidence against Meneloto?'

'As you said, for every item the eyes and ears of the Pharaoh produced, Meneloto produced another. It was like a game of Senet where both players have blocked each other.'

'And the witnesses?' Amerotke asked. 'Peay?'

'He has an unsavoury witness. He lives in the shadow lands between day and night.' Asural moved his head from side to side. 'Peay consorts with whores and prostitutes down near the quayside. He also has a predilection for pretty boys' bottoms. A man who drinks from many cups: some clean, some soiled.'

'But a good physician?'

'He is a wealthy man. I don't think he would lie.' Asural smiled thinly. 'Commit perjury in the Hall of Two Truths. Peay certainly would not like to spend years working in the gold mines of Sinai.'

'And Labda?'

'He dwells in a cave deep in the Valley of the Kings. He is a keeper of a small shrine to the goddess Meretseger. A man of integrity.' Asural paused.

From the trees in the courtyard came an owl hoot, long and mournful.

'It's time we were gone,' Amerotke said. 'Ensure the shrine and my chamber are safe.' He put his hand on the latch.

'You should take care.'

Amerotke turned. 'What do you mean?'

'Don't act the innocent with me,' Asural teased. 'All of Thebes is in turmoil. The Osiris and Isis regiments now camp outside the city. Five chariot squadrons have been moved up from the south. It may be the season of the planting but it is also the season of the hyenas.'

'Oh, come, come, Asural, you are a chief of the temple police, not a riddler and soothsayer. Spell out your dire warnings and portents.'

'There have been plenty of them,' Asural replied. 'Astrologers in the House of Life saw a star falling from the skies. The dead have been seen walking in the streets and alleyways in the city across the Nile. Pharaoh's heir is only a boy. There are those who would like to seize the throne. Well, at least, until he is a man.'

'I am a judge,' Amerotke reminded him. 'I only dispense Pharaoh's justice.'

And, opening the door, he walked out into the Hall of Two Truths.

The courtyard beyond was now deserted. The sacred shrine had been closed, a wreath of flowers placed at its foot. The old priests, the pure ones, had sprinkled its doors with incense. The scribes had cleared away the books of judgement, the cushions and chairs. The hall was bare and empty. Amerotke always thought it looked more majestic that way. He knelt before the shrine, hands extended, muttered a short prayer of thanks then rose and left the temple. Its doors of burnished copper were open and closed by the guards. Amerotke walked down the hall of columns and out through the great soaring pylons. The Way of the Sphinx, the Dromos, was now deserted. A refreshing breeze had sprung up and the dying sunlight caught the roseate sphinxes and gave them a strange life of their own.

A group of novice priests were leading great oxen, streamers fixed between their horns, up to one of the slaughterhouses for the morning sacrifice. A few weary pilgrims clustered around a stela of the dwarf god Bes at the end of the causeway. Under the grimacing figure of the dwarf god, sacred hieroglyphics had been carved. The stela was washed by a fountain, the water splashing over it and trickling down into a granite basin. The pilgrims were filling leather skins with water, a sure protection, or so it was claimed, against scorpion and asp bites.

Amerotke brushed by them. He was now in the great forecourt of the temple. He paused. Should he really go straight home? Or journey to the north of the city and visit the funeral priest in the temple of Amun-Ra whom he'd paid to pray for his dead parents? Amerotke breathed in: that was the place where divine Pharaoh had died. Perhaps they would think he was there on official business.

'My lord Amerotke?'

He turned. 'Ah, kinsman Prenhoe!'

The young scribe came shuffling towards him. One of the thongs on his sandal was broken.

'I do not wish to discuss the case,' Amerotke warned.

Prenhoe hid his disappointment.

'One day, kinsman,' he asked, 'would you support me in being appointed as a judge? I mean, in the minor courts?'

'Of course. You are a member of the School of Scribes. You have taken its examinations.'

'Good.' Prenhoe's thin face broke into a smile. He blinked. 'I thought today was a good day. I had a dream last night.'

'Prenhoe,' Amerotke warned. 'Now is not the time for your dreams though it is perhaps the hour to prepare for sleep.' He stretched out and clasped Prenhoe's wrist. 'Go home!'

His kinsman shuffled off. Amerotke walked down towards the palm trees where he had seen Shufoy selling amulets earlier in the day. The dwarf was leaning against a tree fast asleep, his master's walking stick and parasol lying beside him, a beer cup cradled in his lap. Of the amulets, or the money Shufoy must have earned, there was no sign.

Amerotke crouched down. He put his mouth near the dwarf's ear.

'Sleep only during the hours of night,' he declared sonorously, quoting one of Shufoy's proverbs. 'But while Ra rules the day, use it for life; use the light for happiness, health and prosperity.'

Shufoy startled awake. 'Oh master! You were longer than I thought.'

He scrambled to his feet, thrusting the beer cup into the little sack he carried. He handed Amerotke his white walking cane, its head carved in the shape of an ibis bird. He would have prepared the flabellum but Amerotke patted him on the head.

'How much beer did you drink?' he teased. 'The sun's strength is fading, I have no use for that.'

Shufoy grimaced and, turning, bellowed in a deep voice, 'Make way for the lord Amerotke, chief judge in the Hall of Two Truths! The divine servant of beloved Pharaoh! Scribe of justice! Holy priest! Blessed and touched by Ra!'

'Shut up!' Amerotke seized the dwarf by the shoulder. Every evening they went through this parody.

'But, master.' Shufoy's disfigured face broke into a sly smile. 'I am your most humble servant. My task is to sing your praises so that all we approach know who you truly are.'

'I am a judge,' Amerotke replied. 'A very tired one! The last thing I need, Shufoy, is you bellowing across the marketplace.'

Shufoy tried to look hurt. He loved this tall, enigmatic priest, this objective judge who seemed so harsh; Shufoy knew him to be kind and gentle, even though a little too solemn.

'I am only doing my job,' he whined playfully.

'And I do mine.' Amerotke began the usual arguments.

They left the forecourt and entered the marketplace.

'And what is your job, master, really?' Shufoy leaned on the parasol as if it were a staff of office.

'To watch, to listen, to judge.' Amerotke kept his face straight. He pointed across to a swarthy, gaudily dressed man with gold amulets on his wrist and rings in his ears: he lounged beneath a palm tree where a grey-haired woman was selling cups of bitter Nubian beer.

'Now, take a man like that,' Amerotke said. 'Look at him, Shufoy. What do you think he is?'

'A Syrian?' the dwarf replied. 'A merchant?'

'Lounging under a tree, drinking beer!'

Shufoy looked again.

'I shall tell you who he is,' Amerotke continued. 'His face is weatherbeaten, burned dark by the sun, so he works in the open. He wears no sandals; his feet are hard and coarse-skinned yet he is no beggar, as he dresses well. The dagger he carries in his sash is curved and not made in Egypt. He sits with his back to a tree on hard ground yet he is relaxed and comfortable. I would wager he is a Phoenician, a sailor, a man who has brought his craft down the Nile, sold whatever cargo he has and allowed his crew the run of the city for the night.'

'How much?' Shufoy asked.

'A deben of silver,' Amerotke replied, stony-faced. 'Go and ask him.'

The dwarf waddled across. The stranger looked him up and down but answered his questions. He turned, smiled at Amerotke and said something else. Shufoy angrily waddled back.

'You are correct,' he said, tucking his chin against his chest and looking up under bushy eyebrows at Amerotke. 'He's a Phoenician sailor! He's here for two days and he sends you his regards. He knows the lord Amerotke!'

The judge burst out laughing and walked on.

'You are a cheat!' Shufoy gabbled, coming up behind him. 'I don't owe you any silver!'

'Of course you don't. I mean, how would my humble servant be able to afford such a wager? I pay you well. But you are not a merchant, are you Shufoy? You have nothing to sell. No trade?'

Shufoy blinked and looked away.

'I'm hungry,' he grumbled. 'My stomach's rumbling! It's a wonder I don't charge you for letting it beat like a drum to let everyone know you are approaching. Perhaps that's what I should do. Let it rumble away and everyone will say: "Here comes poor old Shufoy, the starving servant of Amerotke, the chief judge must be close behind!"'

'You eat well enough,' his master replied. He patted the dwarf on his balding head. 'In fact, I'm fattening you up as a sacrifice.'

Amerotke walked on, down the basalt-paved alleyway. Shufoy trailed behind, now angry at his master's teasing. He was quoting proverbs about: 'Those who laughed would soon mourn and those who mourned would soon laugh while empty bellies would have their fill!'

Amerotke walked through the marketplace. It was still busy. Barbers armed with curved razors were clustered round their stalls under the trees, shaving heads, making them as smooth as pebbles washed by the river. Sailors, drunk on cheap beer, staggered about looking for a pleasure house, a brothel, where they could spend the rest of the night in revelry. They were closely shadowed by the police, armed with thick cudgels, watching for any sign of disturbance.

The market filled every available place in the small open squares and along the narrow lanes. Amerotke sensed no tension. The shops were open. The fleshers and sellers of meat had long finished trading as anything that was fresh at the beginning of the day had now turned putrid in the heat.

However, other traders still had their awnings stretched over poles. A group of the unclean clustered around a cookshop, waiting for bread baked in the hot sand in the garden behind the house. Another stall sold onion seeds, a sure way, the stall-owners bawled, to block snake-holes. Other 'delicacies' lay on the board: gazelle dung to keep off rats; giraffe tails to serve as whisks next to honey pots and boxes of caraway seeds to serve as sweeteners.

The crowd was cheerful and noisy. Children ran around screaming and playing, getting in the way of oxen-pulled carts piled high with produce, hurrying down towards the city gates before the conch horns blew and the curfew was imposed. Powerful merchants, squatting in their makeshift litters slung across two donkeys, shouted and gestured with their fly whisks for the crowd to stand aside. Two Nomachs, governors from the provinces, also tried to make their way down to the House of Silver. The crowd ignored the banners carried before them displaying the Nomachs' insignia, one a hare, the other two hawks. They were more interested in the teller of tales from the border town of Syena, a small, wizened man who had trained two monkeys to hold firebrands on either side of him as he told of his wanderings across the great sea to lands the people could only marvel about. His rival, a female dancer and contortionist a few paces away, was trying to attract the crowds with her clacking castanets and the bells which jingled all over her body. She turned and twisted while a young girl beat a drum and another played a flute. A crowd of men gathered round, sitting down on their haunches, clapping their hands. The teller of tales, frightened that his stories would be ignored, became more fanciful.

Amerotke smiled and passed on. He turned, expecting to see Shufoy trailing disconsolately behind him, but the dwarf had disappeared. Amerotke bit back his impatience. He'd threatened to put a collar round his waist and lead him like a pet monkey. Shufoy was constantly distracted and he kept wandering off. Amerotke was secretly fearful for him; with his disfigured nose and stunted size, the sellers of flesh might well kidnap the little man, bundle him on to a barge and sell him to some rich merchant, a collector of the curious. Time and again, in the Hall of Two Truths, Amerotke had seen such cases. Using his stick he pushed his way back through the crowds.

'Shufoy!' he shouted. 'Shufoy, where are you?'

He espied the little man, at the front of a crowd which had gathered round a tamarind tree. From one of its branches hung a sign extolling the exploits of a physician, a specialist, a 'guardian of the anus'.

Muttering under his breath, Amerotke pushed his way through. The physician had his patient lying down on a reed mat, legs extended, and was about to treat a fistula between his buttocks. Amerotke closed his eyes. He could never understand Shufoy's deep interest in the workings of the human body. He grasped the dwarf by the shoulder.

'The lady Norfret will be waiting.'

'Aye.' Shufoy took one last look at the physician as he bent down over his patient. 'So she will!'

He followed his master back through the crowd and on to the trackway which wound down to the great city gates, two huge pillars dominated by soaring towers.

For the first time that evening, Amerotke noticed a difference. Usually city watchmen lounged about, more interested in their games of chance than who passed or when the gates were closed. Now a corps from the crack regiment of Amun stood on guard, their leather greaves and breastplates shimmering in the light of torches lashed to spears thrust into the ground. Officers stood by scrutinising all who journeyed out. One of them recognised Amerotke and bowed slightly, waving his hand for the chief judge to pass untroubled.

Amerotke and Shufoy passed through the gates and on to the basalt-paved causeway. To his right Amerotke could see the Nile glinting and the stretched sails of a ship; children were playing down among the papyrus reeds. To his left sprawled the mud-baked dwellings of peasants who flocked to the city. These were unable to afford or build a house within the walls so they dug mud from the banks of the Nile and built their own: a jumbled maze of mean, one-storey tenements which housed not only workers from the quarries or the city but also fugitives from the law. It was pleasant enough, people sitting outside their front doors chattering and joking, watching naked children play. The air was pungent with the smell of salted fish, cheap beer and the hard bread these people cooked. A few got to their feet as Amerotke passed, studying him carefully. The chief judge heard his name mentioned. The men sat down. Soon he was through the Village of the Unclean. The causeway rose steeply. Amerotke stopped on the brow to revel in the cool breeze. Across the river he could glimpse the lights from the City of the Dead, its workshops and funeral houses.

Amerotke thought of his own parents' tomb on the other side of the rocky cliffs; he vowed he would visit it as soon as possible. He must check all was well and that the funeral priest he'd hired still left food before the entrance and went there daily to say the prayers. Amerotke also thought of the thefts. How skilful the thief must be! Most grave-robbers simply broke in but, in doing so, soon roused the suspicions of others. In the end they were always caught and cruelly punished. However, according to Asural, these thieves were different: slipping in and out like shadows. The judge wondered if these robbers had found the grave of the Pharaoh at whose court he had been raised, the old warrior Tuthmosis I. Amerotke shivered as he remembered the stories. How Tuthmosis had driven hordes of slaves and criminals into a lonely valley where the tomb had been secretly dug, its entrance cleverly concealed. The workmen were later barbarously murdered so they couldn't betray the secret to anyone else. Was it true, Amerotke wondered, that the Ka, the spirits of these dead, moved across the Nile at night to visit the homes of those they had loved and left?

'Master, I thought we were in a hurry? And, by the way, did you see those soldiers?' Shufoy had apparently forgotten his sulks at being dragged away from the physician.

'What soldiers?' Amerotke asked.

'Those at the gates. Is it true, master, that the House of War will soon replace the House of Peace?'

'Divine Pharaoh has gone to the far horizon,' Amerotke replied. 'His son Tuthmosis III is his heir. There will be some tension over who controls the regency but, in the end, all will be well.'

He tried to sound confident but, even though Amerotke turned his face away, Shufoy knew his master was only reassuring him. Sitting under his palm tree selling his amulets, Shufoy had listened to the chatter and the gossip. The royal circle, those close councillors round the young Pharaoh, were divided. A leader would emerge and seize power but who would it be? Rahimere the Grand Vizier? General Omendap, commander of Pharaoh's armies? Or Bayletos from the House of Silver? Other names had been mentioned especially dead Pharaoh's wife and half-sister, Hatusu. The merchants were worried and had voiced their concerns for all to hear. Chariot squadrons and infantry battalions were being pulled back from the borders. And what would happen then, they asked? Would the sand-dwellers, the Libyans, the Nubians, interfere in their trade? If the war galleys were moved up to Thebes would pirates once again prowl the Nile?

'I think you should be very careful.' Shufoy drew alongside Amerotke and, moving the parasol, grasped his master's hand. 'I heard about your judgement. People are wondering how a Pharaoh can be bitten by a viper but not die until he enters the house of Amun-Ra.'

'And what do the people say?' Amerotke teased.

'That all this is a judgement. The gods are going to deal out justice.'

'Then we'll have to see.' Amerotke sighed. 'But for the moment, Shufoy, I am tired and I am hungry.'

They walked on, passing the high walls of other palatial residences, their great wooden gates locked and sealed for the evening. Every day new houses were being built in this pleasant, lush area, only a short distance from the Nile where water could be brought in by canals and garden wells were plentiful.

Eventually they reached Amerotke's house. Shufoy knocked at the small door built into the great wooden gates.

'Open up!' Shufoy shouted. 'Make way for the lord Amerotke!'

The door hastily swung open. Amerotke stepped inside. He always loved this time of the day. Once that door closed behind him, he felt as if he were in a different world. His own paradise, spacious gardens, vineyards, beehives, flowers and trees. The porter was grumbling at Shufoy. Amerotke glanced around. Everything seemed in order. Alabaster jars full of oil had been lit and placed in their stone holders. He glimpsed the summerhouse, its roof in the shape of a small pyramid, which overlooked the tiled lake and the statue of Khem the god of the gardens.

He walked down the avenue of trees which ringed the main house, a great three-storeyed building, then climbed the steps, went through the painted columns and into the hallway where rich cedar beams spanned the pink ceiling. A frieze of fluted flowers ran along the top and bottom of the red walls. The air was sweet with the perfume of myrrh and frankincense.

Servants brought a jug and basin for Amerotke to wash himself. He sat on a stool and took off his sandals. As he washed his feet in the basin and dried them with the rough linen towel he could hear his two sons laughing and shouting from the floor above him. Shufoy handed him a cup of white wine to wash his mouth and clean his teeth. He heard a sound and looked up. Norfret had come down the stairs. He marvelled at her beauty. How much she reminded him of the statue of Ma'at: her sloe eyes sparkled, emphasising the dark rings of kohl around them, her full lips were painted with red ochre. She wore a pleated robe with fringes and an embroidered shawl clasped at the front by a cluster of precious stones. She walked across, her silver thonged sandals slapping on the floor. She had put a new wig on, plaited and oiled, interspersed with gold strips. At her neck hung a collar of blue and yellow stones, which shimmered in the light from the oil lamps. Syrian servants clustered behind her. Amerotke caught the gaze of one of them, Vaela, who glanced away; the girl's hot-eyed stares always made him feel uncomfortable. She wasn't impudent or forward but, now and again, he would catch her staring at him, studying him closely. Norfret stood on tiptoe and kissed his cheeks, then his mouth. She pressed her body close to him.

'I expected you earlier, what happened?'

Amerotke looked over her head at the servants. Norfret turned and snapped her fingers. The servants, apart from Shufoy, disappeared. Norfret led him into the huge banqueting hall, its columns painted a light green and decorated at their top and base with yellow lotus flowers. Dishes of bread and fruit had been placed on the small polished tables. At the far end, the huge wine vats built into the wall gave off a pleasing fragrance. The furniture, of the best cedar and sycamore and inlaid with strips of ebony and silver, included couches with headrests, chests with curved lids and chairs and stools cunningly carved. Coloured matting hung on the walls and rugs of dyed wool covered the shiny floor.

The doors closed behind them. Once again Norfret kissed him on the lips and ushered him to a chair near one of the tables. She served him a goblet of wine, light and refreshing.

'What happened?' she repeated. 'I've heard rumours . . .'

Amerotke glanced into the wine cup. Was she so eager to find out, he wondered? Did it mean so much to her?

'Meneloto is innocent,' he told her. 'Only the gods know the truth behind Pharaoh's death.'

He took a sip and tried to ignore Norfret's long but hasty sigh. Was it relief?

'He looked well,' he continued. He raised his cup and smiled over the rim at her. 'He bore himself well. He had the courage of a lion. But he was always like that, wasn't he?'

Norfret just smiled. Amerotke wanted to pinch himself. She didn't seem at all disturbed or alarmed. He realised how stupid he was. The case brought before him had been the talk of Thebes. Why shouldn't his wife be interested! What proof did he have, apart from rumour and gossip, that she had been close to Meneloto? And, even if she was, did that mean that they had lain together?

'Father! Father!'

There was a pounding on the doors, which were thrown open. Amerotke's two sons, Ahmase and Curfay, naked except for loin cloths and pursued by Shufoy pretending to be a baboon, raced into the room.

'Have you eaten?' He tugged on each of his son's side locks. Were there really two years between them? If Ahmase wasn't a few inches taller, he'd find it hard to tell the difference.

'We will eat upstairs,' Norfret announced. 'We will be able to catch the breeze.' She smiled dazzlingly at Shufoy. 'You can join us!'

They went to the upper room where servants had laid out roast goose, pots of honey and dishes of vegetables. Oil lamps were lit. Their master's favourite high-backed chair was placed near the open doors which led to a balcony. The sky was clear, the stars so bright Amerotke felt he could stretch up and touch them. The boys were chattering. Norfret sat, head close to Shufoy. Amerotke could never understand their relationship. He knew Shufoy made her laugh with his descriptions of the marketplace, the guile and tricks of the merchants and traders.

'Tell us a story!' Ahmase demanded, once they'd eaten. 'Father, you promised us a story!'

'Ah yes.'

'You did promise,' Shufoy echoed, eyes gleaming as he rubbed the ugly gap where his nose had once been. 'I can smell a good story!'

The boys and Norfret laughed.

'There was once a Pharaoh,' Amerotke began, 'who built a very, very strong treasury. It had secret doors which only he could unlock, but no secret passageways or windows. He poisoned the architect, the man died and the wicked Pharaoh ignored the plight of the poor widow and her two sons.'

'Which Pharaoh was this?' Curfay demanded.

Five years old, Curfay was always inquisitive.

'A long time ago,' Amerotke replied. 'Anyway, once the architect was dead, Pharaoh moved his gold and silver into his new treasure house. However, on the morning after he had moved it in, he discovered some of the gold and silver had gone missing.'

'And the door was not open?' Ahmase asked.

'The doors remained locked and sealed. I have told you: there were no windows, no secret entrances.'

'But what happened then?'

'Pharaoh took counsel with his wise men.' He smiled. 'But I'll continue the story tomorrow night. Come on, it's time for bed.'

Shufoy grabbed his charges and marched them out of the room. Amerotke stared out into the night down towards the Nile and wondered how his judgement in the Hall of Two Truths had been received at the royal palace.

Nephthys: 'Lady of the house': a goddess often depicted as a young woman.

CHAPTER 5

In the hall of columns of the House of a Million Years, the royal palace near the great mooring place on the Nile, Hatusu, wife of the great god Tuthmosis II, who had now journeyed to the far horizon, took her place in the royal circle. She sat on a chair before the table provided and gazed quickly about her. This was the throne room, the source of all power; the great chair, the throne of the living one, with its gorgeous canopy bearing the red-gold figure of Horus, its arms carved into sphinxes, was empty. Its footstool, embroidered in cloth-of-gold and inscribed with the names of Egypt's enemies, lay rather forlornly to one side. Hatusu gazed at the throne's carved legs, shaped in the form of leaping lions, and bit her lip. That throne should be hers! Next to the great chair, on its special pedestal, stood the red and white double crown of Egypt, encircled by the glittering Uraeus, the lunging cobra with its red jewelled eyes, spitting terror at Egypt's enemies. Along the mother-of-pearl-topped table in front of this lay the insignia of Pharaoh, the crook, the whip, the sickle-shaped sword, and beside them the chepresh, Pharaoh's war crown.

Hatusu, dressed in a simple white sheath dress, a jewelled necklace round her throat, sought to hide her feelings. By rights she should still wear the vulture headdress, the crown of the Queens of Egypt. However, the keeper of the diadems, that dough-faced servant, that creature in the pay of Rahimere the Vizier, had told her this would not be acceptable. Others had sided with him. The keeper of jewels, the royal fan-bearer, the overseer of the royal ointments, all had pointed out that her stepson, Tuthmosis, was, in fact, Pharaoh and the royal circle would decide who would be Regent.

'How old are you?' the keeper of the diadems had simpered.

'You know my age,' Hatusu had replied tartly. 'Not yet nineteen years.'

She tapped her throat. 'But I bear within me the mark of the god. I am daughter of divine Pharaoh Tuthmosis, wife to the god his son.'

The keeper of the diadems had turned away, but Hatusu was sure he had mouthed to the other sycophants, 'Were you now?' which provoked giggles and laughter behind raised hands.

I know where you'd like me, Hatusu thought, staring round the circle. You'd have me in the House of Seclusion, in the harem with the other women, growing fat on honey, bread and wine, stuffing my mouth with the choicest meats until I am as round as a beer vat. Who among these men could she trust? She was only here because of whose daughter she was and whose wife she had been. She must think coolly, clearly. At the far end of the circle sat Rahimere the Grand Vizier, thin-faced, deep bags under his eyes. That crooked nose suited his character! With his shaven head and constant look of piety, Rahimere always reminded Hatusu of some petty priest. He was a sly one! He controlled the scribes of the House of Silver so he could dig deep into the chests of gold and silver, precious jewels and necklaces. Hatusu had soon learned that every man had his price. Had Rahimere bought them all? The court officials who sat wafting their perfumed fans or stiffened ostrich plumes in front of their faces. The fragrance created some coolness while the fans hid their expressions. She did not trust any of them! They were like water, they'd simply go the way the board was tilted. Further down the circle, however? Hatusu wafted her own perfumed fan. These were different: Omendap, commander-in-chief of the army. He always looked kindly upon her though, most times, he seemed more interested in her breasts and neck than he did in her brain. Could she buy him with her body? And the other soldiers? The commanders in charge of the crack regiments, the Amun, Osiris, Horus, Ra and Ibis. These military men looked decidedly uncomfortable in their white linen robes, grasping small silver axes, the symbols of their office. What had her father said?

'Soldiers, Hatusu, can rarely be bought by gold and silver. They will always fight for Pharaoh and the royal blood.'

Hatusu felt uncomfortable. She looked to her left. A tall, shaven-headed young man was staring at her. He wore a close-fitting skull cap and had a nervously expressive, rather wrinkled face with plump cheeks and full lips. His white robe looked rather soiled at the neck. He carried a fly whisk which he was tapping against his cheek but it was his eyes which held her. Hatusu would have smiled at the lust in that gaze. All etiquette and protocol forgotten, the young man sat undressing her with his eyes. His tongue came out, licking the corner of his mouth. He didn't seem the least discomfited that he had been noticed or change his gaze or expression. He was finding it difficult to sit still; as the rest took their places and the clerks placed documents in front of them, his hot gaze never wavered.

Now there's a man, Hatusu thought, I could buy body and soul, but who was he? She turned and talked to the divine father on her immediate right, one of the chief priests from the temple of Amun-Ra.

'Who is that young man?' she whispered. 'The one who looks uncomfortable?'

'Senenmut,' he growled. 'An upstart born and bred.'

'Ah yes!' Hatusu turned away and glanced sideways, smiling faintly. Senenmut! She had heard of him. A man who had risen from nothing. A brave warrior, an outstanding soldier. He had left the army to join the court and risen quickly to become overseer of Pharaoh's works, in charge of monuments and temples. She would remember his name!

She heard a cough and turned to see that Sethos had joined them. He was smiling openly at her and winked. Hatusu smiled with relief. It was good to see a friendly face. She and Sethos had known each other for years. She would need the support of this powerful, wealthy lord, a high-ranking priest, the royal prosecutor, the eyes and ears of Pharaoh. Sethos had been one of her dead husband's closest friends. His voice would carry sway in the royal circle. Hatusu breathed in, nostrils flaring as she composed herself. She must not lose her temper, let these enemies see how weak and vulnerable she really was. One day they would kiss the earth before her! Until then, Hatusu reflected as she closed her eyes, she had other dangers to face. Time and again she had been summoned to the small chapel of Seth, to pick up another letter full of threats, of cunning blackmail. If these secrets, it mentioned, were published, Rahimere would close like the crocodile he was and the House of Seclusion would be a welcome alternative to the other fates he could threaten.

'Let it be known!'

Hatusu started and looked up. The cedar doors had been closed and guarded, the scribes and clerks had gone. The oil lamps glowed brightly;

the council was in session. A priest was now standing, turning towards the empty throne. If Tuthmosis were alive he would be sitting there but his heir was now fast asleep in the House of Adoration, Pharaoh's private quarters.

'All hail!' the priest intoned, hands extended. 'The King of Upper and Lower Egypt, speaker of truth, beloved of Ra, the golden Horus, lord of the diadem, lord of the cobra! The great silver hawk who protects Egypt with his wings!' the priest continued, despite the fact that he was talking of a boy too young to hold a sword, never mind go to war. 'Strong bull against the miserable Ethiopians! His hooves trample the Libyans!'

On and on went the divine paean of praise. Hatusu stifled a yawn. Eventually the priest finished his psalm and withdrew. Rahimere clapped his hands and leaned forward, his eyes smiling a welcome.

'We have business before the royal circle, this council is in session.' He looked to his right at Bayletos the chief scribe. 'The matters before us are secret.'

Hatusu schooled her features. First, there were the usual reports about the state of crops, visiting envoys from abroad; silver and gold ingots in the House of Silver, the health of Pharaoh's sisters. Only when Senenmut gave a short and incisive report on the royal tombs did Hatusu look up. The young man's voice was soft but clear. He did not look at Rahimere but down at the table. Hatusu gripped her hands in pleasure. She could feel it deep in her breast. Here was a man the Grand Vizier had not bought. Omendap, strangely silent since the death of Pharaoh, then delivered a short, pithy report on the deployment of troops and the state of fortifications on the borders, along the Nile and near the First Cataract. He spoke in short, abrupt sentences. Hatusu's stomach tingled. Omendap painted a dire picture. Spies and scouts were reporting movements along Egypt's borders. In the Red Lands, the great wastes to Egypt's east and west, the Libyans could be massing troops. From the southeast scouts were reporting stories told by desert wanderers, how the Ethiopian tribes had heard of Pharaoh's death and were openly advising all and sundry among the sand dwellers to ignore Egyptian border patrols and customs posts. If there was no Pharaoh, they agreed, no tribute should be paid. Finally, beyond the Horus road, which ran through Sinai to Canaan, Egypt's great rivals, the Mitanni, watched and waited.

'It is important,' Omendap concluded, 'that this council name a Regent who acts in the name of Pharaoh.'

'Let me march!' Ipuwer, commander in charge of the Horus regiment, struck the table with his fist. 'Let us choose our foe! Let us bring our enemies back to Thebes where their heads can be smashed and their bodies hung from the walls as a warning to all!'

'Against whom should we march?' Omendap replied. 'Libyans? They have done no wrong. The Nubians? They may plot mischief but they are quiet. How do we know that all our enemies are not in one great secret coalition? That they are not waiting for us to lash out? They will take that as a sign of weakness as well as a pretext for war.' His words created a chill.

Ipuwer stirred restlessly on his chair.

'Two matters must be addressed,' Omendap continued remorselessly. 'The death of Pharaoh is a mystery and that must be clarified. Secondly, a Regent must be named.'

He glanced across at Sethos. The royal prosecutor looked quickly at Hatusu who smiled sympathetically.

'Well?' Rahimere glanced at Hatusu, malice glittering in his eyes. 'How is the case going against Captain Meneloto?'

'It is not,' Sethos replied tersely. 'Everyone here knows what happened in the Hall of Two Truths. Amerotke, the chief judge, instead of solving the mystery, created more. He has adjourned the case until tomorrow morning.'

Hatusu sat and listened as Sethos gave a short description of what had happened in the court. The royal prosecutor did not look at her and Hatusu gripped the table with her hands. There was silence after Sethos had finished. Rahimere will strike now, she thought. The Chief Vizier had picked up his fly whisk and was tapping it against his cheek.

'Was this wise?' he simpered.

'Was what wise?' His sycophant and placeman, Bayletos, chief scribe of the House of Silver, spoke up.

Rahimere's crooked face broke into a smile and his eyes, lizard-like, slipped towards Hatusu.

'Divine Pharaoh has travelled to the far horizon,' the Vizier declared. 'His going has caused us grief and anguish. The citizens of Thebes cover themselves in dust, sprinkle ashes on their heads. Lamentations are heard as far north as the Delta and south beyond the First Cataract. Yet, he has gone! Why investigate the reason for his going? A viper struck his heel. That was the will of the gods!'

Hatusu remained silent. She would not tell them what she had been instructed to do. The person writing those blackmail letters had clearly stipulated how Pharaoh's death must be portrayed. She could not forget that terrible morning when her husband had collapsed in front of the great statue of Amun-Ra. How his body had been taken into a side chapel. While mourning there, she had found another letter addressed to her in the hieratic hand. It laid down stark instructions on what was to happen. What choice had she but to obey? Hatusu's flesh prickled with cold. The blackmailer must be here, one of these men. Rahimere himself? It must be a member of the royal circle. Hatusu had thought she could discover it herself. Hadn't the letters arrived before her husband's return? There again, most of the royal circle had been sent on in advance to Thebes, well ahead of Pharaoh's arrival.

'My lady?'

Hatusu's head came up. She wished the trickle of sweat down her forehead had not appeared but she dare not raise her hand and rub it away.

'I beg your pardon, my lord Vizier. I was lost in sweet memories of my dead husband.'

Hatusu was pleased when some of the army commanders nodded wisely, a look of distaste in their faces. Perhaps Rahimere had overstepped the mark? After all, she was the grieving widow. Her husband, divine Pharaoh, had died in mysterious circumstances! She had every right to order such an investigation.

'My lady.' Rahimere pressed his point. His lizard eyes blinked as they always did when he was sarcastic. 'Do you think it was wise to open this matter for the gossips in the marketplace? Is it true, my lord Sethos, that as royal prosecutor you were most reluctant to take the case up? Did you not advise as much?'

'My lord Vizier.' Senenmut raised his right hand. 'My lord Vizier, if the lady Hatusu, if her highness,' he emphasised the last word, 'wishes to investigate this matter then let it be so. No one here has spoken against it.

No one here raised an objection. The lord Amerotke is well known as a man of integrity. There is a mystery behind divine Pharaoh's death and consequently it should be investigated.'

'I agree,' Sethos put in. 'I advised her highness not to pursue the case as a matter of state. However, as a Queen who demands justice . . .'

His words created a murmur of approval. Hatusu relaxed. Rahimere, however, refused to give up the advantage. He's circling like a jackal, Hatusu thought. He wants the regency and he's determined to control this council. He's determined to prove I'm empty-headed, feckless! Sweep me into the House of Seclusion! Grasp young Tuthmosis by the shoulder and proclaim himself as Pharaoh's Regent. And how long would she survive in the House of Seclusion, bereft of money, power, influence?

Rahimere now opened the silver-lined leather bag he carried, as did all the council, where private papers and documents could be stored.

'I have heard Omendap's opinion about the state of our borders,' Rahimere said. 'And the reports we have from our spies. This is the reason for this meeting. However, the news is more ominous. I have, how can I put it?' He smiled and drew out a document. 'Proof that the princes of Libya and Ethiopia are considering an alliance against Egypt.'

'That's all to the good.' Senenmut spoke up, an impudent tone in his voice. 'But, my lord Vizier, to whom may the gods grant health, wealth and prosperity! We were, I believe, discussing my lord Sethos' report on the case before my lord Amerotke in the Hall of Two Truths.'

Hatusu glanced sideways. Sethos was grinning, head down. Some of the generals had covered their faces with their hands. Rahimere had been so malicious, so eager to strike, he had in fact offered great insult to the royal prosecutor, passing from one business to another without a by-your-leave. Rahimere's face mottled with fury. He breathed heavily, gestured with his hands that his own placemen did not get drawn into this quarrel.

'My apologies, my lord Sethos, what do you advise?'

'That we let justice take its course,' Sethos replied airily. 'Let my lord Amerotke issue his judgement. We will have to await that.' Sethos spread out his fingers on the small table in front of him. He gazed across at the painted wall frieze, a glorious scene in blue, green and gold depicting the victories of Egypt's armies over the sea people. 'May I add that I suggest my lord Amerotke be invited to join the royal circle. He is, as you know, a man of integrity and wisdom. He may well ask questions which, perhaps, would be better answered here than in the Hall of Two Truths. Moreover,' Sethos added slyly, 'we might need his good counsel and wisdom in the months ahead.'

'Be that as it may,' Rahimere snapped. 'The hour grows late.' He tapped the piece of parchment. 'We shall adjourn for a while and then discuss the matter in hand. We must send an army south as far as the First Cataract.'

'Why?' Omendap asked.

'Because the attack will come from there,' Rahimere continued. 'We must decide which troops, which members of the royal circle attend the commander-in-chief.' His gaze brushed Hatusu. 'Who will lead Pharaoh's armies?'

The Grand Vizier put down his fly whisk.

'I have brought some wine, the finest of Moeretia. Let us drink that and return to these discussions.'

The meeting was adjourned. People rolled up the papyrus parchments, putting them into the small leather bags on the back of their chairs. Hatusu polished the table with her hand. The red henna on her fingernails gleamed in the light from the oil lamps and torches. So red, so liquid, it looked as if she had steeped the tips of her fingers in blood. If necessary, she thought, I'll do that. They treat me like some pet cat but claws I have and claws I'll use.

She knew what Rahimere was going to recommend. He would have Omendap and some of the other generals out of Thebes: send the crack regiments south. Rahimere would also advise that she should go with them, for that was always the case. If Pharaoh the god did not go, because of his youth, then why not the widow of the god Tuthmosis? The troops would demand that. Hadn't her own grandmother marched against the Libyans? And, while Hatusu was gone, Rahimere would plot. Worse still, Hatusu thought as she tapped her fingers, what if the army was not victorious? Would she come back to Thebes to an empty house? Or worse? Imprisonment in some chamber? Her mind teemed. She couldn't object. She couldn't recommend Rahimere to go: he was Grand Vizier. His task would be to stay at home and hold the reins of government.

'My lady?'

Hatusu glanced up. The rest of the royal circle had risen. Sethos, talking to two of the scribes, was staring at her strangely. The doors had been thrown open to allow clerks and servants in. She glanced to her left. Senenmut was standing next to her holding two brimming glass goblets.

'My lady, you still grieve?'

Hatusu took the goblet from his hand.

'My lady still grieves,' she answered but she smiled at Senenmut with her eyes. 'I thank you for your support.'

'If you don't feel well,' Senenmut raised his voice, 'then, my lady, I'd take the night air, it will refresh you.'

Cradling the goblet between her hands, Hatusu followed Senenmut out on to the balcony. The air was rich with the perfume from the flowers below. It brought back bittersweet memories of her shy husband, Tuthmosis. How he would love to take her walking there, discussing some project or wondering about religion. Yes, Tuthmosis always thought about the gods, about their nature and their function. She used to listen to him with half an ear, but Senenmut? She would watch this man intently.

'A soft, balmy night,' he began. 'One dedicated to the goddess Hathor.'

'The goddess of love,' Hatusu replied, not turning her head. 'Well, she's a goddess I've not paid much homage to.' She glanced sly-eyed. 'At least, not for the moment.'

'And that is wise, my lady. This is the season of the hyena, the year of the locust.' Senenmut was talking fast. 'Out beyond the borders, in the Red Lands, Egypt's enemies prepare. More dangerous are the snakes coiled and ready in your own house.'

Hatusu looked at him quickly. Did he know anything about what was going on? Was Senenmut the blackmailer?

'You talk of snakes.' Her voice was cold.

'That is appropriate, your highness.' Senenmut deliberately enhanced her title. He stepped closer. 'Your highness,' he whispered hoarsely. 'You must trust me.'

'Why?'

'Because you can trust no one else.'

'Has Rahimere bribed you?'

'He tried to.'

'And why did you refuse?'

'For three reasons, my lady. Firstly, I do not like him. Secondly, I like you. And, thirdly, the bribe wasn't big enough.'

Hatusu burst out laughing. 'So, tell the truth.' She moved her wine cup from one hand to another, her fingers brushing his. 'Just how can I bribe you?'

'With nothing, my lady. But, if I succeed, with everything.'

'Everything?' Hatusu teased. She smiled up at him from under half-closed lids. She felt a flush of excitement. Here was a man who wanted her; desperately wanted her and was prepared to play for the highest stakes. 'So, tell me, my clever overseer of works, what is Rahimere really going to recommend?'

'He's going to recommend an army be sent south. Omendap will lead it.'

'Were you with my husband at Sakkara?'

Senenmut shook his head. 'What would an overseer of royal works have to do with the army?'

'But you were a soldier once. A captain in the chariot squadrons, I understand?' She looked at him from head to toe, deliberately imitating a woman studying a wrestler before she lays a wager. 'Your wrists are strong, your legs firm, your chest broad and you have no fear.'

'I am the overseer of Pharaoh's works,' Senenmut continued drily. 'As I have said, Rahimere will recommend the army move south and you go with it.'

'I guessed that already.'

'You must not refuse.' Senenmut now drew closer, staring over her head as if discussing something of little importance. 'Go with the army,' he urged. 'You'll be safe there. Stay in Thebes and you'll die. I will go with you.'

'And if I fail?'

'Then I fail with you.'

'And if I win?' Hatusu teased.

'Then, my lady, I gain everything.'

'And you'll wait till then?'

His clever eyes crinkled in amusement.

'My lady, that's a matter for you. Yet heed my advice. If you can, bring this matter before the lord Amerotke to a close. Bury it, forget it.' His eyes grew puzzled. 'Only the gods know why you began the business in the first place!'

Senenmut was about to continue when the clerks announced the councillors must retake their seats. They went back inside and the doors were closed. Hatusu started. An oil lamp had fallen from its niche, causing a little chaos and some nervous laughter. The flame caught one of the rugs but a quick-thinking servant stamped the flame out. The oil lamp was replaced. A psalm was chanted to divine Pharaoh. The officiating priest had scarcely withdrawn when there was the most heartrending scream. Hatusu whirled round. The commander Ipuwer was on his feet staring in horror at his arm. On the table before him lay his writing bag, documents spilling out. Hatusu, appalled, saw the viper curling among the papyrus sheets.

Dagger out, General Omendap lunged at the snake. He missed. The snake struck again, this time taking Ipuwer in the thigh. Omendap was on his feet lashing out with the dagger. The council chamber was in uproar. The doors were thrown open, soldiers rushed in. Ipuwer had collapsed to the floor. Members of his regiment were around him. Omendap had killed the snake, picked it up with his dagger and hurled it down the council chamber. They watched helplessly as Ipuwer entered his death throes, body shaking as the venom sped through his blood. Eventually he gave a strangled cry, a final convulsion, then his head fell sideways, eyes glazed, mouth drooling.

'Have him taken out!' Omendap ordered. 'The news of his death, leave that to me!'

Hatusu sat rigid as a stone. Ipuwer's sudden death brought back memories of those terrible convulsions of her husband before the statue of Amun-Ra! The priests taking his corpse into a small side chapel and the dreadful events which had followed.

Rahimere had the chamber cleared. The rest took their seats once more. No one spoke but everyone moved gingerly; cloaks, bags, belongings were carefully searched with the point of a dagger, walking sticks or fly whisks.

'A terrible accident,' Bayletos intoned.

'Accident!' Senenmut scoffed. 'My lords, my lady Hatusu, do you

81

think that was an accident? Did Commander Ipuwer put a viper in his sack? If he did, why was it not there at the beginning of this meeting?'

'Ipuwer was murdered,' Sethos declared. 'Someone put that viper there. An assassin who intends to kill and kill again! Divine Pharaoh's journey to the far horizon will not be alone!'

'I agree.' Rahimere's hard eyes studied Hatusu. 'Murder has been done and I call upon the god Thoth, the speaker of truth, to unmask this assassin and bring him,' he paused, 'or her, to merited destruction!'

Wadjet: guardian goddess, often depicted as a cobra.

CHAPTER 6

The assassins, the Amemets or devourers, sat in a circle in the small palm grove near the temple of Hathor, a deserted, secluded spot. Their leader had felt confident enough to light a small fire against the evening chill. The city had fallen silent. Only the occasional faint cry of a guard or sentry was carried on the night breeze. Sometimes from the river they heard the roar of a hippopotamus or the sudden flights of birds from the papyrus thickets. The air was pungent with the sweet smell of rottenness from the Nile. The river was beginning to fall, leaving vast areas of rich mud which dried in the sun and, baked hard at night, gave off its own strange perfume. The Amemets were confident. Their leader had told them exactly what they were going to do. Nothing dangerous, just the removal of a few guards, followed by the abduction and execution of Captain Meneloto.

The Amemets whiled their time away, telling stories until one of them had produced their pet cat, a huge, horn-eared, half-wild animal they regarded as their amulet, their mascot for good luck. Someone else had captured a scorpion, carefully imprisoned in a piece of hardened papyrus. A small circle of fire was created. The scorpion was placed in its centre and the cat put down. Wagers were laid and taken and one of the Amemets began the usual count. The wager was to see how long it would take the cat to kill the scorpion. The animal moved quickly, trained to kill and be rewarded with choice pieces of meat. It delicately avoided the small ring of burning charcoal, hit the scorpion on the side, turned it over and, with one swipe of a powerful paw, removed the poisoned tail before crunching the rest in its jaws. A sigh went round the onlookers. The cat had moved quickly and only a few had won. The rest forfeited their hard-earned debens of copper until the next time.

'A true killer,' the Amemet leader declared.

He picked up the cat, held it to him and stared up at the sky. He had received his orders. They had come as secretly and mysteriously as the last. Yet the gold had been paid; whoever was hiding him must be a great Egyptian lord.

'It's time, yes, it's time,' he said softly.

He handed the cat to his lieutenant. The fire was quickly doused. The Amemets donned their black cloaks, hiding their faces as if they were sand wanderers. They drew their daggers and padded quietly as the cat they worshipped across the open space and up an alleyway.

Meneloto's town house was a small, two-storeyed building surrounded by a garden and a curtain wall. The guard in front was fast asleep on the cheap beer he had drunk. He was disposed of immediately, his throat sliced from ear to ear. The soldier guarding the postern gate at the back was more alert. However, before he could cry out, the Amemets were on him, stifling his mouth, pushing him down to the earth, their daggers moving in and out until his body stopped jerking. Hands covered in his hot blood, the Amemets scaled the wall and flowed like a wave of darkness across the moonlit garden. Two more guards were killed. The seal on the side door was broken, the lock forced. A sleepy-eyed officer staggered round a corner into a hail of arrows. He died immediately. The Amemet leader scurried ahead. The rest of his followers dispersed, intent on stealing anything valuable. A few minutes later Meneloto, still drowsy from a heavy sleep, was quickly forced to dress, pushed down the stairs and out into the garden. The night air revived him; shadowy figures gathered round. Meneloto grasped the cloak pushed into his hands and glanced across the garden: in the corner the buttress was decayed. If he reached it, he could climb over the wall and hide in the warren of alleyways beyond.

'You are to come with us,' a voice grated.

'Where?'

'To a safe place!'

Meneloto realised he was going to be killed; he swung the cloak round as if to put it across his shoulders but threw it at his captors. At the same time he burst into a run, knocking aside the hands that grabbed out. He reached the wall and was up and over before the first arrows whirred above his head.

*   *   *

Amerotke sat in the chair of judgement in the Hall of Two Truths and stared in disbelief at Sethos.

'Captain Meneloto has escaped?'

'Apparently.' The royal prosecutor spread his hands. 'Certainly with the support of others. The soldiers guarding him were killed.'

Amerotke looked down at the floor. He ignored the murmur of consternation from the scribes and witnesses. The life of Thebes, he reflected, was like the Nile. It swirled and changed. Even as he walked into the city this morning, Shufoy loudly complaining behind him, Amerotke had noticed the change. A tension hung in the air. The guards at the gate had been doubled. Trade in the marketplace was not as brisk at it should have been. Crowds clustered round the beer shops and wine booths. Shufoy had brought him the gossip: how at the meeting of the royal circle in the House of a Million Years, the popular and ambitious Ipuwer, commander of the Horus regiment, had been bitten by a snake. Publicly, it was proclaimed as an accident; privately, people whispered murder and drew similarities between the commander's death and that of divine Pharaoh.

On the one hand Amerotke felt relieved by Meneloto's escape, on the other angry that his time had been wasted and justice had been thwarted. He had reached his decision, the only logical conclusion. Divine Pharaoh may have been bitten and killed by a viper but that snake was not the one whose desiccated corpse lay on the floor before him. Somehow or other he must have been bitten by another viper. If that was the case? Amerotke sucked on his teeth. Was it an accident or was it murder?

'These matters should be adjourned.' Khemut, his chief scribe, spoke up. 'My lord Amerotke, the prisoner has gone, so a judgement cannot be delivered.'

Amerotke touched the pectoral of Ma'at. He felt a spurt of anger. Justice was Pharaoh's, a tool of the gods, not the plaything of a faction in the royal circle.

'Judgement can be deferred,' Amerotke declared hotly. 'But I, as chief judge in the Hall of Two Truths, have the right to comment on the case before me. There are matters here which deeply concern me.'

The court fell silent. Amerotke placed his hand on his knees. Keeping his head rigid, he regarded a symbol painted on the far wall, the all-seeing eye of Horus.

'First,' he began, 'I find it difficult to believe that Pharaoh's death is not connected to the blasphemous and sacrilegious desecration of his tomb which took place as divine Pharaoh journeyed down the Nile.'

A loud sigh greeted his words, a stir of excitement.

'Secondly, I find it difficult to believe,' Amerotke continued remorselessly, 'that Pharaoh's death was caused by the viper found on the *Glory of Ra*. Thirdly, I accept the opinion of witnesses, both those produced by the eyes and ears of Pharaoh as well as those by the now-absent Meneloto. All spoke the truth, as they saw it. However, in the end, divine Pharaoh's death conceals a dark mystery.'

Sethos leaned forward as if to interrupt but Amerotke made a cutting movement with his hand.

'Judgement will not be given. The case will be adjourned.'

Amerotke did not move from his judgement chair. Sethos sighed in exasperation and clambered to his feet. He bowed to the judge then to the shrine and padded quietly out of the Hall of Two Truths. Amerotke snapped his fingers, indicating the court would remain in session and other cases would be heard. Sethos would have loved to take him aside and discuss what he had said but Amerotke was determined not to be drawn into the subtle intrigues of the royal circle. Amerotke would also have liked to comment on Commander Ipuwer's death but he had the good sense to bite his tongue. If he was placed on oath for his opinion, then he would give it. He suspected divine Pharaoh had been murdered and Commander Ipuwer's death was connected to it. And who had freed Meneloto? Was it the royal circle? Had some order been passed down that this embarrassing trial be brought to a sudden conclusion, that the matter be brushed aside and quickly forgotten? Or had Meneloto, fearful that he might not receive true justice, conspired with friends to effect his escape?

Amerotke accepted the small cup of watered wine Prenhoe offered. He sipped and handed it back, then looked at the scribes, still restless and fidgeting.

'The court is still in session,' Amerotke announced. 'Bring in the next case!'

The scribes would always remember that morning. Chief judge Amerotke moved quickly but ruthlessly. A woman who had killed her child was ordered to carry that child and sit in the marketplace for seven days in public view. Five drunkards who had urinated in the sacred pool of the temple of Hathor, the goddess of love, were summarily dealt with and taken down to the House of Darkness to be stripped and flogged. A merchant who had sold putrid meat, causing the death of two of his customers, received a heavy fine and banishment from the city markets for a year and a day. By noon Amerotke believed that he had emphasised divine Pharaoh's justice enough. The court was adjourned. He rose from his judgement chair, tense and angry, and walked into the small side chapel. He took off the pectoral of Ma'at but started as a figure stepped out of the darkness. The man was dressed like a priest. Amerotke noticed the strength of his wrists, the arrogant tilt of his head.

'You have no right to be here.' He turned away.

'Come, come, my lord Amerotke, is your memory fading?'

Amerotke turned and smiled. 'You've put on a little weight, my lord Senenmut, but those eyes and that voice. How can I forget them?'

They clasped hands.

'However, this is my chamber, my private chapel,' Amerotke reminded him.

'That's why I'm here,' Senenmut replied. 'My lord Amerotke, I bring greetings from her highness the lady Hatusu, widow of divine Pharaoh.'

'I know who the lady Hatusu is!'

Senenmut pushed a small scroll of papyrus into his hand. Amerotke unrolled it. He noticed the cartouche sealed at the bottom and kissed it. The summons was short and succinct.

'Lord Amerotke and the lady Norfret are invited to a banquet at the royal palace this evening where lord Amerotke will receive the official ring and seal, tokens of his promotion to membership of the royal circle.'

'A surprising honour.' Amerotke raised his head but Senenmut had gone.

* * *

The sun was slipping into the west, bathing the city with its dying rays, when Amerotke, Norfret in the chariot beside him, made his way down to the House of a Million Years on the banks of the Nile. Norfret had been quietly pleased by the great honour bestowed on her husband.

'You must take it,' she had urged, grasping him by the hand. 'Whether you like it or not, Amerotke, you are caught up in the politics of the court.'

'They want to shut my mouth,' Amerotke had replied tersely. 'To silence or buy me. Meneloto's escape, not to mention Commander Ipuwer's sudden death, is enough embarrassment for one day.'

'Neither of these things has anything to do with you. Meneloto was a capable soldier. He has escaped and can take care of himself.'

He had studied her face for any sign of upset or consternation. Norfret had gazed icily back.

'You know the truth,' she had added firmly. 'The gods know the truth. If we know the truth, Amerotke, why care what others say?'

In the end, as always, she had her way. Amerotke was flattered and gratified by his wife's quiet ambition. True, Norfret admitted, she loved her visits to court, the dinner parties where she could listen to the gossip, an occasion not to be missed. Amerotke had kissed her on the forehead.

'You remind me of a beautiful shadow,' he had declared, grasping her hands.

'A shadow!' she had mocked and, putting her lovely arms round his neck, stood on tiptoe and kissed him on his nose.

'You like to go on such occasions, but not to be seen. You love to sit, listen and watch.'

'That's how I found you.'

'And that's how I found you. Remember? We spent that evening watching each other.'

Norfret had laughed and hurried away, calling out over her shoulder that he should dress in his finest.

Amerotke, the reins of the chariot wrapped round his wrist, glanced sideways. He'd put on a new pleated robe, and his ring of office; as always, he refused to wear a wig. He recalled how, when he had served in the chariot squadron, the soldiers used to ridicule the popinjay officers who tried to maintain the height of fashion even when patrolling the Red

Lands. Norfret, however, as usual looked as lovely as the night. She was dressed in a spotless robe of goffered linen, her long black wig shot through with strands of gold and silver. Rings of amethyst hung from her ear lobes, a beautiful gorget of lapis lazuli circled her throat. She was busy leaning over, talking to Shufoy who followed the chariot, a parasol in one hand, his walking cane in the other.

'You are welcome to join us, Shufoy,' she teased. 'There is room here.' She tapped the wooden wickerwork. 'It's not a war chariot so the horses are geldings without a spot of fire in them.'

'I don't like chariots,' the dwarf answered. 'I don't like feasts and banquets. People always stare at my face and ask ridiculous questions like, "Where has your nose gone?" I always want to reply, "Up your bum!"'

Norfret laughed and turned away.

Amerotke grabbed the reins. He watched the crimson plumes of his horses rise and fall and looked about him. The quayside and the banks of the Nile were always busy, whatever the hour. Beer shops were open. The alleyways thronged with sailors and soldiers visiting the pleasure houses or staggering about, cups in their hands, eyeing the girls and shouting good-natured abuse at each other. Of course they glimpsed Norfret but one look at Amerotke, not to mention the two soldiers who were escorting him down to the palace, and they went looking for easier prey.

A scorpionman ran up, a self-confessed magician, offering amulets and magic sticks against ill-fortune. Shufoy, nimble as a monkey, drove him off.

At last they reached the causeway which led into the palace. The crowds, eager to see the comings and goings, thronged here, held back by archers and foot soldiers from the Isis regiment. Amerotke rattled the reins and the horses moved a little faster. They swept through the gates and into the broad, well-watered gardens of the palace, a beautiful paradise with shaded walks, ornamental pools and great open lawns where trained gazelles and sheep grazed. The guards led them round. Amerotke helped Norfret out of the chariot, while issuing instructions to the grooms to unhitch the horses, dry them off and feed them before they were stabled. They were escorted through the main door, past huge paintings on the walls depicting the glories of Pharaohs in battle, along the hall of columns while squads of soldiers guarded the entrance to the House of Adoration, the private quarters of the young Pharaoh. At last they reached the great banqueting hall, a great lofty chamber where the columns were painted dark red, their capitals shaped like golden lotus buds. Pure alabaster lamps, painted different colours, provided soft light which shimmered across the frescoes which adorned the walls: trees, beautiful birds of plumage, flowers, butterflies all drawn on the smooth plaster in a gorgeous array of colours. Above them the rafters were painted with hieroglyphics which promised health, life and prosperity to those who congregated below.

Amerotke gazed round at the throng of bare-shouldered women and dark, heavily wigged men. He recognised some: Sethos, Rahimere, General Omendap. As each caught his eye they nodded imperceptibly and turned back to their companions. Servant girls, wearing practically nothing except wisps of fabric about their loins, moved round the guests offering a lotus flower in welcome as well as small dishes of dainties and jewelled cups of wine or beer. Norfret took one of these cups and walked away to greet an acquaintance. Amerotke stayed near the doorway. The babble of conversation died as the far doors swung open and Hatusu entered the room. Amerotke was surprised at how Hatusu had changed during the period of mourning since her husband's death. He had always regarded her as a woman of the shadows, but now she walked majestically, hands clasped before her, a vision of beauty in a clinging robe of almost transparent linen. Her long, glossy wig shimmered with oil and was bound round her forehead by a coronet displaying the vulture goddess, a reminder to all that she was a Queen of Egypt. A silver pectoral about her neck bore the same design, while broad gold bands, ornamented with a spitting cobra, clasped her wrists. Her finger and toenails were dyed a rich henna and those dark sloe eyes were made even larger, more elongated, by the striking green-blue eye paint she had applied.

She caught Amerotke's stare and smiled faintly. Others came up but she politely gestured with her fingers and came across to greet him. On her bare left shoulder a tattoo had been delicately drawn, depicting Sekhmet, the lion goddess, the wreaker of vengeance. She dresses as a princess, Amerotke thought, but she gives a warning like a warrior. She stopped before him and extended her hand. Amerotke would have gone down on one knee as courtesy dictated but Hatusu shook her head slightly, her eyes full of impish good humour.

'My lord Amerotke.' The voice was low, rather deep. 'How many years is it now? Ten, twelve, since you left my father's court?'

'I believe twelve, my lady.'

'Then welcome back to it.'

Amerotke gazed over her shoulder. The other officials, commanders and scribes pretended to be locked in deep conversation but they were watching intently. Further down the hall, near a column, Sethos was holding Norfret's hand, chattering to her, making some joke. Norfret's head came back and her laugh echoed around the chamber.

'I watched you arrive,' Hatusu continued. 'The lady Norfret is as beautiful as ever.'

'In which case, beauty beheld beauty,' Amerotke replied.

Hatusu sighed. Amerotke wondered if she was laughing at him, as her carmine-painted lips tightened. She lowered her head flirtatiously.

'You'll never make a courtier, Amerotke. Your flattery is so obvious.'

'I am a judge,' Amerotke replied. 'Flattery comes hard.'

'With you it always did, Amerotke.' She gazed at him softly. 'Are you still madly in love with the lady Norfret? I saw you standing here, just glowering at everyone.' She laughed behind her hand. 'Ah, Senenmut.'

The overseer of the royal works came up. Amerotke was surprised how familiar he was, standing beside Hatusu as if he were a member of the royal kin, a prince of the palace. Amerotke clasped the outstretched hand.

'I am sorry,' Senenmut apologised, 'that I did not stay long this morning. I thought you might refuse and that would be embarrassing for everyone.'

He produced a small embroidered leather pouch. Hatusu opened it and shook the gold ring into the palm of her hand then, grasping Amerotke's finger, slipped the ring on. Amerotke studied it. The broad band of gold was engraved with hieroglyphics which proclaimed to the world that he was now one of 'Pharaoh's friends', a member of the royal circle with a seat on the council and a duty to advise Pharaoh.

'It's not a bribe,' Hatusu whispered, her eyes cold and hard. 'I need you, Amerotke. I need your powers of reflection, your good counsel. And, I'll be honest, your commonsense.'

Amerotke wanted to ask her why but the servants were already setting out the cushions and matting before the small tables arranged for the royal supper. Hatusu touched Amerotke lightly on the hand and moved away.

Slave girls came up. One put a wreath of flowers round his neck. Another offered him a cake of perfume. Amerotke refused this but those who wore wigs took the cakes and placed them on top. In a little while it would grow hot and these would melt and drench their heads in the most fragrant of smells. As was customary, the men sat at one side of the hall, the women at the other. Cups of wine were circulated as the feasting began. Dishes of roast beef, chicken, goose, dark pigeon and many varieties of bread cut in different shapes were served. Wine jars, set up in metal stands, each marked as a vintage year, were opened and servants ensured the jewelled bronze cups were regularly filled. Napkins and finger bowls were brought. Next to Amerotke sat General Omendap. He turned, dipping his fingers in a bowl, and winked at Amerotke.

'Welcome to the royal circle,' he murmured.

Amerotke smiled back. He had met the general on a number of occasions, and knew him to be a good, honest man, stout-bodied, fleshy-faced but with a bluff good humour which hid a sharp brain and keen wits. A brave warrior, Omendap wore round his neck the golden lotus given to him by Pharaoh for courage in battle. Omendap leaned closer.

'We have all heard your judgement about poor Meneloto.' He checked to ensure no servants could hear. 'You spoke the truth! The case should never have been brought.'

'So why was it?' Amerotke asked. 'Wasn't it discussed in the royal circle?'

'The wife of the god insisted!' Omendap turned and stared across the chamber to where Hatusu sat on a small throne-like stool above the other women. 'I thought she had more sense than that. Anyway, you'll soon sense the politics of the royal circle. Basically, there are two factions.' Omendap took his wine cup and slurped from it. 'Rahimere.' He gestured down the table to where the Vizier, in all his jewelled splendour, sat talking to the chief scribe Bayletos. 'He wants to be Regent and so does Hatusu.'

'And who will win?'

'Probably Rahimere. He controls the treasury, the chancery and the temple of Amun-Ra.'

'And the lady Hatusu?'

'She has three supporters. Sethos, Senenmut and now the lord Amerotke.'

'I belong to no faction.'

'Don't you?' Omendap grinned. 'You accepted her invitation and took that ring. We are all part of the dance now.'

'And you?' Amerotke gestured with his cup at the military commanders.

'We haven't made our minds up. We are soldiers, we take orders. We've heard the rumours in the marketplace. Pharaoh's dead, gone into the blessed west, his successor is a boy, the council is divided. The jackals think the guard dogs are gone so they'll try to rob the hen coop.'

'And whom will you support?'

Omendap moved the cushions a bit closer.

'My sympathies are with the lady Hatusu. She has the blood of Tuthmosis in her and I don't like Rahimere. But you know us soldiers. Our first rule is never give battle when you know you are bound to lose. So, drink up.' He clinked his cup against Amerotke's. 'And let's pray for more fortunate days.'

Amerotke turned back to his food. He was trying to see where Norfret sat when a messenger entered carrying a small chest bound with copper bands. He knelt at the entrance to the banqueting chamber waiting to be noticed. Rahimere's steward, standing behind his master's chair, beckoned the man forward.

'What is it?' Rahimere looked up.

'A present, my lord. From Amenhotep.'

The Grand Vizier's lip curled. Amenhotep was a chantry priest, chaplain to the dead Pharaoh Tuthmosis II.

'Amenhotep should be here. As a priest in the temple of Horus, it is his duty to attend to the royal circle.'

Rahimere was making his power felt and the banqueting hall fell silent. An invitation to such a meal was really a royal summons and only sickness or some serious calamity should prevent attendance. Amerotke was surprised. He had met Amenhotep a number of times: a busy, pompous little man full of his own importance. It was most unlike him to avoid such an occasion.

'Perhaps it's a peace offering,' the chief scribe joked. 'A fitting apology, my lord, for his non-attendance at our meetings.'

Rahimere shrugged and gestured at the servant to draw closer. Amerotke looked over his shoulder. Hatusu sat pale-faced, her eyes blazing with fury. The present really should be given to her. She was the host, the lord of this palace, but Rahimere's intervention was a public snub and an eloquent reminder that he held the reins of power. The servant brought the chest forward.

'It was delivered, my lord,' he explained, 'by a man cloaked in black.'

Amerotke dropped the piece of goose he had been nibbling on. The reference to black robes stirred memories. In reports which had come before the court, Amerotke had learned about the guild of assassins, the devourers, professional killers. Time and again in criminal cases, references had been made to this bloodthirsty band who worshipped a ferocious feline goddess Mafdet, and were garbed in black from head to toe.

'I accept the gift.' Rahimere clapped his hands in irritation. 'Open the chest!'

The seals were broken, the lid thrown back. Amerotke turned to say something to his companion when he heard the scream. The servant had taken the gift out of the chest, holding it up like a man in a dream. The blood still dripped from the neck. The guests stared in horror at the severed head of the priest Amenhotep.

Sekhmet: the lion goddess; the destroyer.

CHAPTER 7

The banquet ended in chaos. Two ladies fainted. Some of the male guests, covering their mouths with their hands, left the hall for the privies to vomit and purge their stomachs. The head was thrust back into the coffer, guards despatched to find the bearer, but he had long gone. Hatusu, supported by Senenmut and Sethos, imposed order.

'My lords!' Hatusu clapped her hands for silence. 'My lords and ladies, there is little point in continuing these festivities. The banquet is over. The royal circle will meet in the hall of columns!'

Servants came in to take away the dishes and wine jars. Those not members of the council were only too pleased to make a sign against the evil eye and leave the palace. Amerotke arranged for Shufoy to take Norfret back to their house. Omendap kindly volunteered two of his officers to accompany them.

Once she had gone, Amerotke went back into the banqueting hall. The blood-stained chest still lay open on the floor. Amerotke crouched down: the ghastly face stared back, its eyeballs rolled up, the tongue protruding. Amerotke studied the severed neck: the cut had been clean and sheer. He noticed how the skin of the face was puffy and discoloured.

'What are you searching for?'

Hatusu, with Senenmut and Sethos on either side of her, was looking down at him.

'My lady, I suspect Amenhotep was dead when his head was severed. The cut is clean, a professional heavy blow. The messenger who brought this was clothed in black. This is the work of the Amemets, a group of professional assassins.'

'But why kill Amenhotep?'

Senenmut crouched down and peered curiously at the severed head.

99

'That prattling mouth is now quiet,' he declared. 'And those arrogant eyes will never again look at me from head to toe.'

Amerotke glanced quickly at this new right-hand man of the lady Pharaoh: his dislike of the dead priest was apparent. Hatusu lifted one sandalled foot and kicked the chest closed.

'In the Hall of Columns!' she snapped.

The council chamber had been prepared, seats and small tables arranged in an oval. Rahimere was already there, taking the place of precedence. The scribes and priests who supported him flanked him on either side. Hatusu sat where she had the previous evening, Senenmut and Sethos on either side.

Amerotke took the chair nearest to the door. He felt uncomfortable and wished he wasn't there. Despite the wine and the gaiety of the first part of the banquet, the atmosphere in the chamber was oppressive. The hatred and jealousy which seethed there were almost tangible.

The priest hurriedly intoned a psalm, likening the young Pharaoh's face to that of the god Horus. How his hair was as tender as the skies; his left eye the sun in the morning, his right eye the sun in the evening. How the glory of Ra filled his body, providing light and warmth for the people of Egypt. Once the priest left, however, there was no sign of this light and warmth. Hatusu seized the initiative.

'My lords.' She sat so imperiously, her chair seemed like a throne.

Rahimere went to interrupt but she raised her hand.

'My lord Vizier, this is a royal palace: the House of a Million Years. Our glorious Pharaoh is in the House of Adoration. I am his stepmother. So, what do we have here? My husband collapsed in front of the statue of Amun-Ra, bitten by a snake. General Ipuwer died in this chamber, bitten by a snake. And now, during a banquet, the severed head of Amenhotep is sent as a grisly reminder or, perhaps, as a warning to the rest of us?'

'What are you implying?' the chief of the House of Silver whined. 'Three men have died.'

'No,' Senenmut intervened. 'Three men have been murdered.'

'Murdered?' Rahimere cocked his head. 'So you are now saying the death of divine Pharaoh, who has travelled to the blessed west, was no accident?'

'General Ipuwer's certainly wasn't,' Hatusu pointed out. 'And I don't think Amenhotep fell downstairs.'

'My lord Amerotke.' Rahimere beamed down the council chamber. 'We have all heard of your judgement.' He spread beringed hands. 'You established, at least to your own satisfaction, how the viper on board the *Glory of Ra* was not responsible for the death of divine Pharaoh. Now we all know that the divine Pharaoh was carried to the temple on a palanquin where he was met by his lady wife.'

There was a hiss of intaken breath. Senenmut would have leapt to his feet but Hatusu restrained him, one hand on his wrist.

'I did not say,' Amerotke answered quickly, 'that divine Pharaoh was murdered: that was not the case before me. I ruled that the viper which killed Pharaoh was not the one found on the royal barge.'

'But you also talked about the desecration of Pharaoh's tomb?' One of Rahimere's scribes spoke up.

'All of Thebes knows about that,' Amerotke replied. 'I speculated, as I have every right, that someone had a blasphemous grudge against divine Pharaoh.'

'And Commander Ipuwer?' Sethos asked. 'How do you account for his death?'

Amerotke pointed to one of the writing bags hung on the back of a scribe's chair.

'From what I can gather, and this is gossip, the royal circle met here, yes?'

'A fact,' Rahimere replied tersely.

'And Ipuwer brought papers?' Amerotke continued.

'Yes, he did,' Omendap agreed.

'And then the council meeting adjourned?'

'Yes,' Sethos said. 'We collected our papers and put them into the writing bags. What are you saying, Amerotke, that while we all moved around someone took a viper and put it in a writing bag?'

His words created a spiteful giggle from some of the scribes.

'There is a possibility,' one of the priests taunted, 'that the snake crawled into the bag.'

'And there's a possibility,' Amerotke flashed back, 'that snakes can fly!'

He ignored the laughter.

'The solution is quite logical. If a snake crawled into a council chamber, or into a temple, it would be seen. If a viper had been on the palanquin of divine Pharaoh, that viper would have been noticed. If a viper had been on the steps, or in the entrance hall, of the temple of Amun-Ra it would have been seen and destroyed.'

'Yet Pharaoh died of a snake bite,' Rahimere said.

'I agree. But how, when and why is a great mystery. I ask you.' Amerotke swallowed hard. 'Has anyone ever heard of or seen a human being, with crowds around him, being bitten, killed by a snake and the actual serpent never detected?'

Members of the royal circle murmured agreement.

'There's the mystery,' Amerotke insisted. 'And the same is true of General Ipuwer. Did anyone here see the viper which killed him before he put his hand in that bag? Any priest, scribe, soldier, member of the royal circle? My lord Vizier, if I may?'

Rahimere nodded. Amerotke got up and walked round the council chamber. He picked up the writing satchels where the different members had slung them on the backs of their chairs and moved them about, then gestured at Sethos.

'My lord, you are the eyes and ears of Pharaoh. I have changed writing bags around. Could someone, as sharp and observant as you, now tell me which bag belongs to which person?'

Hatusu smiled. Senenmut tapped the top of the table.

'On the night Ipuwer died,' Amerotke said as he returned to his seat, 'during the adjournment, the assassin, that follower of red-haired Seth the god of destruction, brought the viper into the council chamber in a writing bag. My lords, my lady Hatusu, go down to the market. Talk to the scorpionmen, the snake-charmers, those who use such reptiles to astonish the crowd and earn a few debens of copper. A snake can be carried in a bag or a basket. The very movement soothes and calms it. The snake lies curled. If it is recently fed, it is even more passive.'

'Until Ipuwer,' Omendap spoke up, 'put his hand in the bag.'

'Such a movement would rouse the sleeping viper to fury,' Amerotke replied. 'It would strike and strike again. Yet, would anyone notice or remember who had removed a writing bag from one chair to another?

Or, indeed, if the chairs themselves had been moved round? Did anyone here,' he asked carefully, 'ever establish that the viper actually came from Ipuwer's bag?'

'No, no, we did not.' Sethos pointed at Omendap. 'You took care of the corpse and had it transported to the City of the Dead.'

'I also took Ipuwer's papers,' Omendap replied hotly, his fat face now red with embarrassment. 'But, at the time, I did not know what was what.'

'Of course you didn't.' Senenmut spoke up, his voice tinged with sarcasm.

Omendap, supported by his commanders, would immediately have objected. Sethos intervened smoothly, wary of offending the soldiers whose support was so essential for Hatusu.

'My lord Amerotke, you seem to know a lot about snakes?'

'And about murder,' Rahimere added spitefully.

'My lords,' Amerotke replied. 'Death by snake bite is on the lips of everyone in Thebes. I have reflected on the stories. What I now suggest may not be the truth but it has a logic of its own.'

'And your conclusions?' Hatusu asked. 'If, my lord Amerotke, you are correct, that the bags were exchanged?'

'Then, my lady, the assassin must be in this room. You all know that. It was not a soldier or a servant. The bag was brought in here and protected by someone before being hooked over the back of Ipuwer's chair.'

'Continue!' Rahimere ordered.

'We know the assassin must be a member of the royal circle.' Amerotke played with the ring of Ma'at on one of his fingers; he quietly prayed for her help, that his heart and lips would be brushed by her divine feather of truth and wisdom. 'The next question must be why.'

He was about to continue when there was a furious hammering on the door. The captain of the guard entered, a half-caste Nubian dressed in a leather kilt. On the sword belt across his bare chest hung the emblem of the brigade of Osiris. He ignored both Hatusu and Rahimere and bowed towards General Omendap.

'I followed your instructions, sir.'

'And?'

'I sent search parties out along the riverside down near the old temple.

The rest of Amenhotep's corpse was discovered floating in the reeds. The torso was naked except for a loin cloth and the armlet which identified it.'

'There's more?' Omendap demanded.

'Yes sir. One of the soldiers, he trained for a while in the House of Life, was a physician. Well, the body was swollen and discoloured . . .'

'It's a wonder the crocodiles didn't get it!' Bayletos scoffed.

'Amenhotep had been bitten five or six times in the leg by a viper,' the soldier finished.

'Have the corpse and the head taken across river to the Necropolis,' Rahimere ordered. 'Amenhotep was preparing himself a tomb. Tell our overseer in the City of the Dead that Amenhotep's body is to be given proper burial, the cost will be borne by the House of Silver.'

The soldier withdrew.

'The season of the locust,' one of the priests murmured. 'Death and devastation. Sekhmet the destroyer now walks the Kingdom of the Two Lands. Chaos within, threats from without.'

As if to echo his words the sunlight faded, as clouds covered the setting sun. Amerotke wondered if the priest was telling them the truth. He recalled the stories his grandmother had told him. How every day Amun-Ra rode across the sky in his golden chariot. At night the sun god entered the Duat, the underworld where his great adversary the formidable snake god Apep waited to destroy him. Was that about to happen now, Amerotke wondered? Would these murders by viper turn the Two Lands into a theatre of destruction and bloodshed, like those nightmare years when the Theban kings had struggled to drive out the Hyksos?

'We all grieve for Amenhotep.' Hatusu spoke up. 'But, my lord Amerotke, you have not finished?'

'No, no, I haven't.' Amerotke pushed the table from him. 'We have three deaths: two are certainly murders. All apparently caused by a viper. We do not know who is responsible or why they act. So, we must turn to the victims and ask what they have in common?'

'I think that's obvious,' Bayletos drawled.

He waved his fly whisk as if Amerotke's words were irritating, something to be wafted away. If Bayletos hoped to elicit the support of the Grand Vizier with his sarcasm he was disappointed. Rahimere was staring intently down the hall at Amerotke.

'It's obvious that all the victims, including divine Pharaoh, are members of the royal circle,' Rahimere commented. 'But what else?'

'These deaths, and the desecration of Pharaoh's tomb, all coincide at one point. Divine Pharaoh's return after his victories over the sea people on the Nile Delta. His voyage to the Great Sea,' Amerotke continued, 'was victorious and splendid. Tell me, Ipuwer was with him?'

A chorus of agreement greeted his words.

'And so was Amenhotep?'

'What are you implying, Amerotke?'

The judge pulled a face.

'Did something happen on Pharaoh's journey from the Delta to Thebes?'

'Such as?'

'Was there any calamity or crisis? Did divine Pharaoh open his mind about what he planned when he returned to Thebes? Or, there again,' Amerotke looked at Hatusu, 'during his absence, did anything happen here in Thebes? I am only making a conjecture. I haven't proof, even a shred of evidence that anything did.'

A murmur of conversation broke out. Senenmut leaned across, whispering to Sethos, who kept shaking his head. Amerotke noticed that Hatusu looked concerned, even frightened, lost in a reverie, lips moving wordlessly, eyes blinking. He recalled some of the gossip he had heard about Pharaoh's wife as well as his own memories of the royal court.

'Too sweet to be wholesome,' was how a royal page had once described her.

Amerotke recalled the gossip that Hatusu had soon brought her half-brother and husband Tuthmosis II under control. Indeed, according to protocol, Hatusu should have accompanied Tuthmosis to the Delta but, instead, as a mark of confidence, he had left her in charge of Thebes, controlling the government and the city. Was Hatusu responsible for all this? She and that wily Senenmut? Involved in some subtle game to seize power? Control Thebes, the kingdom and the empire beyond its borders?

'I recall nothing untoward happened.' Rahimere thrust out his hands for silence. 'Divine Pharaoh sailed down the Nile in the *Glory of Ra*. He stopped off at Sakkara where he visited the pyramids and the mortuary temple of his ancestors. He made offerings to the gods, slaughtered some of the captive princes and continued his journey.'

'And there was no change in his mood or demeanour?' Amerotke asked.

'Divine Pharaoh was a man who kept his own counsel,' Rahimere pompously stated. 'He was not a man to chatter or gossip. He was pale, sometimes sickly. He said he felt unsteady, but he did suffer from the falling sickness. He was touched by the gods and, in trances, saw visions.'

'My lady.' Amerotke glanced at Hatusu. 'Your highness.' He emphasised her title. 'Did your husband write anything to you in his letters?'

'How Ra had smiled on him,' she said. 'How his victories had gone before him. How he crushed his enemies under his heel and how much he missed his wife and family.'

Amerotke put his head down. Hatusu had told him nothing but reminded the royal circle how close she and divine Pharaoh had been.

'He was silent.' Omendap spoke up. 'He did not suffer from the falling sickness on his journey but he was quiet and withdrawn.' He held up his silver axe of office. 'But, on reflection, something did happen. Remember, we left Pharaoh shortly after the *Glory of Ra* set sail for Thebes.' He pointed down at the scribes and priests. 'Most of you, like me and his excellency the Vizier and my lord Sethos, were sent ahead to prepare for his arrival in Thebes. I cannot recall Pharaoh sacrificing to any of the gods; I remember, on the day he disembarked, some of the royal guard commented on that as well.'

'But that is nonsense!' A priest of Amun sitting next to Bayletos raised his hand.

Rahimere nodded as a sign he could speak.

'I accompanied divine Pharaoh from Sakkara. True, he did not offer sacrifice but, there again, until he reached Thebes, he never left the royal barque.'

'So, he didn't visit any other temples or shrines?' Omendap asked.

'No,' the priest replied. 'He stayed on the ship, remaining in the royal cabin, though sometimes he came out to pray. Ask the guards.

He often went into the poop, had matting and cushions put there and sat cross-legged staring up at the stars, hands extended.' The priest smirked. 'Indeed, divine Pharaoh, on his return to Thebes, was in a constant state of prayer. I do not know what my lord Amerotke is implying. I am one of the royal chaplains. I saw nothing untoward during divine Pharaoh's absence from his city and court.'

Rahimere would have intervened but Hatusu abruptly rose to her feet. Senenmut and Sethos followed. Amerotke had no choice but to do likewise. Hatusu stood in silence. She folded her hands across her chest, the same gesture Pharaoh used before he spoke. It was a challenge to the rest of the circle. Hatusu was reminding them that she was Pharaoh's widow, a member of the royal blood; ritual and protocol demanded that they all stand with her. Rahimere sat back in his chair as if to refuse the challenge. Omendap, however, grinned and winked at his commanders, who rose slowly to their feet. The scribes and chief priests followed. Rahimere had no choice. He stood up, taking his time, grasping his rod of office. He kept his face impassive yet hatred seethed in his eyes.

'This talk of divine Pharaoh,' Hatusu said as she lowered her hands, 'has troubled my heart and grieved my soul. The council meeting is adjourned but it is our wish that the deaths of Commander Ipuwer and the high priest Amenhotep be investigated by the lord Amerotke, chief judge in the Hall of Two Truths.' Her kohl-rimmed eyes blinked prettily. 'He is to report directly to me. I and my advisers will now take close council with him in my private chambers.'

'And the other business?' Rahimere enquired.

'What other business? There is nothing, Grand Vizier, which will not wait until the morning. General Omendap, are the regiments outside Thebes?'

'The Isis, the Osiris, the Horus and the Amun-Ra are,' he told her. 'But the Seth and Anubis are bivouacked in an oasis to the south.' Omendap played with the handle of the silver axe. 'Grand Vizier Rahimere, however, has command of the mercenary troops which police the city of Thebes. I believe,' Omendap added slyly, 'they camp in the meadows and fields of the House of Silver as well as those of the temple of Amun-Ra.'

'They are there,' Rahimere intervened, 'for the protection of the city during these troubled times.'

Hatusu pursed her lips and nodded.

'For all our protection, Grand Vizier?'

'Yes, my lady, for all our protection.'

The rest of the royal circle fidgeted, pretending to adjust robes or pick things up from the table. Nevertheless, they all knew the armed might of Egypt was now congregated around the city. The swords were being drawn. It was only a matter of time and opportunity before these swords were used, the royal circle divided and the city, the kingdom and the empire plunged into civil war.

'It might be best,' Bayletos suggested, his fat, oily face creased in a smile, 'if divine Pharaoh was shown to the troops, taken in solemn procession through the city. The priests of Amun and the mercenaries would provide an effective guard.'

Hatusu smiled back, her upper lip curling like that of a dog about to snarl. She looked at Rahimere and Bayletos, trying to calm the turbulence in her heart. I know what you want, she thought: once the boy Pharaoh is out of the palace, the mercenaries and the priests of Amun will take him elsewhere.

'Divine Pharaoh.' She paused. 'Divine Pharaoh will reflect upon your request but he is young and there is disease in the city. I think it's best if he stays in the House of Adoration. Nevertheless, I heed your advice, chief scribe. The gods know we live in turbulent times. General Omendap, I want you to move an entire brigade into the grounds of the royal palace: its officer will answer directly to me.'

Omendap looked stubbornly back, about to refuse. Hatusu clicked her fingers and Senenmut, pushing by the table, went across and thrust a papyrus scroll into the general's hands. Omendap opened it, saw the royal cartouche and kissed it.

'It is not my desire,' Hatusu added sweetly. 'But that of divine Pharaoh. His word has gone forth.'

Omendap bowed. 'What divine Pharaoh wishes shall be done,' he answered quickly. 'Naturally, I will visit the palace daily to ensure my troops are in good health.'

'You are always welcome here.' Hatusu smiled. 'My lords.' And with this Hatusu left the royal circle, Senenmut and Sethos behind her.

The council meeting immediately broke up. Amerotke noticed how many gathered round Rahimere, whispering and murmuring. Omendap stayed away but two of his commanders were immediately drawn into hushed conversation by Bayletos.

It will be civil war, Amerotke thought. Hatusu and Rahimere hate each other. One of them will have to die.

If the troops were fighting, he knew what would happen. The crowds, the mobs who thronged the tenements down near the quayside, would run riot. I'll move Norfret and my children, he decided. I'll send them north, to sanctuary in the temples at Memphis. If the sword is drawn, there'll be no room for justice in Thebes.

'My lord Amerotke?'

He looked up. A page stood near the doorway, gesturing at him. Amerotke would have ignored such a discourtesy but Rahimere and the rest were looking at him, so he had to make a decision. If he walked away he would be the enemy of both factions. If he stayed, Hatusu would reject him and, if he went, Rahimere would mark him down as Hatusu's adherent. He glanced at Omendap. The general made a movement with his eyes towards the door. Amerotke pushed back his chair and followed the page out.

Neit: an ancient goddess associated with hunting and warfare.

CHAPTER 8

Amerotke followed the page boy along the gallery. On either side the walls were decorated with huge frescoes of Egypt's victories over its enemies. Chariots, painted in blue and gold, thundered over fallen Nubians, Libyans and warriors from the Land of Punt. Asiatics gazed up in shock and horror at the glory of Pharaoh and the power of Egypt's army. Along the edge of the painting ran words of praise.

'He has stretched out his arm. He, the golden falcon of Horus, has swooped upon his enemies. He has broken their necks. He has shattered their heads. He has taken their gold and treasure. He has made the earth tremble before his name.'

Amerotke wondered if the inscriptions would be an epitaph on Egypt's glory. A boy Pharaoh at home, a divided royal circle, and now a murderous hatred had broken out among those who governed Thebes.

The page boy padded ahead of him then turned right. The guards at the door were dressed in full ceremonial armour: red and white striped stiffened headdresses, corselets of bronze, leather kilts. The soldiers, from one of the crack regiments, stood, shields slung across their arms, swords drawn. When the page boy whispered to one of them the bronze doors were opened and Amerotke was led into Hatusu's private chambers, which were cool and well lit. Pastel shades on the walls provided a welcome relief from the warlike scenes outside. The air was heavy with the smell of cassia, frankincense and the most fragrant perfume from flowers in pots or wreaths around the room. The chamber was sparsely furnished with some beautiful figurines of gold and silver, chairs and stools of polished wood inlaid with ebony and ivory.

The page boy left him in the antechamber and went through a small side door. Amerotke tried to relax, admiring the paintings of fishermen on the Nile throwing out clap nets and lithe dancing girls with their thick, rich wigs and sinuous naked bodies. In the shifting light these seemed to move gracefully, lifting their sistra and clapping in eternal, ever-moving dance.

'My lord.'

The page boy was beckoning imperiously. Amerotke followed him into the chamber beyond and stifled his astonishment. It was a small room, the paintings on the walls hidden because there were only two lamps on either side of the great throne-like chair under a cloth-of-gold canopy. Hatusu sat, hands grasping the arms carved into the shape of snarling leopards. Her feet rested on a footstool covered with cloth-of-gold depicting the goddess Ma'at sitting in victory over one of the terrible demons of the underworld. On either side of Hatusu sat Senenmut and Sethos.

Amerotke was sure that Hatusu had chosen this chamber to convey the sense of her own royal power. If she had worn the blue or double crown and carried the flail and rod, she would have looked like Pharaoh himself sitting in judgement. Her face had changed, no longer soft and flirtatious. Now her jaw was tensed in fury, her eyes blazing. Amerotke glanced at Sethos, then genuflected. He was affording her no more dignity than she deserved yet he recalled Omendap's warning. Hatusu was making it very clear she was to be Regent. Secretly he wondered if she also wanted to be Pharaoh.

'Your highness.' Amerotke spoke firmly. 'You have summoned me here.'

'If you do not want to stay, my lord Amerotke, you may go!'

Hatusu's voice was tense and clipped. Amerotke sighed and got to his feet, folding his arms across his chest. Sethos' eyes now looked guarded. He shook his head imperceptibly, a warning for Amerotke to heed his words. Amerotke felt a spurt of rebellion.

'I am chief judge in the Hall of Two Truths,' he said. 'I represent Pharaoh's justice.'

'You were always stiff as a pole.' Hatusu leaned forward, smiling now. 'Do you remember, Amerotke? You used to have a b . . . bi . . . bit . . .' she mimicked, 'of . . . a stammer. Do you remember that?'

'I remember the teasing, your highness. How can I forget? You and your pet cat, grey wasn't it? With soft eyes and sharp claws.

Sometimes it was difficult to tell between the two, the pet or its owner.'

Sethos' hiss of breath was audible but Hatusu surprised him. An impish gleam appeared in her eyes.

'You were always blunt, Amerotke. You've overcome your stammer but you have the same secretive face, the same passion for the lady Norfret and the same determination to do what is right. Don't you ever get bored?'

'Your highness, I was trained at your father's court, so if I do I have the good manners to hide it.'

Amerotke could feel his anger. He found it difficult to control his breathing. He wanted to walk about, give vent to it. At the same time he felt childish; was he angry or simply frightened?

'Some people would say you were impertinent.' Senenmut spoke up. He was lounging sideways, one arm on the throne. He caressed it so lovingly Amerotke wondered if Hatusu's henchman wanted to sit there himself.

'I beg your pardon?' Amerotke cocked his head as if he couldn't understand Senenmut's words.

The overseer of the royal works moved his hand, tapping his fingers on his thigh.

'My lord Amerotke,' he said again. 'Some people would call you impertinent.'

'In which case, sir, many people would say we have a lot in common.'

Hatusu laughed and sprang to her feet. She went and leaned against Amerotke, her face staring up at him. In the poor light Amerotke felt as if they had gone back years and he was a young man being teased by a little imp in Pharaoh's household. As she pressed her body against his he caught her sweat, the costly perfumes and oils from her gown and body. She kissed him on one cheek and walked elegantly back to the throne where she slouched with a petulant cast to her lips.

'What do you want, Amerotke?'

'To be left alone.'

'No, as chief judge?'

'Life, health and prosperity for divine Pharaoh. Peace in his household.'

'Amerotke,' Sethos broke in. 'Don't play the foolish prude with us. To put it bluntly, a line has been drawn. Which side do you stand on?'

Amerotke raised his eyebrows. 'I am afraid, my lord, I stand where I did before any line was drawn.'

'You are a liar!' Senenmut broke in.

Amerotke took a step forward and Senenmut raised his hands.

'I apologise. I withdraw that. You are many things, Amerotke, but you are not a liar. Indeed, unless you are a fool, I think you are a man of integrity.' He smiled crookedly. 'A little prudish, rather stiff. But, if the kingdom slides into civil war?'

'I will support Pharaoh against his enemies,' Amerotke replied.

'And who are Pharaoh's enemies?' Hatusu asked, her voice loud and strident. She stretched out her arm and opened her hand.

Amerotke saw the royal cartouche of the boy Pharaoh, the unmistakable hieroglyphics displaying Thoth the god of wisdom, Pharaoh's royal name and the double crown of Egypt.

'Well, what is the law?' she demanded.

'Whoever holds the cartouche, the seal of Egypt,' Amerotke replied, 'manifests the divine power of Amun-Ra.'

'I hold it,' she said. 'Those fools in the council think that my stepson hates and rejects me. He does not!'

Amerotke leaned down and kissed the cartouche.

'What do you want of me, your highness?' He pointed at Sethos. 'There sits the eyes and ears of Pharaoh. If enemies are to be searched out . . .'

'Ah, so that's it!' Hatusu smiled. 'You think you are here to be Pharaoh's dog, to bark and show your teeth?' Her voice became matter-of-fact. 'I simply want these deaths investigated.'

'Why?'

'Because the assassin may have marked down anyone in this chamber for destruction.'

'Why?' Amerotke deliberately repeated.

'Pharaoh is still a boy.' Sethos spoke up. 'Perhaps there is a member of the royal circle who believes he can wade through a sea of blood to control the throne of Egypt.'

'I don't think so,' Amerotke replied. 'Your highness, I believe the deaths are somehow connected with that of your husband. He was the first to die. Immediately, on his return to Thebes, the other deaths quickly followed.'

'But why?' Hatusu asked.

Amerotke now regretted his earlier hostility. Hatusu looked vulnerable, mystified, her eyes full of fear. She knows something, Amerotke thought.

'But if you trap the killer?' Senenmut spoke up.

'If I trap the killer then we will have the perpetrator, the cause, the motive. Yet it will be a difficult task. If I began with divine Pharaoh's death, then I would rule Captain Meneloto was innocent.'

'Do you accept my commission?' Hatusu insisted.

'I do.'

'And you will report directly to me?'

'Your highness, if you wish. But, there again, if I accept this commission, my lady, I must begin by questioning you.'

Hatusu sat back in her chair. 'But . . .' Her stammer was genuine. She smiled in self-mockery. 'I know nothing. I received divine Pharaoh on the steps of the temple of Amun-Ra. We walked in. He collapsed and died in my arms.'

'And he said nothing?'

She shook her head. 'He said nothing!'

She's lying, Amerotke thought. He glanced at Senenmut and wondered how much he knew.

'I was in the crowds outside the temple,' Senenmut declared. 'I was not a member of divine Pharaoh's entourage.'

'I was even further,' Sethos joked. 'I was down in the city, overseeing the crowds along the quayside.'

'Divine Pharaoh died at noon,' Amerotke continued. 'My lady, what happened then?'

'Divine Pharaoh's golden flesh was taken to a nearby mortuary temple. A physician was called.'

'Which one? Was it Peay?' Amerotke asked.

'No, no, an old man from the House of Life. He felt for Pharaoh's life beat in his neck and chest and held a mirror to his lips. He said the soul had gone.'

'And then what?'

'There was consternation and chaos outside.' Hatusu shrugged. 'Prisoners had been executed. Signs and portents in the courtyard – doves had fallen from heaven.'

'Ah yes, I heard of that. What was wrong?'

Hatusu pulled a face. 'Some people claimed it was a portent. Others that hunters had injured the birds. They had flown in across the city but the attempt to fly over the high walls of the temple proved too much.'

'Was a search made? I mean, for the hunters? Were there other birds?'

Hatusu shook her head. 'I don't know. I stayed with my husband's corpse in that mortuary temple until after dusk. I couldn't believe he was dead. I couldn't accept that he had flown to the far horizon. I thought it was some dreadful mistake.'

'But people came in to see you?'

'A few. Rahimere, General Omendap, others of the royal circle. They asked me questions, I forget now.'

Amerotke nodded. What Hatusu had told him was court protocol. A Pharaoh died, his Queen would grieve alone. The process of embalming, preparing his body for the royal funeral rites, would not begin until after dusk.

'And then Peay was called?'

'I stripped the body,' she replied. 'Divine Pharaoh's crown had fallen off but that had been brought into the mortuary temple with him. I removed his kilt, his cuirass, pectoral and sandals and covered the body in a linen sheet. After dark Peay and the embalmers came to remove the corpse.'

'And then the snake bite was discovered?'

'Yes, on Pharaoh's left leg just above the heel.'

'Who saw it first?'

'Peay. He had this ridiculous idea that Pharaoh might be in a deep swoon.' Hatusu spread her fingers. She watched the light catch the rings carved in the shape of snakes. 'The rest you know. I called Sethos, who was in attendance. He ordered troops down to the royal barque. The viper was found, curled up beneath the royal throne. So small, yet it caused such chaos.'

'And why were the charges levelled against Meneloto?'

'My lord Sethos counselled against that,' Hatusu replied. 'But I was distraught, angry. I truly believed, and still do, that Meneloto's carelessness had cost Pharaoh his life.'

'I would have given the same advice as Sethos,' Senenmut growled. 'But at the time I was never asked.'

Hatusu's hand slipped over the arm of the chair, the back of her fingers grazing Senenmut's knee.

'Meneloto was put under household arrest,' she said. 'And the case was brought before you.'

'Has a search been made for Meneloto?' Amerotke asked.

'Spies and scouts have been sent out, but, for all I know, he could be with the sand-dwellers or the troglodytes in the Red Lands.'

Sethos got up and carried a stool forward, gesturing Amerotke to sit. The judge did. He felt uncomfortable but, at the same time, secretly pleased. This is what I am good at, he thought, solving a problem, sifting the evidence. But how much of it is true? And, if I unpluck a loose thread, how much will it unravel, how far will it go?

'Meneloto is a sand wisp,' Senenmut jibed. 'My lord Amerotke, do you wish some wine?'

The judge shook his head. 'I drank enough at the banquet.'

'In the council hall?' Sethos asked. 'You implied, Amerotke, that Pharaoh's visit to the pyramid of Sakkara was significant. Surely you didn't pluck that from the air?'

'I didn't pluck it from the air,' Amerotke replied. 'Remember, before Meneloto's trial, I read the evidence, the depositions. Nothing remarkable happened after Pharaoh's great victories in the Delta. It was more something Meneloto had said in his written admission to the court. How Pharaoh was jubilant at his great victories but, after Sakkara, became more quiet, withdrawn. Reference was also made to that at the meeting of the royal circle.'

'It's true,' Sethos agreed. 'Though, after Pharaoh rejoined the *Glory of Ra*, I and others were sent ahead of him into Thebes.'

'My lady, your highness.' Amerotke smiled. 'Why did divine Pharaoh stop at Sakkara? Surely not just to see the pyramids?'

'In a letter to me,' Hatusu said, 'written just after his victory, he said he had received a letter, a special missive from Neroupe, chief custodian and priest of the mortuary temples around the great pyramids at Sakkara; Neroupe was one of my father's most loyal retainers.'

'I've heard the name,' Amerotke told her. 'A scholar. He was writing a history of Egypt's past. I met him once in the Hall of Light in the temple of Ma'at.'

'Neroupe fell sick,' Hatusu went on. 'He was a very old man. By the time divine Pharaoh had reached the mortuary temples around Sakkara, Neroupe was dead.'

'And what happened there?'

'The royal barque was taken into shore,' Sethos continued. 'General Omendap will confirm these details. Divine Pharaoh travelled inland.'

'Did you go with him?'

'No, I stayed with the Vizier, Bayletos and the others on the royal barque. Divine Pharaoh always asked me to keep an eye on his chief officials.'

'And then?'

'Divine Pharaoh went by himself. No.' Hatusu raised a finger. 'He was accompanied by Ipuwer, Amenhotep and a detachment of the royal bodyguard, no more than five men. They were away three days at Sakkara.'

'And Meneloto?'

Sethos pulled a face. 'Yes, Meneloto went as well. It was his duty to guard Pharaoh's body. From what I can gather very little happened. Divine Pharaoh stayed in Neroupe's house. He visited the temples, shrines and tombs of his ancestors. Afterwards he returned to the royal barque.'

'And did he tell anyone of what had happened?' Amerotke asked.

Sethos shook his head. 'The following day I was despatched in a barge down to Thebes. I brought letters for her highness and other members of his family. I, and others, were told to prepare for divine Pharaoh's entrance into Thebes.'

Amerotke crossed his arms. He recalled Sakkara, its great tombs and mausoleums built hundreds of years ago as monuments, signs of Egypt's power and glory. Now, since the royal court had moved to Thebes, it had become a desolate, crumbling place, wedged between the green fields of the Nile and the hot, burning sands of the Red Lands. He felt a glow of pride, for he was correct: Tuthmosis, Amenhotep and Ipuwer had visited those shrines. All had died while Meneloto had faced serious charges and had now disappeared. Or had he been killed? But who was behind this? Rahimere and his faction? Or Hatusu and Senenmut? Was he Hatusu's lover? Had their liaison begun when divine Pharaoh was away fighting Egypt's enemies?

'My lady?'

Hatusu was now whispering to Senenmut. She turned.

'Yes, my lord Amerotke. I thought you had gone asleep.'

'Did divine Pharaoh write to you? Or, in the few minutes when you met in the temple of Amun-Ra, intimate that anything was troubling him?'

'I received one letter just after he left Sakkara,' Hatusu said. 'It proclaimed his great victories. It contained messages for myself and his son. How much he looked forward to his return to Thebes.' She maintained her poise to hide the lie. 'But nothing else.'

'And so what now?' Senenmut asked harshly. 'My lord Amerotke, we wish you to investigate all these deaths. Of Ipuwer, you know as much as we do. The man put his hand in a bag and was bitten by a snake. How that happened we don't know. Of Amenhotep.' He spread his hands. 'That is a matter for you to unravel. You have our authority to act.'

Senenmut, Amerotke reasoned, was using the words 'our' and 'we' as if he were now Hatusu's chief Vizier, her principal minister of state. He stared at Hatusu, who held his gaze coolly. You were a mischievous minx, Amerotke thought, and, in my arrogance, I had you wrong. You are more dangerous and subtle than I thought. There are things you are not telling me. You don't really want me to investigate. This is simply a pretext, a sop, a public gesture. The real game will be played out here in the palace. Once power is seized, what will you care? And, if you fail, what will it matter?

'You have our permission to retire.'

Amerotke rose, bowed and left Hatusu's chamber, entering the now empty hall of columns. The cushions and chairs were pushed back, goblets and plates still littered the table. He glanced towards the balcony and noticed darkness had fallen. From outside he heard the clink of armed guards. He hoped Norfret was home and wondered whether to join her. He remembered Amenhotep's severed head and, of course, poor old Shufoy would be somewhere near the gates waiting for him.

'My lord Amerotke.'

The judge, startled, noticed Omendap standing in the shadows almost hidden by a column.

'I didn't think you were a cat, my lord general,' Amerotke said as he bowed mockingly, 'to watch stealthfully from the shadows. What are you doing? Waiting for me or a quiet word with the lady Hatusu?'

Omendap held the silver axe of office nervously, passing it from one hand to another. He grasped Amerotke's elbow, pushing him gently towards the door.

'You have decided which faction to support, my lord Amerotke?'

'No, I have not. I am here to investigate deaths, including that of one of your senior officers.'

At the door Omendap stopped. 'We are safe here,' he whispered. He tapped the door. 'The wood's thick and we are well away from any spy on the balcony or in the garden below.'

'What have you to tell me?'

'Your words about the divine Pharaoh's journey to Sakkara. He went there for about three days. You know that, don't you? Well,' he hurried on, 'I asked Ipuwer on his return what had happened. Ipuwer said nothing except that Pharaoh had gone out at night. Ipuwer stayed, only Amenhotep and Meneloto accompanied him.'

'Did Meneloto's or Ipuwer's behaviour change after Pharaoh's return?'

Omendap shook his head. 'I speak to you man to man, Amerotke. Divine Pharaoh suffered from the falling sickness. He had visions and dreams. I am a soldier. I fight his enemies and he can do what he wants. If he wishes to go out at night to sacrifice or pray to the stars that is his business.'

'So why should Ipuwer die?'

'I don't know. And that's why I'm here. He was one of my officers. Brave as a lion. Loyal and big-hearted.' Tears started in Omendap's eyes. 'He should have died with a sword in his hand, not bitten like some old woman in a council chamber!'

'And is that all you have to tell me?' Amerotke asked, wary of being drawn into any treasonable conversation.

'No, I've come to tell you two things.' Omendap sucked in his lips. 'Or rather three.' He drew so close Amerotke could smell the beer on his breath. 'And, before I do, my lord Amerotke, let me make it clear, my loyalty and that of my officers is still divided. However, if I discover who slew Ipuwer, that will decide us. And, if it comes to blood-letting,' Omendap tapped the silver axe against Amerotke's chest, 'no high office, no pleasant conversations at dinner parties will save anyone.'

'You said you had two things to tell me,' Amerotke replied coolly. 'Then you changed it to three. My lord general, I am in a hurry.'

'I didn't mean to threaten.'

'I didn't think you did. The three things?'

'First, Ipuwer did not change after his visit to Sakkara but Amenhotep did. He rarely attended the meetings of the royal circle. When he did he was unwashed, dishevelled. On one occasion I even thought he was drunk. Secondly, Ipuwer reported nothing except this.'

Omendap opened the small leather bag which hung from his sash. He took out a small red figurine and handed it to Amerotke. The judge took it over to one of the alabaster lamps to study it more carefully. It was no more than a fingerspan high. A figure of a man, of a prisoner with his hands tied behind his back with red twine and the same around the clay ankles.

'The red ribbons of the war god Montu,' he observed.

'Yes, that's right,' Omendap replied. 'As when the priests bind the ankles and wrists of captives before they are slaughtered.'

'Witchcraft.' The work of a scorpionman or amulet-seller.'

'It's a token,' Omendap explained. 'A warning from the red-haired Seth, the god of destruction. It's not just clay. It's probably mud taken from a grave, mixed with menstrual blood and fly-dung. An offering to a demon.'

'And Ipuwer received this?'

'No, something like it!' Omendap snatched the figurine back. 'That's the third matter! As I entered the palace tonight, this obscenity was thrust into my hand!'

'Do you know why it was sent?'

'No.' Omendap put the figurine away. 'I'll have it destroyed over a sacred fire. Much good that will do.' He swallowed hard. 'It's a curse as ancient as Egypt, a summons by the angel of death!'

Isis: principal goddess of Egypt, often depicted as a young woman with the hieroglyph for a throne.

CHAPTER 9

Amerotke left Omendap and went out of the hall, down into the great courtyard before the palace. Here mercenaries milled about, dressed in their distinctive armour. The Shardana with their lean, sharp faces under horn helmets; the Dakkari in their striped headdresses, round shields slung on their backs; the Radu in long cloaks and embroidered belts, earrings and necklaces glittering in the torchlight, their dark skins covered with blue tattoos; Shiries, in caps, armed with short horn bows; Nubians black as the night in their leopardskin kilts and feathered headdresses. All these lounged in porticoes or beside the walls, weapons piled beside them. They looked surly-eyed as Amerotke pushed his way by them but he smiled politely, excusing himself. The mercenaries glimpsed the pectoral and ring of office and reluctantly stood aside.

The tension was tangible. The regular troops were under Omendap, and would march when he gave them the sign. However, these mercenaries were controlled by Rahimere and he was slyly pushing them forward, placing them closer to the palace. While the regular troops remained loyal, the guards regiments and the chariot squadrons, these auxiliaries, who fought only for profit, would not lift a finger.

Amerotke reached the gates and gazed back. If Rahimere struck, he reasoned, the palace would be overrun. The revolt would spread. The poor would swarm out of their hovels down by the quayside. And what would he do? No justice would be dispensed and the mob would certainly attack the villas and mansions outside the city. No sanctuary would be safe. Amerotke thought of friends in Memphis, or even garrison commanders further down the Nile; he must make plans.

Amerotke left the palace and entered the great concourse which stretched before it. Blazing torches, lashed to poles, drove back the darkness, enhancing the light of the full moon which hung like a silver disc in the blue-black night sky. He sensed no tension here. The midnight crowds, as usual, were more concerned with bartering and trading, taking advantage of the good weather and the rich harvest it promised. A group of white-robed priests went by, the standard of Amun-Ra borne before them. They were escorted by some of the mercenaries. Amerotke paused to let by a funeral procession. A family who had lost their household cat had, as custom dictated, shaved their eyebrows and were now taking the mummified animal in a casket down to the river Nile for transport to the cat necropolis of Bubastis. The family had hired professional mourners who sprinkled ashes on their heads and went before the funeral procession, digging up clouds of dust and throwing it over them. These wailed incessantly at their sad loss and prayed to the gods that the cat would journey to the west and eventually be reunited in paradise with its owners.

Amerotke looked about, searching for Shufoy. He was distracted by a group of slaves clustered under an olive tree: recently purchased by their owner, they were now being branded on the forehead, with black powder rubbed into each open wound. The slaves were held fast. Their owner ignored the screams; the powder ensured that the scars never healed and so they were marked as his property for life. Amerotke glanced away. He hated such sights. There was no need for it, not when you looked at poor Shufoy's disfigured face. A group of whores sauntered by, red paint rubbed in their cheeks, their eyes made more lustrous by rings of green and black kohl. They wore filmy white gowns which left little to the imagination and their braided, oil-soaked wigs swung provocatively. One of them caught Amerotke's eye and stopped. She made an obscene movement with her hands, beckoning him towards her, but Amerotke shook his head. The whores would have persisted in their bartering but a group of young men, probably priests, their bald heads now disguised by straw hats, ambled up and drew them into conversation. The whores turned away with high-pitched squeals and noisy giggles as they bargained for a night's entertainment at some house of joy.

The great marketplace was busy with traders and hucksters, sailors from the ships, officials from the Nomachs coming up to render their accounts. A cooking stall had been opened. Fresh gazelle and ibex, bought from the hunters, had been gutted and cleaned and were now being packed into strips on a grill over glowing charcoal. The sweet smell seeped through the night air, hiding the more distasteful odours from the public latrines and the beggars who sat in their own dirt, sightless eyes gazing around, bony fingers stretching out for sustenance and alms. A group of singers from a temple's House of Song wound their way through, practising a hymn to a god Amerotke had never even heard of. Their singing was rudely interrupted by a furious quarrel between a snake charmer and a purveyor of songbirds. Apparently a cobra had escaped from its basket, slipped up to one of the cages and, sticking its long tongue through the bars, had killed a bird and had dragged it out without the owner noticing until it was too late. Both men started to push each other. One was sent sprawling, knocking into one of the singers; a fight would have broken out if the market police had not appeared, beating about with their staffs.

Amerotke, cursing quietly, moved on looking for Shufoy. Revellers appeared, drunk. They were moving from one house to another carrying before them a mummy casket belonging to a former friend whom they wished to commemorate. They espied Amerotke and tried to entice him into their revelry but the chief judge ignored them. One of them became raucous, staggering towards Amerotke, slack mouth drooling, fists clenched. A policeman, who had noticed Amerotke's seal of office, came between them, and gently pushed the man back among his companions.

'Can I help you, sir?' The policeman came back, tapping his staff against his bare leg. He narrowed his eyes. 'You are lord Amerotke? Chief judge in the Hall of Two Truths?' He bowed his head. 'You shouldn't be here, sir. This is a night of revelry.' He glimpsed the puzzled look on Amerotke's face. 'A feast of the god Osiris,' the policeman explained.

Amerotke sighed. 'Yes, yes,' he apologised. 'I forgot. I'm looking for . . .' He paused. 'Well, my manservant. He's a dwarf. Shufoy. He has a disfigured face. He . . .'

'He has no nose.' The young policeman grinned. 'An amulet man?' He pointed to the far corner of the marketplace. 'He's over there doing a roaring trade!'

Amerotke thanked him and pushed his way through the crowd. There were more trees in this part of the marketplace: a few acacias, some olive, the rest palm trees, their outstretched branches providing comfort and shade during the day and a useful meeting place at night. Shufoy was under one of these, a cloak spread out on the ground before him. The little man was standing on a barrel proclaiming himself to be a great scorpionman, a seller of true amulets which would provide sure protection against demons and witches as well as the spells and magic of enemies and rivals.

Amerotke stared in astonishment. Shufoy's stall was full of merchandise. Small statues of the dwarf god Bes, carved scarab seals, amulets covered in magic hieroglyphics such as the eye of Horus; ankhs, wooden crosses looped over the top; small stelae of the goddess Taweret with ears round the rim, a sure sign that this goddess would listen to any prayers. Shufoy was holding these up, bellowing at the open-mouthed crowd.

'I have journeyed across the Black Lands and the Red Lands!' the dwarf's powerful voice boomed. 'I bring you luck and good fortune! Amulets and scarabs! Shrines and statues, all tokens of good luck and sure protection against the demons. I have sacred wax.' He crouched down, his grotesque face pulled in a grimace. 'Put this in your ear at night,' he told one gaping peasant, 'and it will prevent a demon ejaculating in your ear. All these,' he intoned, standing up again, 'will protect you against the arrows of Sekhmet, the spear of Thoth, the curse of Isis, the blindness caused by Osiris or the madness inflicted by Anubis!'

Amerotke moved closer. 'And will it protect you,' Amerotke shouted, 'from the lies and tricks of charlatans?'

The transformation in Shufoy was wonderful to behold. He jumped down from the barrel and, in the twinkling of an eye, the amulets, scarabs and all his curios were wrapped up in a great blanket while he shooed the crowd away. He then sat on the barrel and looked plaintively up at his master.

'I thought you'd gone home,' he moaned. 'Taken your chariot and left poor Shufoy to his own devices. A man has to work. A man must labour,' Shufoy quoted one of the sayings of the scribes, 'from dawn to dusk and earn a crust by the sweat of his brow.' He sighed. 'My face is pale, my belly is empty. My purse is thin and full of dust.'

'Shut up!' Amerotke crouched down before him. 'Shufoy, you have your own chamber in my house. You eat and drink like a scribe. You have fine clothes.' He grasped the dwarf's threadbare cloak. 'But you insist on dressing like a Syrian, found wandering in the desert.'

Shufoy's eyes gleamed at Amerotke's quoting of a famous proverb.

'Aye, you can remember that one as well,' Amerotke observed. 'But it does not hide the truth. Why all this?' He tapped the makeshift bag of amulets. 'You are not a wizard, a scorpionman!'

'How did the council meeting go?' Shufoy asked, head to one side, a dreamy look in his eyes.

'Don't change the subject!' Amerotke rasped. 'Where did you get all this rubbish? Where do you hide it? And where do you put all the profits?'

'I dreamed last night,' Shufoy said as he rocked backwards and forwards. 'I dreamed last night that I captured a hippopotamus and was carving it up for a meal. That means you and I will dine in palaces. I later dreamed I was copulating with my sister.'

'You haven't got one,' Amerotke broke in.

'Yes, but if I did, she would be like the girl I dreamed of; that means my wealth will grow. I also dreamed, master, that your penis became large and you were given a golden bow: a sure sign your possessions will multiply and you will hold high office.'

'Prenhoe!' Amerotke got to his feet and dragged Shufoy to his. 'That's the first time you've talked about dreams. You've been talking to Prenhoe, haven't you? That's where you keep your sack, in his house! And you divide the profits. I wondered why I had never caught you. Because when Prenhoe goes home he tells you I'm coming and you hide all this or he takes it with him.'

Shufoy scratched his ragged beard. 'It's a good trade, master. We do no one any harm and we do live in sore times.'

'What do you mean?' Amerotke asked.

'I may have no nose, master, but I've got ears, eyes and a brain which curls like a snake. It's all over the city. War is coming, isn't it?' He looked expectantly upwards. 'But the heart is violent; plague will stalk through the land and blood splash everywhere. Dead men will be buried in the river,' Shufoy continued sonorously. 'And the crocodiles will be glutted with what they have carried off.'

'Have you been drinking?' Amerotke asked sharply.

'Just a little beer, master.'

Amerotke sighed. 'I will look after your bag of trinkets. Go and find where the priest Amenhotep lived.'

Shufoy scurried off, only too eager for a diversion. He came back a short while later, picked up the sack and heaved it over his shoulder.

'Come with me, master.'

He led Amerotke out of the marketplace and down the winding streets. On either side stood the mud-walled cottages of peasants and workers, their small, unshuttered windows and doors flung open, men, women and children squatted outside around the cooking fires. They rose as Amerotke passed, eager to sell trinkets. Shufoy loudly announced who Amerotke was and the shadows slunk away. They crossed another open stretch of ground and went along a narrow, dark alleyway. Here the houses were more spacious, surrounded by high walls protected by bronze-studded gates. Shufoy stopped at one of these and hammered. Amerotke stepped back and looked over the wall. The shutters of the three-storeyed house were closed and he could see no light.

'Who is it?' a woman's voice whined.

'Lord Amerotke, chief judge in the Hall of Two Truths! Friend of divine Pharaoh!' Shufoy thundered. 'Open up!'

The gates swung open. An old woman carrying a small oil lamp in an alabaster jar peered out at them, her grimy, seamed face wet with tears.

'Have you no respect?' she moaned. 'My master is dead! Foully murdered!'

'That's why we are here.'

Amerotke pushed by Shufoy and stepped through the gate. He took the old woman by the elbow and gently led her back through the acacia trees to the main house. He smelt the fragrance of the flowers, the sweetness from the wine press, the odour of newly baked bread and the tang of fruit and cooked meats.

'Your master was a wealthy man?'

'He was a priest in the temple of Amun-Ra,' the old woman quavered. 'Personal chaplain to divine Pharaoh.' She dabbed the tears which stained her painted face.

'What happened?' Amerotke asked.

They walked into the entrance hall. The walls and pillars were freshly painted, depicting hunting scenes and the life of the gods, yet the floor was unwashed. The air smelt dank and sour. Potted plants in the corner had been allowed to wither, their leaves turning yellow-black. A dish of food lay on a chair, flies buzzing above it. The room had been shuttered and the whine of the mosquitoes, as they danced round the oil lamps, was irritating, heightening the sense of desolation and despair. It was almost as if Amenhotep had known he was going to die and had lost all care for living.

'Your master was well?'

'No.' The old woman shook her head. She let the embroidered robe round her shoulders fall to the floor. The linen sheath dress beneath was shabby and hung loose, exposing flaccid breasts and a scrawny throat. 'He just stopped everything.' Her voice became sad. 'Kept to his chamber. Sometimes he'd eat and drink. Oh yes, he'd drink all right! I warned him it was wrong, strong wine on an empty stomach, but he never went out, either to the palaces or the temples. He received no visitors.'

Amerotke pinched his nostrils at the sour vegetable smells from the kitchens.

'He wouldn't let me clean,' she wailed. 'He dismissed his servants and slaves. Even the young girls who used to dance and entertain him.'

'And his death?' Amerotke glanced over his shoulder. Shufoy hadn't entered the house. Amerotke hoped his manservant wasn't getting up to any mischief in the darkening garden beyond.

'A messenger came,' the woman replied. 'I didn't like the look of him. Well, I didn't see much of him, he was swathed in black like one of those desert wanderers. He claimed to have a message for my master. I took it off him and he disappeared.'

'When was this?' Amerotke asked.

'Earlier today. I took it up to the pure one's room.' The old woman used the title often given to a high-ranking priest. 'He opened it and, well, he became agitated. He waved his hand at me to go. He was muttering to himself. He had a sour temper, did the pure one. He'd thrown things at me. Ever since divine Pharaoh's death he became a recluse.' She peered up. 'You are lord Amerotke, aren't you, the judge? You've been sent here to investigate?'

133

Amerotke nodded. 'And you didn't know, well, what changed your master's mood?' he enquired.

'At first I thought it was divine Pharaoh's death but he never talked to me. He never talked to anyone. Come, I'll show you.'

She led him through the darkened house, out across a courtyard where a fountain splashed and the air was sweeter with the fragrance from the flower pots. They went down a corridor. The old woman shuffled ahead carrying the oil lamp, a moving shadow in a pool of light. She stopped at a door and Amerotke recognised a small chapel, very similar to one in his own house. Inside, the chapel was as shabby and as dirty as the rest of the house. Pictures of Amun-Ra, arms outstretched, accepting the worship of his priests adorned the walls. Beside him was represented the hawk-headed god Horus bearing a plate of offerings. The cupboard of the Naos, containing the shrine, hung open; the small statue within seemed rather pathetic and beneath it lay a plate of offerings which looked as if it had been there for days. The sand strewed across the floor was scuffed and disturbed, the incense holder cold, the resin within hard and black. The situla of holy water, which the priest would use to purify himself, lay cracked upon the floor. In any other circumstances Amerotke would have thought the shrine had been desecrated. In the flickering light of the lamp it seemed as if Amenhotep had either forsaken his gods or believed those gods had forsaken him.

The old woman had gone back to the door and was standing there peering out at the night. Amerotke went across.

'Amenhotep said nothing to you?'

'Nothing at all, my lord. He ate little, drank a lot of wine, sometimes he slept; other times he would just sit in his room muttering to himself.'

Amerotke recalled the severed head delivered to Rahimere at the banquet. The head was not shaven, the cheeks and chin were covered in stubble. Amenhotep had not even bothered to purify himself, the first duty of every priest.

'And he read that message?' Amerotke persisted.

'He read it.' The old woman's voice quavered. 'Then he went across and I saw him drop it into one of the oil lamps. Later in the afternoon he took a cloak, his walking cane and left without a word.'

'Let me see his chamber?' Amerotke asked.

She took him back into the house and up the stairs. Amenhotep's private rooms were dirty and smelt rank as if the priest had not even bothered to use the latrine but urinated in the corners. The bedchamber was littered with scraps of food. Amerotke grimaced as two rats, perched on a cushioned stool, scurried off. He waited while the old woman lit more oil lamps. Amenhotep in his prime had certainly enjoyed a luxurious way of life. The bed was of pure sycamore with a gold encrusted headrest. Chairs and stools covered in precious stuffs inlaid with ivory and ebony were plentiful. Gold and silver cups stood on tables and shelves. Pure woollen rugs covered the floor; tapestries hung on the bare walls. Amerotke opened a small coffer full of turquoise and precious stones from the mines in Sinai. Another held debens of silver and gold, bracelets, armlets, pectorals and necklaces containing precious stones.

'This all meant nothing to him,' the old woman lamented. 'Nothing at all. He used to go down to the Lake of Purity. It's in the garden. He would wash and bathe three times a day. In the days before his death, however, he wouldn't even change his robes.'

Amerotke picked up a papyrus roll and undid the clasp. It was a beautifully copied version of the Book of the Dead which every priest knew and studied carefully. It contained the prayers and preparation a soul would need as it journeyed through the chambers of the underworld to be judged by Osiris and the other gods. It was written in beautiful hieroglyphics, the 'Medu Netfer', the language of the gods. Amenhotep had apparently taken a stylus, splattering red and green ink, disfiguring the symbols and exquisitely depicted paintings. Time and again he'd scrawled in the margin the hieroglyphics for the numbers one and ten.

Amerotke threw the roll back on the bed and went across to the window. He moved carefully, watching the floor; a chamber such as this, littered with scraps of food, attracted snakes and other dangers. He stared out at the night sky. What had caused this transformation, he wondered? Had Amenhotep's mind become unhinged? It would appear so. But why should a rich, arrogant priest turn in on himself? Give up even the most superficial of rites, neglect the gods and his temple duties? Was it because of Pharaoh's death? Or something else? Something which had happened while the Pharaoh had journeyed down from Sakkara? He looked over his shoulder. The old woman had picked up a jewelled-edged gold plate and was poking disdainfully at the scraps of food.

'And this change, it occurred after his arrival back in Thebes?'

'Yes. And I don't know the reason.' She sniffed. 'He would only eat mutton and onions, you know.'

'But that's forbidden to priests. It taints them, renders them impure.'

'I told Amenhotep that but he just laughed. He said he wanted to fill his belly with mutton and onions and eat nothing else.' She lifted her tear-stained face. 'Why did he die, my lord? Oh, he was a braggart,' she added. 'But he could be kind. He brought me presents.'

'Did he receive any visitors?' Amerotke asked.

'Just one. No, no.' She dropped the plate. 'Where is it?' She went over to a darkened corner. 'Early this morning. I sleep very little and I love to watch the sun rise. It is glorious to see the lord Ra in his boat begin his journey across the skies.'

'You found something?' Amerotke intervened.

'Yes, I went to the gate. I opened it to see if anything had been left there: fresh food, provisions, especially wine. My master always insisted that his cup be full. I found a linen cloth tied with red twine.' Her voice sounded hollow as she stooped and searched in the shadows. 'I brought it to my master, he opened it. Yes, here it is!'

She came over and thrust the wax figurine, the hands and feet tied with red twine, into Amerotke's hands.

'You don't know what this is?' Amerotke asked.

The old woman narrowed her eyes in the poor light.

'It's a doll. A child's plaything.'

Amerotke put it down on the table.

'Yes,' he sighed. 'It's a plaything.' He tapped the old woman on the shoulder. 'But burn it,' he said quietly. 'Clear this chamber and burn that!'

He went downstairs and out into the garden. Shufoy was crouched by the gate, clutching his precious bundle.

'A man's heart is purified by waiting in patience,' the dwarf intoned.

'As it is,' Amerotke retorted, 'by a good night's sleep. Come, Shufoy.'

His manservant opened the gate and followed him out. Shufoy kept his head down. He didn't want his master to notice he was distressed by what had happened. Shufoy had intended to look round the garden, see if there was anything worth picking up. He had heard a knock at the gate and scrambled back, fearful for the bundle he had left there. The person waiting on the other side was clothed in black. He'd thrust a small linen parcel into Shufoy's hands.

'For your master!' the voice had hissed through the darkness.

Then the figure had disappeared. Shufoy, curious, had loosened the red cord and stared in horror at the figure it contained, the ankles and wrists tied like a prisoner being led to sacrifice. Shufoy had recognised it immediately for what it was, a threat: a token of the god Seth. His master was marked down for destruction! Shufoy had ground it under his heel. As the Book of Proverbs said: 'Curiosity cannot be explained' and 'It is not a servant's duty to shatter the harmony of his master's heart.'

In the great, yawning cavern which lay at the far end of the Valley of the Kings overlooking the dusty, crumbling wadi, the assassin, the devotee of Seth, sat cross-legged, staring out into the night. The cavern was an ancient one, its walls covered in strange signs. It was known as a shrine to the goddess Meretseger, the ancient snake goddess, but now it was empty. The old priest, the one who had spoken so clearly before Amerotke, lay in a corner, his throat cut, his head stoved in, the blood gushing in thick, sticky pools around his thin, dusty corpse. The assassin built up the fire, piling on pieces of dried dung. He would have to keep the fire strong because beyond the rocky outcrop stretched the great Red Lands, the haunt of lions, jackals and the great ruffed hyenas whose howls now seared the night. He looked at the spear, horn bow and quiver of arrows beside him. The fire might keep the hyenas away but the arrows were extra surety, protection against these voracious killers of the night.

The assassin shuffled a little closer to the fire and stared up at the stars beyond the cave mouth. He bit into a piece of water melon and stared at the corpse. He had made his sacrifice, a heron sacred to Horus and now this old priest. The assassin closed his eyes and breathed in deeply. He called on those grotesques of the underworld: the blood drinker from the slaughter-house; the devourers by the scales; the great strider; the swallower of shades, the breaker of bones, the eater of blood, the announcer of combat. He prayed that Sekhmet, the lion goddess, and Seth the god of darkness, death and destruction, would hear his prayers and send their demons to his assistance.

Beyond the old priest's body sprawled the corpses of the two baboons also sacrificed by the assassin to the killers in the shadows. He recited a list of enemies, begging that these would be inscribed in that scroll held by the gods of the underworld listing those who would die before the year was out. He had to do this. If he did not, Egypt would not be saved, the gods would not be protected. What matter if a little chaos was caused? Yet he had to be cunning as well as ruthless. Especially with Amerotke! No sudden snake bite for him! The assassin gazed round at his destruction and bowed his head in thanks. He listened to the yapping bark of the hyenas. It was an answer to his prayer, how to destroy the righteous, ever-inquisitive chief judge from the Hall of Two Truths!

Osiris: principal god of Egypt; husband of Isis. Died but resurrected due to her; depicted as a man dressed in a tight-fitting white garment, grasping the crook and flail.

CHAPTER 10

Hatusu rolled over and stared round her private bedchamber. The guttering flames of the oil lamps made the shadows jump and the figures depicted on the walls come to sudden life. She picked up an ostrich fan and gently wafted it, feeling the perfumed coolness against her face and neck. The sheets of the ebony-inlaid bed were tumbled and sweat-stained. She kicked them away and swung her long legs off the bed. She pushed back the cups of gold, the wine jar of blue porcelain. The floor was strewn with tunics sewn with gold, robes embellished with thousands of rosettes. Her eye caught an unguent perfume jar. Hatusu smiled at the inscription written in gold around its rim: 'Live for a million years oh darling of Thebes! With your face towards the north and your eyes filled with love.'

Hatusu took off her wig bound with a jewelled diadem necklace, the lapis lazuli gorget, the gilded castanets. She looked over her shoulder to where Senenmut lay stretched out on the bed fast asleep, his strong, thick body coated in sweat. He had proved to be a veritable bull of a lover, potent and strong. They had drunk wine from gold vessels and she had danced for him, wearing the jewels and robes of Pharaoh's wife. Afterwards, Senenmut had taken her roughly, cruelly, twisting her on to her front, stretching her out, thrusting in as if he wished to fill her body with his seed. She rolled back on the bed and gently touched Senenmut's nose with the tip of her finger. Did he love her? Was that why he had taken her time and time again? Or was it because she was a princess of the royal blood, Pharaoh's former wife so, in conquering her, he had seized Egypt, possessed its lands and status, all this ambitious, wily courtier hungered for? And could he be trusted? Was he the blackmailer? Was he the one who had left the small scrolls of sealed papyrus with their threats, warnings and clear instructions? If it was . . . Hatusu leaned closer and ran her finger across Senenmut's throat. If this man ever betrayed her, she would dance for him, fill him with good foods and costly wines, fight like a cat beneath him and, when he was asleep, cut his throat! Hatusu smiled at such dramatic thoughts. She remembered the slaughter of the prisoners on divine Pharaoh's return from the Delta. She felt as if she were going to swoon yet now she would walk through a sea of blood to grasp what was hers. She would take the heads of Rahimere, Omendap and the rest and place them in the House of Skulls.

Hatusu rolled over on her back and stared up at the star-spangled ceiling. What had caused the change? Was it the threat? Was it being alone? Was it the prospect of being thrust into the House of Women, the House of Seclusion? To grow fat and watch the years roll by while she painted or embroidered and listened to the scurrilous gossip of the court? Or was it something else? Was she a man in a woman's body? She recalled the slave girl she had been friendly with, close and intimate in those years before her marriage to Tuthmosis. Or was it because she really believed she was Egypt? That's what her father had called her. That gruff old warrior would scoop her up, hug her close and call her his Little Egypt.

'For you represent,' he would tell her, 'all its glory, its beauty and its grandeur!'

Hatusu waved the ostrich fan. But that was all in the past. Father, husband all gone into the west, to the House of Eternity, and she was alone. And what were the threats? Who was this blackmailer? How, in the name of all the gods, could he have learned the secret her mother had whispered to her when she lay racked with fever on her death bed! And why was the threat being posed now? Just as Tuthmosis returned to Thebes, the warnings had begun. Did the blackmailer wish to control her and, in time, control Egypt? Or was it to drive her deeper into the shadows? Was this the work of Rahimere, Bayletos and those smiling, sanctimonious priests who gathered in the secret chambers of their temples and plotted treason? Or could it be the soldiers led by Omendap? Divine Pharaoh always had a weakness for soldier boys. And what would happen now? It was like a game of chess. Each side had moved its pieces. She controlled the palaces, Rahimere controlled the temples while the soldiers refused to move.

Hatusu put the fan down. It was like waiting for a storm to loose, those sudden violent rains when the clouds boiled black over Thebes. Senenmut here had told her what was happening. Spies and scouts were coming in; Libyan horsemen had been seen out in the Red Lands much further east than they had ever been glimpsed. The Viceroy of Kush had complained how the Nubians no longer sent tribute, that the castles and fortifications beyond the First Cataract were becoming isolated. Patrols were being ambushed but was there worse? Senenmut kept talking of the north from where his spies and scouts had not returned. He had described, in clear, succinct phrases, the real dangers facing Egypt. The Ethiopians, Libyans and Nubians were an irritation, vexatious like the flies which now buzzed around the oil lamps. But the Mitanni, the great Asiatic power which lusted after the rich fields of Canaan. What happened if they moved west? Sending an army across Sinai, capturing the mines which provided Egypt with its gold, silver, turquoise and other precious stones. If they moved fast they could reach the Delta then ravish the northern cities. And what would happen then? Senenmut had smoothed out the piece of papyrus on which he had drawn a crude map.

'Rahimere will demand an army to be sent north or south. Its commander, of course, will be Omendap but he will insist that you go.'

'And what then?' she had asked.

'What do you think?' he jibed.

'I'll be defeated! Either a prisoner of the Mitanni or come sloping back to Thebes like a beaten dog.'

'Bitch,' Senenmut joked. 'Like a beaten bitch ready to be led off to the kennels.'

'And while I am gone,' Hatusu prompted him.

'While you are gone, his mercenaries will get closer and closer to the palace. His officials will find constant excuses to visit your stepson.'

Hatusu sighed and rolled over on to her side. Was that why the murders were occurring? But they didn't make sense. Ipuwer was a good commander but he could be replaced. Amenhotep, so important in life, who would mourn him? She thought of Amerotke. Could he be trusted? Hatusu closed her eyes. She should tell someone about that dreadful evening when she had knelt beside her husband's corpse and found the message rolled up in a piece of red twine. She had to break free! She had to trust someone. She leaned over and blew gently on Senenmut's face.

*   *   *

Amerotke had risen long before dawn and, in doing so, had roused Norfret. She had come out of her chamber, her eyes heavy with sleep, her mouth full of questions. Amerotke had embraced her, feeling her smoothness, her exquisite fragrance. She had asked him about the previous evening and he had told her what he thought he should. Norfret had stepped away, her eyes bright with laughter.

'You are the worst liar I have ever met, Amerotke! It's serious, isn't it? It will be a time for drawn swords. And you will be part of it.'

He had nodded.

'Don't send me away.' She came closer, her face beseeching. 'Don't send me away, Amerotke.'

'My little fighting cat.' He smiled. 'But what about the boys? If the mob runs riot they'll spill out of Thebes.'

'Troops are in the city?'

'The troops will act on orders and there might be no one to give them. Even worse, they may join in.' He grasped her hands. 'Promise me one thing. If the worst happens, do exactly what Shufoy tells you.'

'Shufoy!' she exclaimed.

'Shufoy could take blood out of a rock,' Amerotke replied. 'And there's not a hole he can't clamber out of. He'll be worth a regiment of soldiers. He will have you out of here to a place of safety.'

Norfret gave him her word and returned to her bedchamber. Amerotke visited his writing room and went up on the roof of the house to watch the sun rise. He had purified his face and hands with water, his mouth and lips with salt. As the sun rose he knelt, hands extended, eyes closed, praying for both wisdom and protection for his family. He then turned to his left, gazing north, feeling the cool breezes, the breath of Amun. Afterwards he went down and joined the children scampering around the banqueting room while the servants tried to make them eat and drink before they went out to play. Amerotke absentmindedly replied to their questions and returned to his writing desk at the top of the house.

The sun had now risen, greeted by the temple trumpeters in the city, their shrill blasts carried on the breeze as the sun's rays caught the gold-topped obelisks in shimmering circles of light. Amerotke sat and worked, going through the accounts of the temple of Ma'at: provisions bought, flowers planted, the profits of his share in the incense trade with the land of Punt. Shufoy now joined the children, chasing them round the garden then lecturing them solemnly on treating him with more dignity. Amerotke had decided not to interfere with his servant's trade in amulets and scarabs. He knew it would be impossible to stop and Shufoy, when he wanted, would listen obediently while his mind and ears remained firmly closed.

'Mock not the blind, nor deride the dwarf!' Shufoy bellowed at the two imps. 'Don't tease a man made ill by a god!'

'There's nothing wrong with you,' Amerotke said to himself.

Norfret came and sat with him for a while. They talked about their eldest entering the House of Life as a scribe. Norfret could see Amerotke was distracted so she kissed him on the brow and went downstairs.

Prenhoe arrived and, forewarned, ruefully confessed to being Shufoy's accomplice.

'We share a deep interest in dreams,' he explained plaintively. 'And the trade in amulets,' his eyes held those of his kinsman, 'supplements the rather meagre income of a scribe.'

'You are well paid, Prenhoe,' Amerotke said. He opened a small coffer and threw across a leather purse. 'That's for you.' He smiled. 'Prenhoe, you are a very good scribe. You are sharp, incisive. I watch your hand move across the scroll. Your summary of the court is one of the best I read.'

Prenhoe's face beamed with satisfaction.

'I thought this day would be fortunate. I dreamed last night that I ate the flesh of a crocodile . . .'

'Yes, yes,' Amerotke broke in. 'But at least that's better than Shufoy. He dreamed he was copulating with his sister.'

'But he hasn't got one!'

'I know,' Amerotke said despairingly. 'Now, listen, Prenhoe, write up the account of Meneloto's trial, have it with me as soon as possible.'

The next visitor was a woebegone Asural. He walked into the house like a god of war in his leather kilt, cuirass and rather ridiculous helmet held under his arm. Amerotke quietly gave thanks that the children were not present, otherwise Asural would have had to draw his sword and display for the millionth time how he had fought single-handed against a Libyan champion. The chief of temple police eased himself down in a camp chair and gratefully accepted a cup of beer.

'More robberies?' the chief judge asked.

'Aye. Figurines, small objects. You know the sort. Perfume jars, needle-boxes, small cups and plates.'

Amerotke thought of the story he was telling his children.

'And the doors were undisturbed?'

'The doors are always undisturbed! It's only when they open the tomb to place another corpse that the thefts are discovered. There are no other secret entrances or tunnels, only very small air vents.' Asural shifted in his seat. 'Oh, by the way, before I left, one of the junior priests from the temple said this had been delivered for you.'

He handed across a scroll. Amerotke undid it.

'It's from Labda!' Amerotke exclaimed. He looked up. 'He wants to see me, just before dusk, at the snake goddess's shrine in the Valley of the Kings. He says he cannot come to me and begs my indulgence.'

'It's a lonely place,' Asural said. 'On the edge of the desert; you should be careful. Why does he want to see you?'

Amerotke looked at the cursive writing, the professional hand of a scribe.

'He claims to have information about divine Pharaoh's death, something he has learned.'

'Oh, I've also come to congratulate you,' Asural teased. 'On your promotion to high office, a member of the royal circle . . .'

'And what else?' Amerotke asked.

'It's beginning to happen.'

'For truth's sake, Asural, what are you talking about?'

'Refugees have arrived in the city, a few merchants from Memphis and other towns to the north. It's only gossip, the Vizier's men took them away, but there's rumours that a large army has moved across the Sinai and is raiding the Delta.'

Amerotke went cold. As a boy he had heard about the Hyksos, fierce charioteers, who had swept into Egypt spreading famine, war, plague and devastation. His father used to whisper about their cruelty and Amerotke knew enough about military strategy to realise the terrible danger now unfolding. If the hostile army seized control of the Delta, then the northern towns, it would divide Egypt in two.

'Perhaps it's just gossip,' he countered.

'I don't think so. You should go into the city, Amerotke. Discover what is really happening!'

'There'll be time enough for that,' Amerotke replied. 'If refugees come flooding in, the House of Secrets will take over. They won't want any panic to spread, not while the royal circle is divided.' He could have bitten his tongue at the quickening in Asural's eyes.

'So, there is division?' the chief of police whispered. 'The stories are true?'

'Go back to the temple, the Hall of Truths,' Amerotke told him. 'Have the guard doubled, the doors locked. The court will not sit for a few days, no pressing case awaits us.'

Asural got to his feet.

'Any news of Meneloto?'

Asural turned at the door and shook his head.

'Like incense smoke.' He smiled. 'There's a fragrance left but, of Meneloto, neither sight nor sound.'

Amerotke listened to Asural's heavy footsteps down the stairs. He felt a tremor of stomach-clenching panic but he was determined not to give way to it. He must keep occupied. He pulled across a newly cut sheet of papyrus and spread it out. He opened the pallet box containing brushes, inks and styli from which he picked out a stylus, dipped it into the red ink and wrote quickly from right to left, using the script he had learned in the House of Scribes. He closed his ears to the distant cries of his children playing among the tamarind and sycamore trees, frightening the black-tipped hoopoe birds which always clustered round the ornamental lake. When he finished the introduction, he picked up a small knife and sharpened another stylus. What sense could he make of all this?

Amerotke made the sign for Tuthmosis II, divine Pharaoh, mystic, epileptic. A brave general and a clever strategist. He had marched north and brought Egypt's enemies under the whip. All had been well. His chief officers were with him while his half-sister and wife Hatusu stayed at home and governed Thebes. Amerotke drew a pyramid. Divine Pharaoh then returned south. He'd stopped at Sakkara, visiting the great pyramids and mortuary temples of his long-dead ancestors. Tuthmosis had left the royal barge with Commander Ipuwer, Captain Meneloto and the priest Amenhotep. He'd visited the pyramids, secretly, by night. Amerotke wrote the word 'why?' and stared up at the sunlight pouring through a window.

'Why?' he muttered.

Because Pharaoh had received a letter from that old priest Neroupe? He continued with his writing. What did that message contain? Why was it so important? Had Pharaoh discovered something there? Had he shared a secret with Amenhotep? Was it a question of faith? Tuthmosis had always been the most devout of men. He had continued with his prayers and offerings but privately, not visiting any temples, while Amenhotep appeared to lose all purpose in life or any belief in the gods. Why did Amenhotep scrawl the hieroglyphics for one and ten? Amerotke recalled from his own learning that those were sacred numbers for the essence of God and the climax of all things.

Finally, the murders. How had divine Pharaoh died? Undoubtedly he had been bitten by a snake. But was that the real cause of death? All the evidence demonstrated it was not. And why use a snake? Amerotke drew the hieroglyphic for a viper. Was there some ritual significance in the weapon the assassin used? Was the snake supposed to represent the great leviathan of the underworld, Apep the lord of chaos and eternal night, who constantly struggled against the lord Amun-Ra and the forces of light? Or did the snake represent Uraeus, the spitting cobra, the diadem on Pharaoh's helmet, the symbol of resistance to all of Egypt's enemies? Or was it just an easy tool to use for murder? The assassin definitely knew a great deal about snakes. If handled properly, and Amerotke had seen the snake charmers in the markets, serpents could be easily controlled, carried about with no real harm to their owner. Amerotke smiled grimly. In a sense Ipuwer was an easy victim. During the busy council meeting, or rather during its adjournment, someone simply had exchanged bags. To thrust a hand close to a viper would bring instant death.

And poor Amenhotep? He must have gone out to meet someone he knew, someone he trusted. The fat old priest would be an easy victim. He had been lured to that derelict temple on the banks of the Nile, killed, his head severed then delivered to Rahimere by some paid assassin. The only description was that they were dressed in black. Amerotke put his stylus down.

'The Amemets!' he exclaimed.

Were the clay figurines delivered by them? Was it part of their ritual, to break the harmony of their victims? Amerotke always dreamed that one day those sinister killers would be captured and brought before him in the Hall of Two Truths. He would relish that. He would love to put them to the question and discover the true litany of their crimes. Yet that would be as easy as trapping sunbeams or catching the divine breath of Amun-Ra. So who was the assassin?

Amerotke went back to his writing. Was it Hatusu? Her lieutenant Senenmut? Or Rahimere with his coterie of sycophants? And what was the purpose? Revenge? To conceal a secret? Or simply to cause chaos and mayhem? Amerotke sighed and pushed the parchment away. The task was frustrating. No one would tell the truth. Divine Pharaoh's wife could say more but kept her own counsel. He was only being used as a sop, a public gesture for the deaths which had occurred. Amerotke rose and stretched. The day was drawing on. Silence from the garden. He went and lay down on his bed, his mind seething with pictures and memories. He heard Norfret calling but his eyes were growing heavy. Then he was shaken awake by Shufoy. The dwarf grinned down at him.

'The burdens of high office, eh, master?'

Amerotke got up and swung his legs off the bed. He took the cup of cold beer Shufoy pushed into his hand and saw the platter of newly baked bread and strips of roast goose on the table.

'You should join us in the garden.' Shufoy studied his master carefully. 'The sun is beginning to dip, it's cool and refreshing under the sycamore trees.'

'I must go out,' Amerotke said. He went to the table and picked up the plate.

'Why?' Shufoy asked.

'Because I have to,' Amerotke replied evasively. 'Business of the royal circle.'

'I met Asural,' Shufoy said. 'So, set your heart upon hearing my words, oh master. You will find them profitable.'

'My heart is sick of taking your advice,' Amerotke quipped, quoting another proverb.

'You are like a sandpiper,' Shufoy jibed. 'One of those birds which, when the crocodile suns itself on a mud bank, and opens its jaws, hops in to pick at whatever morsels lie between the crocodile's teeth.' Shufoy drew closer. 'The crocodile may close its mouth and the sandpiper itself becomes a juicy morsel.'

'And who is this crocodile?' Amerotke asked, wishing to keep the conversation light.

'Go into the House of a Million Years,' Shufoy answered. 'The place swarms with crocodiles all hungry for blood.'

Amerotke grinned and finished what he was eating.

'There's another story, Shufoy, about crocodiles. When they sun themselves on a mud bank, their great jaws open, a mongoose can slip between the jaws, go down into the crocodile's stomach, then kill the beast by gnawing its way out.'

'Some mongoose!'

Laughing, Amerotke went to wash his hands and face and put on his robe. He took from a chest a thick woollen military cloak and a bronze-studded war belt, slipping sword and dagger into the sheaths.

'Tell the lady Norfret I'll be back soon. Don't disturb her.'

And, ignoring Shufoy's warning looks and the litany of proverbs he was about to mutter, Amerotke went down the stairs. He paused at the bottom, savouring the sweet fragrance of the flowers from the garden where Norfret was teaching the two boys to write.

'I'd love to stay,' Amerotke thought.

Yet the old priest might be able to tell him something. Amerotke considered taking a chariot but such a dramatic departure would only alarm Norfret and incite the boys to their interminable questioning. He slipped out of a side entrance. The trackway was fairly deserted. A procession came towards him, a group of junior priests escorting a bullock, garlanded and flowered, straining at its embroidered harness. He bowed as the priests passed and looked quickly into the cart. He said a quick prayer to Ma'at that Shufoy or Prenhoe weren't with him. The cart was full of bones, a sure token of ill luck as these priests took the contents of their slaughterhouse into the desert to be buried.

Amerotke was soon within the city gates, making his way along the trackways past the mud-packed houses of the artisans and peasants down towards the quayside. He saw none of the tension Asural had warned him of. The markets and booths were still doing a roaring trade. The air was sharp with the smell of natron which the traders used to coat their stalls against the myriads of flies. A pedlar seized Amerotke's hand.

'Cat fat for sale!' he said. 'Daub this on the lintel of your house and you'll never see a mouse or rat!'

'Not the rats and mice I fear!' Amerotke retorted.

He shook the pedlar off and made his way further along the riverside. The sun was beginning to dip. Amerotke paused at a stall to buy a water gourd and slung it over his shoulder. He had left in such haste but now he recalled previous journeys into the Valley of the Kings where the heat and dust soon clogged the mouth and throat.

Amerotke hurried on past young boys dancing around, fencing with papyrus sticks. Others were picking up animal dung, covering it with straw, to be laid on the roofs of their houses and baked into hard cakes which could be used as fuel when winter came.

A group of Hesets, singing girls in the service of Hathor the goddess of love, had drawn a large crowd and blocked the path. Amerotke paused to watch. The girls were dressed provocatively in long, oiled wigs in which coloured strands had been woven. Around their necks hung lotus blossom, while earrings of the same colour danced and flickered at their every movement. Their bodies were bare, only their groins covered by thick linen kilts which moved enticingly as the singers, clapping their hands, moved in a shuffling, sensuous dance.

> 'How delightful, my beloved!
> To go down with you to the river.
> I look forward to the moment
> When you ask me to bathe before your eyes.
> I shall sink into the water and come up
> Holding a red fish.
> It will lie happy in my fingers.
> It shall lie between my breasts.
> Come with me, my beloved!'

This provocative dance, and even more provocative song, attracted the attention of sailors who roared back the words and eagerly accepted the small scraps of papyrus the accompanying musicians distributed, displaying crude but erotic love scenes. A group of Nubians in pantherskins were taken by the tempo of the fluting music and eagerly joined the Hesets. The market police arrived and, in the consequent confusion, Amerotke slipped round the crowd, following the path overlooking the busy quayside where ships, boats and barges clustered. Merchants, sailors, pimps, prostitutes and the myriad visitors thronged the beer shops and wine stores exchanging gossip, bartering or just enjoying the last few hours of trading but Amerotke avoided these, walking further on past the docks and wharves until the warehouses and houses gave way to a muddy trackway which wound through the great papyrus thickets. Amerotke paused and gazed across at the Necropolis, above which the curiously coloured granite and limestone cliffs fringed the Valley of the Kings. He closed his eyes and played with the ring of Ma'at. He sensed danger; the snake priest might hold valuable information and he had to go, but nevertheless he prayed that Ma'at would bring him safely back.

Meretseger: snake goddess with shrines in and around the Necropolis and the Valley of the Kings.

CHAPTER 11

Amerotke walked further along the river bank. Now and again flocks of birds would burst up and sail out across the river busy with crafts and boats of all kinds and shapes. He heard a squealing from a dense thicket. A group of hunters were beating a pig with sticks while two others cast pieces of pork on the end of great hooks into the river, hoping the bloodied meat and the cries of the pig would attract one of the hunting crocodiles which would swallow the bait and be pulled into shore to be clubbed to death. The men, naked except for loin cloths, stood holding spears and clubs. One of them glimpsed Amerotke.

'You should join us,' he called. 'It's good sport!'

Amerotke shook his head and moved on.

At last he came to a fairly deserted landing quay and went along it. He stood on the causeway looking down at the swollen waters. There was always the danger of crocodiles and, though rare, it was not unknown for them to hunt unwary loiterers by the riverside. Asural believed so many drunks had fallen into the Nile and been eaten, the crocodiles had acquired a taste for human flesh. Amerotke stood there until he attracted the attention of a small fishing dhow which plied as a ferry up and down the Nile.

Amerotke clambered in. The boat crew hardly noticed him but took his deben of copper. They chattered among themselves, turning their craft under Amerotke's directions across the Nile to a small landing quay on the edge of the Necropolis. Amerotke stared up at the warren of streets, houses, shops and booths and, above these, the great rocky outcrop now turning reddish as the sun began to set. This was the peak of the west, dedicated to the serpent goddess Meretseger, lover of silence. Amerotke recalled the warning regarding the valley over which this rocky outcrop kept gloomy guard.

'Beware of the goddess of the western peak. She strikes instantly and without warning!'

Amerotke closed his mind to such gloomy thoughts by wondering what Norfret and his two sons would be doing. He became so withdrawn the ferry men thought he was asleep and shook his knee as their craft bumped into the wooden quay. Amerotke thanked them and clambered ashore.

He took the road which wound through the Necropolis, pausing at the huge statue, a shrine to Osiris, foremost of the westerners, the god of the dead before whom all must appear. Amerotke often visited the Necropolis, to visit either his parents' tomb or those of other members of his kin, and it was always an eerie experience. The close-packed dwellings of the many-streeted town housed embalmers, coffin-makers, chandlers, painters, and the makers of funeral furniture. Through the open doorways Amerotke glimpsed gilt and painted coffins leaning against the wall: show rooms where customers could choose the best designs. Some traders even offered their clients miniature mummy cases to take home and inspect.

Beside these were the embalmers' booths and sheds where the corpses would be prepared for burial. The air reeked with the strong smell of natron, the pungent salt in which corpses were soaked before the embalmers began their work. The smell mixed with others: the entrails, pulled out through the nose; the palm wine, pounded incense, myrrh and casis which were packed into the corpse once it had been gutted and cleaned. Most of the work was for the rich. The corpses of the poor were simply slung on hooks. Amerotke glimpsed some of these turning blue-black waiting to be tossed into huge cauldrons of natron salt to be soaked and cleansed before being collected by their grieving relations.

Beyond the shops and booths were honeycombed tombs carved out of the limestone granite. Amerotke paused to allow a funeral procession to pass. This was led by a priest chanting a prayer to Osiris; behind him came servants carrying alabaster jars containing food, fresh oils and long, decorated wooden chests holding the ornaments, weapons and clothes of the dead man. A covered sled, dragged by two men, marked the centre of the procession. Inside it stood the Canopic jars containing the embalmed entrails which had been removed from the corpse. Behind it a lector priest solemnly chanted: 'We come before thee, oh lord of the west, great god Osiris. There was no evil-doing in this man's mouth. He did not speak untruths. Grant that he may be like the favoured ones who are among thy following. Hail to thee oh divine father Osiris! Oh lord of breath! Oh lord of the palaces of eternity! Grant that this man's Ka may dwell in your courts!'

The words were taken up by other priests accompanying the intricately carved mummy casket resting on a couch beneath a canopy. Behind this trailed the family and friends, as well as a group of professional woman mourners who, weeping, tearing their hair and beating their breasts, intended to give good value for money as they scooped up dust and threw it over their hair and clothes.

The procession passed. Amerotke was about to walk on when he glimpsed the physician Peay scurrying from a house, a pet monkey on his shoulder, one of those small vervin often treated by the rich as a pampered pet. The physician was moving in a hurried, secretive way and Amerotke wondered what business he could have in the Necropolis. He was about to move on when he bumped into someone. He stepped back and recognised the embalmer, the man who had spoken up on behalf of his kinsman during the recent trial in the Hall of Two Truths. The fellow, embarrassed, muttered an apology and, head down, stood back.

'Health and blessing!' Amerotke greeted him.

'Health and blessing to you, my lord Amerotke. Why are you visiting the City of the Dead?'

'Judges and their families eventually come here,' Amerotke said.

'Where are they buried?' the fellow asked.

Amerotke pointed to the far side of the town.

'I can take you there,' the embalmer offered. 'The City of the Dead is not a place for you.'

Amerotke looked through an open doorway. The embalmers were busy on a corpse, the workers stripped to their loin cloths, their bodies glistening with sweat. He heard the clang of hammer, the wails of the receding funeral party while the strange, pungent smells cloyed his nose and mouth. Amerotke had never been here by himself but with his family, servants, guards or officials.

'You should walk careful,' the embalmer observed.

'I walk careful,' Amerotke retorted.

He went to pass on but the fellow didn't stand aside. As Amerotke's hand fell to his sword hilt, the man bowed his head and put his hand up in a sign of peace.

'I thank you, my lord, for the mercy shown to my kinsman.'

'It was a great mercy,' he replied. 'Your kinsman committed a blasphemous, sacrilegious act.'

'I always pray for you, my lord Amerotke.'

The judge tapped the man on his bare shoulder. 'Then do so now,' he requested and went on his way.

At last Amerotke was free of the Necropolis, striding along a dusty path fringed by tough green gorse. The smells and sounds of the Necropolis receded, being replaced by the hot, sandy breath from the desert. At last he was round the rocky outcrop, following the narrow snaking path which ran along the dried wadi into the Valley of the Kings. The cliffs on either side rose dark and forbidding in the dying rays of the sun. Amerotke heard a sound and paused. Just a little way up the cliffside Amerotke saw a bundle of rags move and, grasping his sword, climbed the loose-packed shingle. An old woman had been put there. Her face was yellow and seamed with age, framed by thinning, greasy, grey hair. Amerotke caught the death-rattle in her throat and looked into her milky eyes. He shook her gently; eyelids fluttered, a vein-streaked hand moved as if she wished to cover her face against the sun. Amerotke lifted her carefully. She seemed as light as a feather. He pulled her up into the shade, resting her against a rocky outcrop. The old woman's lips moved but Amerotke could not understand her quick jabber. He knew what was happening. The old woman had been brought here to die, left out in the desert by a family too poor to feed another mouth which had grown useless with age.

'Where are you from?'

The old woman went to speak but shook her head, her breath coming in a dry, croaking rattle. Amerotke took the water gourd and held it to her lips. She drank greedily, then he poured some into his hand and wetted her dry brow and cheeks. Her eyes fluttered open. She suffered from the cataracts, a light film of skin which covered both eyes, but she could make out Amerotke's shape.

'I am dying.'

Amerotke took her hand and pressed it.

'I can take you back,' he offered.

She tried to laugh but her head fell forward. He wetted the back of her neck with more water, which seemed to revive her, for her head came up.

'Will you not stay?' she whispered. 'Will you not stay and say the prayer?'

Amerotke looked further down the valley. He should be going. He could take the woman back but where to? Her skin was already cold and clammy, the death-rattle loud in her throat. He offered the water bottle again.

'I'll stay with you.'

'And you'll close my eyes and say the prayer?'

Amerotke agreed and waited as the shadows grew longer and the old woman became weaker. He gave her sips of water and made her as comfortable as possible. The end came fast. She coughed back some of the water, her scrawny body trembling, then her head fell sideways. Amerotke closed her eyes and, turning to the north, prayed for the special compassion of Amun-Ra, that this old woman's Ka, her spirit, be allowed to dwell in the fields of eternity. He covered her face with a tattered cloak and spent some time placing boulders over the corpse; night was falling and, on the hot blast from the desert, he heard the howls of the scavengers, the jackals, lions and hyenas.

Amerotke reckoned he must have lost at least an hour and hurried down the valley. The deeper he went the more ominous the silence grew. The gorse bushes clinging to the rocky escarpment seemed like hooded watchers waiting to pounce. The night was growing cold. In the blue-black sky the stars were appearing, a myriad of lights. The shadows stretched across and met. Amerotke recalled how this was a haunted place. Somewhere here in this valley lay the secret tomb of Pharaoh Tuthmosis I. The royal grave-digger and architect, Ineni, had boasted that 'eye had not seen, nor had ear heard nor could tongue tell' where the great king had been buried. In other words, dead men tell no tales. The hundreds of convicts and prisoners of war who had worked on the tomb had been massacred. Did the Kas of these men, their ghosts, still wander here?

The track wound round. At the far end of the valley Amerotke could see the great cave, the shrine to the goddess Meretseger, high on the rocky escarpment. A flicker of flame leapt up against the closing night; peering through the gloom, Amerotke glimpsed a figure waving at him to come forwards.

The judge hurried on, sweat coursing down his body as he began the climb. Rough steps had been cut into the cliff face but these were crumbling, covered in shale and shifting sand. The cult of the goddess had declined, being replaced by the lavish temple ritual of Thebes. Amerotke looked up but the mouth of the cave was now hidden by the steep incline.

At last he reached the top. Here, as if scooped out by some giant hand, a dizzyingly deep cleft cut through the rock. Amerotke paused to catch his breath and stared across. The fire was no longer burning nor could he see anybody. Above the mouth of the cave, a carved statue of the slant-eyed goddess stared sightlessly back, her hair a mass of writhing snakes.

'I am here!' Amerotke called out. He glanced behind him, sure he had heard a sound. 'I am here!' he repeated. 'Amerotke, chief judge of the Hall of Two Truths!'

From the rocks above came the yip-yip of the great hairy hyenas. Drawing his sword Amerotke cautiously crossed the wooden bridge which spanned the gorge, nothing more than makeshift planks of wood. He entered the mouth of the cavern and looked down at the trickle of blood coming out of the darkness. Clutching his sword, he went in. Two oil lamps burnt weakly in metal dishes. Water had been poured over the fire, dousing the flame and warmth. The stench of blood and corruption was all-pervasive. Amerotke's hand went to his mouth. He heard a sound and hurried back to the mouth of the cave where to his horror he saw that the wooden planks had been withdrawn, pulled back to the other side. Amerotke screamed in despair. So arrogant, so full of himself, he had not reflected on the possibility of a trap! He went back, picked up the oil lamp and went deeper into the darkness.

He stopped in horror at the scene before him. The old priest lay there, his throat so badly cut the head only hung by sinews of flesh, his skinny body soaked in black blood. Beyond it sprawled the stinking corpses of two baboons. The wind was blowing in the cave and had wafted the smell away but, close up, Amerotke sensed the full horror of the trap. Blood-daubed symbols covered the walls. The stone statue of the goddess had been overthrown. The place had been desecrated.

Amerotke went back to the mouth of the cave, closing his eyes in relief. The cave was dug into the side of a cliff. Surely if he went out on the ledge, he could climb on the rock above, reach the rim of the valley and find his long, dusty way back to Thebes, skirting the rim of the desert? He went out, hands searching for a foothold, and gratefully noticed a narrow, smooth, beaten trackway leading up the rock face. He put down the oil lamp, re-sheathed his sword and clambered up. A low, deep growl shattered the silence and he slithered back, scoring his hands and knees. Further up the trackway a dark shape had appeared, amber eyes glowed in the darkness. A smell of rottenness tinged the night air. Amerotke controlled his panic. The shape, though low and threatening, had not moved. Again the deep-throated growl, this time taken up by others. Amerotke drew his sword and the shape moved, head coming up. Against the blue-black sky Amerotke made out the long ears, ugly head and great maned ruff of a huge hyena, one of those ravening scavengers which hunted the edge of the desert. Amerotke stepped backwards. The hyena, for all its horror, was uncertain. Normally hyenas would never threaten an armed man. However, a hunting pack at night with the smell of blood and rotting flesh luring them on might well close in. They would probe his weakness and attack. Amerotke had heard similar stories from merchants and pedlars, being caught unawares, of wounded men, their cuts and lacerations drawing a pack in on them.

The shape moved, belly close to the earth. The leader of the pack edged forward. Amerotke yelled and screamed, striking his bronze sword against the rock. The threat receded. Amerotke retreated back to the cave where the oil lamp was guttering low. He seized it, burning the tips of his fingers as he tried to build up a fire, the only sure protection against the threat outside. Desperately he tried to make the flames catch the dampened twigs but it was useless. He heard a growl and looked up. A dark, wolf-like shape stood in the entrance to the cave. Even in the poor light Amerotke could make out the full horror of this demon from the darkness. This was no ordinary hyena – the pack leader was probably a bitch in full maturity, its great ruff of hair now on end framing its ugly head, jaws open, eyes like pools of raging fire.

Amerotke screamed and yelled. He picked up the oil lamp and threw it at the mouth of the cave and the shape disappeared. He heard the growls, the pack building to a frenzy. Soaked in sweat, he grasped sword and dagger. Soon they would attack. The fire would provide no protection. He could run, try to leap the gap, but he dismissed it. The gulf was too great and if hyenas could bring down a fleet-footed gazelle, they would catch him.

Amerotke closed his eyes, praying to Ma'at.

'I have done no wrong,' he said quietly. 'Have I not offered sacrifice in your sight? Have I not tried to walk in the truth?'

Again the growl came as the hyena reappeared at the mouth of the cave, another behind it. Amerotke saw an arc of flame through the darkness and something smacked into the rock above the cave followed by shouts and screams. Other fire arrows followed. The hyenas, now alarmed, withdrew.

'Master! Master!'

'Shufoy!'

Amerotke broke into a run then remembered the menace beyond; with his back to the wall of the cave he edged cautiously forward. He peered out into the darkness. He could see a shape moving, a torch was lifted.

'Master, come on! Come on!'

'The planks!' Amerotke shouted.

The shape disappeared. He heard the twang of a bow, one, two fire arrows aimed in the direction of the hyenas. He heard his manservant grumbling, muttering to himself.

'Master, for the love of truth, help me!'

Amerotke went out on to the ledge. The cold night air caught his sweaty skin and made him shiver. He looked to his right. Of the hyena there was no sign.

'They've gone!' Shufoy exclaimed. 'But, master, they could come back. The planks, quickly!'

'Make sure they lie straight.'

Amerotke crouched down and fumbled in the darkness. He found he couldn't stop trembling, he couldn't concentrate. Shufoy threw across the lighted torch, which landed, the flame spluttering but, reigniting the tar and pitch, glowed more fiercely. Amerotke, calming himself, used the light to grasp the edge of the planks and make them secure. Then he was across, crouching beside Shufoy. He allowed his servant to wrap a cloak around him, fighting against the wave of nausea and the burning sensation at the back of his throat.

'How did you know?' he gasped.

'I didn't,' Shufoy declared self-righteously. 'But, master, not here. We must go.'

Amerotke was about to leave but, at Shufoy's insistence, he helped pull the planks back across.

'The hyena is a cunning animal,' Shufoy explained. 'We wouldn't be the first two hapless humans to be hunted through the dark. Are you well? Can you run?'

Amerotke nodded.

'On one condition,' he gasped. 'No proverbs, no maxims, Shufoy!'

'A man's fate is a man's fate,' Shufoy intoned.

'The hyenas don't sound so terrible now,' Amerotke joked.

His manservant put his arm round his waist and the two of them made their way gingerly down the cliffside.

By the time they had left the valley, Amerotke felt weak and sick. His mind teemed with tumbling, terrifying images: the blood-soaked corpses; the baboons with their gaping jaws; that putrid smell and those death-bringing shapes from the darkness.

They skirted the Necropolis, and somehow Shufoy hired a small boat to cross the Nile. On the quayside Amerotke threw all dignity to the wind as he sat down, knees up, arms crossed, eyes closed. He found he couldn't stop shivering.

'What you need is some hot food.'

The invitation was too much. Amerotke began to retch and vomit. He allowed Shufoy to pull him to his feet and to settle him under a palm tree near one of the late-night beer shops. Shufoy put him down on a stool, bawling at the owner not to worry, that they would pay. He then made Amerotke drink a cup of strong white wine.

'You'll feel sleepy but better.'

Amerotke took a deep gulp. He became aware of his surroundings, of sailors in their distinctive attire, laughing and joking with the whores, pimps and pedlars, off-duty soldiers, pompous harbour officials all going about their nightly business. Amerotke felt like jumping to his feet and screaming about the horrors he had seen.

'I can't go back like this,' he warned. 'Norfret will be beside herself.'

'We'll wait here for a while,' Shufoy replied soothingly. 'Some wine and a little food, master.'

'How did you know where I had gone?' Amerotke asked.

He noticed how pale and drawn Shufoy's little face had become. Amerotke stretched and touched the dwarf's cheek.

'You are no servant, Shufoy,' he said quietly. 'You are free and rich. You are my friend to be clothed in the finest linen and sit in a place of honour.'

'No, thank you very much,' Shufoy responded. 'A man's fate is a man's fate. And, if the gods have given you an empty basket, then it's light and easy to carry.' He lowered his head. 'At least I'm not a judge in the Hall of Two Truths being hunted by hyenas in the dead of night. Master, that was a stupid thing you did.'

'I know.' Amerotke leaned back against the tree and wiped the sweat from his neck. 'I am a judge, Shufoy. The thought never entered my head that someone would dare threaten Pharaoh's justice. Tonight I was taught a lesson in humility. I am a man of many limitations and my life is like any other. A flame in the breeze.' He snapped his fingers. 'Which can disappear like that!'

'I wondered where you were going,' Shufoy told him. 'So, as usual, I searched among your papers. I found the snake priest's letter and I followed you.'

Amerotke looked up. 'Where are the bow and arrows?'

'Somewhere in the Valley of the Kings,' Shufoy joked. 'I visited Prenhoe's house and took them. He was gone. Otherwise he would have come with me. Anyway, I took his bow and his quiver. I crossed the Nile and went into the Necropolis. I met that man, the embalmer, the one who was at the trial. He told me he had seen you. So I followed. I saw where you had stopped to help that old woman. Your robe had snagged a rock. I hurried on. It was pitch dark. I couldn't see where you had gone or how to get there until I heard your screams. You had an oil lamp. I caught a flicker of it. I may have no nose but I've two good eyes and ears. Just before leaving the Necropolis I bought,' he smiled and shrugged, 'I stole a pitch torch. The rest you know. I clambered up the rocks.'

'I didn't know about your skill with fire arrows,' Amerotke said.

'I was an archer once,' Shufoy replied proudly. 'One thing I learned on my journeys, no animal will brave fire. A sword, dagger, but fire? Believe me, master, in the desert, in the dead of night, fire truly is the gift of the gods. Now tell me, master, why were you there?'

He refilled Amerotke's cup and listened as Amerotke recounted what had happened since Meneloto had first been tried before him in the Hall of Two Truths. About the rivalries in the council, of his meeting with Hatusu, the deaths of Ipuwer and Amenhotep.

Shufoy recalled that wax effigy pushed into his hands the night before, but he decided not to mention it. If his master had been foolish so had he. He should have warned Amerotke, shown him the waxen effigy and alerted him to the dangers. The dwarf quietly vowed he'd never make that mistake again.

'There's no doubt,' he declared once Amerotke had finished, 'that the assassin struck at you tonight.'

'But why like that?' Amerotke asked. 'Why not a cup of poison or a snake?'

'It was similar to the others. Amenhotep was lured to some lonely place along the Nile and butchered. I tell you this, master. The assassin was at least half successful. For some strange reason that old snake priest Labda had to die. He wanted to silence him. Only the gods know for what reason. But you're different. You were not at Sakkara with divine Pharaoh. You are not to be punished but simply removed. If I hadn't found that note, it might have been weeks, months, if ever, before the bloodied remains found in that cave were traced to you. The assassin simply wanted you to disappear. Those hyenas had been deliberately enticed in, their appetites whetted. Once the fire was gone, they closed in. It would have looked like some dreadful accident.'

Amerotke drained his cup and put it down. He heard sounds from deep in the town, men shouting and yelling.

'Something's gone wrong!' He rose unsteadily to his feet, looking up at the night sky. Was it a fire?

Shufoy grabbed him by the wrist.

'As I followed you, master, a chariot squadron came into Thebes, or what was left of it. The horses were blown, the chariot riders looked bloodied and dusty. I heard whispers, gossip that something dreadful's happened in the north!'

Amerotke walked towards the noise, Shufoy padding behind him. They left the quayside, hastening through the narrow, winding streets into the great enclosure before one of the temples. People milled about, thronging round three young officers. From their insignia Amerotke could see they were from the Isis regiment. He pushed his way through and seized one by the arm. The fellow would have pushed him away, for Amerotke was bloodied and dishevelled, but he held up his ring.

'I am Amerotke, chief judge in the Hall of Two Truths! What's the matter?'

The soldier led him away from the rest, closer to a shop where a pitch torch had been fixed to a crevice in the wall. He studied Amerotke's face and demanded to see the ring again.

'You are what you claim to be, my lord Amerotke.' The soldier bowed.

'Never mind! What has happened?'

'You'll be needed at the palace,' the officer replied. 'I and my companions are rejoining our regiment. The Mitanni and a huge army have crossed the Sinai. They threaten Egypt.'

Montu: falcon god, usually depicted as a man with the head of a hawk wearing a sun disc surmounted by two feathers. He is the Egyptian god of war.

CHAPTER 12

The four great regiments of Egypt's power, the Osiris, Isis, Horus and Amun-Ra, were now advancing north in massed might along the eastern bank of the Nile. Each regiment had its own silver insignia and standards though these were now dulled by the thick clouds of grey-white dust sent up by the tramping feet.

The army had been marching fast for two weeks; the scribes marking off the *iter*, each six and a half miles long, which marked its progress. Provisions and water had been carefully guarded and apportioned out to cover each *iter*. Nevertheless, the men were both hungry and thirsty. They gazed enviously to their left where the royal war galleys with their gilded prows, carved in the shape of snarling animals, cut through the water of the Nile. The marines on board stood to arms, their bronze armour catching the sun. The rowers bent over their oars to the shouts of the overseers and officers striding along the deck in between. The breeze had fallen and it was essential for the galleys to keep close contact with the regiments; in their holds they bore water, precious foods, arms and provisions. Moreover, the war fleet guarded their left flank.

The Mitanni were cunning fighters. Intelligence was difficult to collect and the Mitanni might have crossed the Nile in an attempt to outflank them. Worse still, if the meagre reports they had received were to be believed, the Mitanni could have even seized war galleys themselves and be cruising down the Nile intent on devastation and destruction.

Nevertheless the army was in good heart. From across the water came the faint song of the oarsmen bellowing defiance at their unseen enemy:

'We go upstream in victory!
Slaughtering the enemy in our own land!

Hail to thee, oh great Montu, mighty god of war!
And to Sekhmet the devouress who will ravage Egypt's enemies!
We will come back downstream burning their camps, stripping their
corpses!
Hail to thee, oh great Montu!'

The song rose and fell. Amerotke, marching to the right of his phalanx, also gazed enviously at the water. He lifted his gourd and took a sip then paused, opened the small palette he carried in the bag slung across his back and applied more rings of kohl around his eyes, sure protection against the wind and dust. After putting the palette away he marched wearily on. His white headdress, bordered with the red stripe of an officer, afforded some protection against the sun but his throat was parched, his feet calloused and his legs ached, begging for rest. Yet he had to maintain the cool poise of a senior officer. His men would study his mood. Even now he knew that those grumblers among the Neferu, the new recruits, were watching intently for any sign of weakness or softness in this great nobleman, their officer.

'When will we rest, sir?' a voice shouted.

'When it's dark!' Amerotke shouted back. 'Keep walking, lads! It strengthens the thighs. The women will whistle when you return to Thebes.'

'They'll be admiring much more than my thighs!' a voice shouted back. 'If I don't have a woman soon I'll be walking on three legs, not two!'

The bawdy remark caused a ripple of laughter among the ranks as the badinage was passed on. Amerotke strode on more vigorously. Above him vultures flew, great feathery wings extended, 'Pharaoh's hens', or so the troops called them. They would follow this long column of men waiting for pickings but the soldiers didn't mind. Although scavengers, the soldiers regarded the vultures as a sign of good fortune.

Amerotke shaded his eyes and glanced to the right where the great chariot squadrons, thousands in number, five hundred being attached to each regiment, thundered along in clouds of dust. Among them was his own squadron of two hundred and fifty men for Amerotke bore the title of *pedjet*, chariot commander, leader of the corps nicknamed the 'Hounds of Horus'. His own chariot would be driven by his *skedjen*, or charioteer. It would be easier to travel with him but, although tempting, this would only have slowed the column of march and wearied the horses. The chariots were light, of gilded wickerwork, but they also carried a driver, bow, quiver and throwing spears. The prancing Canaanite horses, with their war plumes dancing in the breeze, had to stay as fresh as possible in case of sudden attack.

Far to the north and east were a line of scouts, mercenaries drawn from the desert wanderers or sand-dwellers. Omendap, the commanding chief, did not trust these. The chariots were a sure defence against sudden attack, a wall of bronze and horseflesh to protect their right flank and allow the regiments to deploy if the Mitanni appeared.

Amerotke gazed up at the sky. It would be just past noon in Thebes. They had been marching for over two weeks. They had passed Abydos and Memphis and now were following the Nile, seeking out the Mitanni, massing, so their scouts believed, somewhere to the northeast. Rumours had swept the regiments, how the sacred shrines of Amun-Ra had been pillaged and burned and now the Mitanni, rested and refreshed, awaited Egypt's army. Once this was destroyed, the rich, lush valley of the Nile would lie unprotected and the Mitanni could take their pickings at ease.

Amerotke just hoped Omendap was right, that they would take the enemy by surprise. Omendap argued constantly, during the long meetings at night, how the Mitanni would not expect this huge host of men hastily organised by the scribes from the House of Battle. These, and the clerks from the House of War, had worked non-stop to bring in arms, provisions, carts, donkeys and all the impedimenta of battle. Amerotke ruefully reflected that, if they surprised the Mitanni, it would be a change for the better. Spies from the House of Secrets had come back to Thebes with news of a great hostile army which had crossed the Sinai desert, keeping well away from the royal highway, the Road of Horus, and the small Egyptian garrison placed there to defend it. The Mitanni had advanced in stealth and now controlled both the road and the desert with its mines of gold, silver and turquoise.

Somewhere in front of the column the trumpeters among the army musicians blared out fanfares to stir the blood of the marching troops. The different battalions answered with roars and cheers before they began to sing songs, usually filthy, about each other.

Each battalion had its own name: 'the Roaring Bull of Nubia', or 'Pharaoh's Raging Panther'. Each corps jealously guarded its reputation and used the long march to exchange good-natured banter with each other. Scouts on foam-flecked horses thundered along the column towards the officers in front. Amerotke watched them go, his mind drifting back to that night when Shufoy had rescued him from the terrors in the Valley of the Kings. They were halfway home when they had been overtaken by royal pages who insisted that he return with them to the House of a Million Years. Shufoy took messages to Norfret, while he hurried to the palace to find the royal circle in uproar. The jealousies and divisions had now come to the surface. Scribes from the House of Battle clashed with those from the House of War though both united in shouting abuse at the scribes from the House of Secrets and their powerlessness in revealing this terrible threat to the kingdom. The councillors were no better. Hatusu, Sethos and Senenmut openly jibed at Rahimere while the Vizier, supported by Bayletos and the priests, laid the blame squarely at Hatusu's door.

'If you had known your place,' Bayletos had sneered, 'and allowed the government of Thebes to be united, we would not be unprepared. Regiments could have been sent.'

'Nonsense!' Senenmut had hurled back. 'Her royal highness is of Pharaoh's blood. If you had not whiled away her time on who does this and who does that . . . !'

Eventually Omendap had reminded them of the threat facing them, laying out in clear, precise sentences the real threat the Mitanni, under their war-like king Tushratta, posed.

'We have only a few troops in the north,' he declared. 'The Mitanni have crossed Sinai. They have probably burned cities and villages and suborned our military garrisons. They will not strike at the Delta or march south, they'll wait and see.'

'For what?' Hatusu asked.

'They'll know about the divisions here,' Omendap added bitterly. 'Perhaps even of the deaths, the terrible murders. They hope we will only send some raggle-taggle army north which they'll annihilate before moving south.' Omendap smiled thinly. 'We have one great advantage. Because, how shall I put it, of the sensitive atmosphere in Thebes following divine Pharaoh's death, four regiments stand outside the city ready to march. A fifth, the Anubis, can follow on behind us. We must strike and strike quickly. The army must be on the move shortly after dawn.'

His statement caused fresh uproar but Omendap coolly and calmly repeated his reasons.

'You will command it,' Rahimere declared, his eyes sliding to Hatusu. 'But her highness should really accompany the army. As the lord Senenmut says, she is of Pharaoh's blood, the troops will demand that.'

Hatusu was going to object but Senenmut whispered in her ear. Sethos, too, murmured his advice. Yet Rahimere had been clever. The campaign could be a fruitless one; the Mitanni might well gather treasure and slaves and re-cross the frontier. Or Hatusu might suffer a setback. Either way she would come creeping back to Thebes to find Rahimere's control over the palaces and temples had only tightened and, of course, he would have personal custody of the divine boy. Hatusu had accepted but she pointed to the war crown, the blue helmet Pharaoh always wore in battle.

'I shall take that,' she declared. 'So the troops know that Pharaoh's spirit marches with them!'

Rahimere had lowered his head.

'And take your councillors with you,' he quipped. 'My lord Amerotke, were you not a chariot commander? General Omendap, you'll need all the experienced commanders you can.'

'I will go.' Amerotke spoke up, his face flushed with anger, the words out before he reflected. 'During this time the Hall of Two Truths will be closed.'

Rahimere merely blinked and looked away. Amerotke knew he was committed. However he struggled, however he tried, he had thrown his lot in with Hatusu who was already pushing back her throne-like chair. The meeting of the royal circle was ended.

Amerotke had hastened home and explained what was happening. Norfret had gone pale, biting her lip. She tried to put a good face on it but Amerotke glimpsed the worry in her eyes. He put his arms round her.

'I'll be safe,' he reassured her. 'I'll come back to Thebes in glory.'

These were the only few moments they had alone. The boys had burst in with a whole spate of questions. Amerotke had reassured them. Prenhoe and Asural were sent for. They were given strict instructions about the custody of the temple and how they were to help Shufoy protect the lady Norfret and her two sons.

'Can't I come with you?' Shufoy had demanded. 'You will need someone to watch your back.'

Amerotke had crouched down and taken the little man's hands in his.

'No, Shufoy, believe me! You must stay here. The custody and care of Norfret and my two sons are your concern. If the worst comes to the worst, and you will know before that happens, protect my family. If you give me your word, I can march a more contented man.'

Shufoy had agreed. Shortly afterwards Amerotke had left to join the regiments already debouching from their camp, forming up in the column of march.

Amerotke heard a cheer and broke from his reverie. He looked along the column. Hatusu in her chariot thundered out of a cloud of dust. The troops clashed their arms, the chariot slowed down as Hatusu accepted the plaudits of her troops. The chariot's huge wheels on the back made it quick and easy to manoeuvre. At the front rose a great standard displaying the vulture goddess, Hatusu's personal emblem. On the sides hung a blue-gold quiver, a large horn bow and throwing spears.

The two black horses were the finest from Pharaoh's stables. Caparisoned in white linen cloths, they strained at their harness, the great white ostrich plumes between their ears dancing with every movement. Amerotke recognised the horses, the Glory of Hathor and the Power of Anubis, two of the fastest chariot horses in the entire four regiments. Their driver was Senenmut, dressed in a white kilt covered with leather straps. Across his naked chest hung a bronze-studded war belt. Hatusu, standing beside him, had her hair bound back in a fillet. She was dressed in body armour, small bronze plates riveted to a linen tunic which fell below her knees. In her belt she carried a narrow-bladed dagger. All around clustered other chariots bearing Hatusu's personal bodyguard.

Between the chariots loped the well-armed Nakhtuaa or 'strong-arm boys', tough veterans from different regiments in their stiffened red and white headdresses. They were armed with rounded, bronzed bucklers, swords and daggers, their bodies protected by linen-padded armour with large oval groin guards.

The royal chariot approached and stopped. Hatusu leaned over the side. Amerotke considered her more beautiful now than when she'd been clad in all her glorious court robes. She was vibrant, her face and eyes full of passion as if revelling in the glory, the might and the power of Egypt's massed armies.

'Your feet are calloused, Amerotke?'

'A little harder, your highness, than they were in Thebes.'

Hatusu laughed deep in her throat and rested her hand on Senenmut's sweat-glistening arm, squeezing it before climbing down from the chariot. The troops marching by gazed appreciatively at her as she walked with a slight swagger towards their commander. She was so slender, so well composed; despite the heat, no sweat glistened on her brow or face. She offered Amerotke a wine skin.

'Just a sip,' she warned. 'It sweetens the tongue and gladdens the heart.'

Amerotke obeyed.

'Keep your face straight,' she murmured, taking the wineskin back, 'but the Mitanni are closer than we think. We camp tonight near the oasis at Selina, there's grass for fodder, water and shade for some of us. Tomorrow we'll know the worst.'

She walked back to the chariot and climbed in. Senenmut bowed, picked up the reins and both chariot and escort went further down the column.

Amerotke watched it go. Omendap, not Hatusu, was technically commander-in-chief, and he carried the field marshal's baton. At first the troops had regarded Hatusu simply as a symbol. They even called her the 'soldiers' mascot' and quietly mocked but, since they had left Thebes, Hatusu's influence and power had grown. She had shown no weakness, asked for no favours. She openly demonstrated that she was a soldier's daughter used to the rigours of camp life. She was constantly on the move, stopping and talking to the men, learning their names and never forgetting. On one occasion one of the strong-arm boys, a large, fat man, had openly jibed at her breasts and how comfortably they sat under the thin padded armour. Hatusu had heard the remark but, instead of striking the man or consigning him to some field punishment, she had pointed to his bare, heavily muscled chest.

'One of the reasons I like talking to you lads,' she cracked back, 'is that I am secretly jealous. If I had tits as big as yours I wouldn't have to wear armour!'

The remark had created surprised delight and guffaws of laughter. Hatusu was seen as one of them, a soldier who did not insist on ceremony, who shared their difficulties and hardships. Increasingly, as the army camped at night, Hatusu and Senenmut would visit the different battalions. Her speech was the same wherever she went: they were going to seek out Egypt's enemies, break their necks, smash their heads, teach them a lesson they would never forget. Those Mitanni who could return home would limp all the way and take back tales of the terrible fury and vengeance of Pharaoh.

In the war council Hatusu increasingly exerted her influence; Omendap, who appreciated her shrewd judgement, always conceded her point of view. Hatusu insisted the army stay together. It was to keep to the Nile and bring the Mitanni to battle on ground of their choosing. Amerotke secretly hoped that Hatusu's judgement would prove effective.

'Are you sun-struck?'

Amerotke started and looked up, shielding his eyes against the sun, to see Sethos, astride a horse. The eyes and ears of the King looked fit, untroubled by the heat or dust. Amerotke smiled.

'No chariot for you, my lord Sethos?'

The royal prosecutor was known as a good horseman, one of the few nobles of Egypt who preferred to ride bareback than in a chariot. Sethos surveyed the column.

'Hatusu is showing the flag again,' he murmured.

Amerotke caught the horse's reins and followed his companion's gaze.

'She mentioned a surprise.'

'I think we are all going to be surprised,' Sethos said. He leaned down and patted Amerotke on the shoulder. 'The Mitanni are much closer. Perhaps, within days, this matter will be decided once and for all. And the other matter,' Sethos continued, 'divine Pharaoh's death, the murder of Amenhotep?'

'It will have to wait. As you say, my lord Sethos, within a week we may all be past caring.'

'When we passed Sakkara,' Sethos said as he stroked his horse's neck, 'you glimpsed the pyramids?'

Amerotke nodded.

'It brought it all back,' Sethos went on. 'Divine Pharaoh's visit and what has happened since he returned and died before the statue of Amun-Ra. Ah well!' He gathered up the reins. 'Tonight, Amerotke, we'll share a cup of wine, yes?'

And, before the judge could answer, Sethos kicked in his heels and galloped after the royal cortège.

They reached the oasis late in the afternoon. The sergeants and drill masters soon had the troops digging a defensive ditch, setting up a makeshift palisade which was reinforced with the shields of the foot soldiers. At first chaos reigned. Horse lines had to be established, water skins filled, latrines dug. Each corps was given a corner of the huge camp. At the far end lay the royal enclosure, defended by another palisade and hand-picked men from the regiments. Inside this stood Hatusu's pavilion as well as those of Omendap and the other senior generals, all clustered round the shrine to Amun-Ra which the priests had set up; their incense-laden offerings already sent a sweet fragrance back into the camp.

Amerotke was always surprised at how quickly the chaos was resolved and order restored. Chariot squadrons were sent out to ensure that the enemy did not launch a surprise attack. The quartermasters soon had large pots of water filled from the springs and irrigation canals which snaked out from the Nile. Camp fires were lit, food distributed; foraging parties went out to nearby villages to requisition stores, animals, anything the army could need.

Amerotke's small tent was set up just within the royal enclosure. It consisted of nothing more than a few poles driven into the ground and covered with sheets to protect him against the night air. He drew rations from the common pot and ate like the rest, cross-legged on the ground. Afterwards he retired, washed and changed and knelt before the small shrine of Ma'at which he had brought. Outside the noise of the camp subsided as darkness fell, broken by the sound of the armourers, the neigh of horses, the shouts and yells of the officers and the ever-present hum from around the camp fires. Amerotke extinguished the oil lamp and went out through the enclosure.

He visited his own chariot squadron. The officer assured him that the horses were well watered and fed, dried off and ready for battle at a moment's notice. Amerotke then crouched under a palm tree. Nearby a physician was cleaning cuts and wounds, distributing small pots of ointment for those soldiers complaining of injuries to their feet or shins after the long, hurried march. Somewhere in the dark a flute started to play. Camp followers swarmed about, the great raggle-taggle which followed the army: whores, tinkers, pedlars. Some had been with them from Thebes; others they had collected on the long march. Long trumpet blasts gave out the hours and passing of the night. Each corps made ready for the dawn sacrifice. Shadows slipped in and out of the camp – lovers, male and female, searching for some quiet place so they could lie in hot, lusty embrace, forget the hardships of the day and the possible threat of tomorrow. Heralds moved through the camp, issuing the orders of march and fresh instructions; scouts crept in and out, carts were wheeled up.

Amerotke wondered what was happening in Thebes. Were Norfret and the boys safe? Had Shufoy followed his instructions? A staff officer approached, announcing that General Omendap sent his good favour and would all members of the war council now approach the royal enclosure. Amerotke sighed and got to his feet. He threaded his way through the camp. Inside Omendap's tent the rest of the war council had gathered, seated on camp stools with small tables before them. Hatusu looked unruffled as ever, seated between Senenmut and the general. The others included Sethos, the principal scribes from the House of War and the commanders of the mercenaries and royal regiments. Clerks distributed rolled sheets of papyrus, covered in calculations of food, water and the line of march. The conversation was desultory. Once the clerks left, Hatusu, picking up Omendap's silver axe, tapped the table.

'The Mitanni,' she declared, 'are much closer than we think.'

'So,' Sethos put in, 'we can't go on marching to the sea.'

'It's not what we expected!' Omendap protested. 'Tushratta is proving as sly and as slippery as a mongoose. We expected to encounter raiding parties, perhaps chariot attacks on our line of march. Nothing has happened. Scouts we sent out have failed to return. One did and said he saw no sign of the Mitanni but he had encountered a group of sand-wanderers. They talked of a great army somewhere to the northeast, thousands of chariots, foot soldiers and archers.'

Amerotke felt the hair on the nape of his neck grow cold. He understood what Omendap was saying. This was no petty raid, the Mitanni were here in force. They intended to bring the Egyptian army to battle and have a settling of accounts.

'So, what can we do?' one of the regiment commanders asked.

'That's the good news,' Senenmut joked. 'We have four regiments. Twenty thousand men, plus perhaps two to three thousand mercenaries, though some of those cannot be trusted. Of that twenty thousand, five thousand are chariots.' He shifted a papyrus roll on the table before him and rubbed his face in his hands.

Amerotke caught his unease.

'The Mitanni may well be twice that number,' he said.

'Twice?' Sethos pressed him. 'If our knowledge is so scarce, why not three times, four times?'

Senenmut just stared at him.

'You may well be right.' Hatusu spoke up. 'Tushratta and the Mitanni will have attracted mercenaries, those who resent Pharaoh's rule. If we keep advancing north we may reach the Great Sea and have no other choice but to turn back. If we leave the Nile and strike northeast we enter the Red Lands where water and provisions are scarce. We could go blundering about for months. Tushratta could fall on us, or worse, simply march round us.'

'And while we are in the north,' Amerotke finished the sentence, 'Tushratta is marching on Thebes.'

'We know they are close,' Hatusu said. 'Undoubtedly our scouts have been killed.'

'Or gone over to the enemy?'

'Tomorrow morning,' Hatusu continued, 'we will send out three chariot squadrons. Each will travel as far as they can and sweep back in an arc. More importantly,' she pointed down the table at Amerotke, 'the Anubis regiment has still not caught up with us. Four thousand men and another five hundred chariots. You, my lord Amerotke, must ride back and tell its commander to hasten on.'

'Easier said than done,' Sethos observed, his head bowed.

Nobody challenged him yet all in the tent recognised the unspoken threat. The commander of the Anubis regiment, Nebanum, was a member

179

of Rahimere's circle, his loyalty and reliability highly suspect. He had left Thebes after the royal army but had persisted in staying two or three days' march behind them. Hatusu got to her feet.

'Until we know more,' she concluded as she handed Omendap his silver axe, 'the army will stay here.' She bowed slightly. 'My lords, gentlemen, I bid you good night.'

Amerotke stayed to discuss matters with the others and accepted Sethos' judgement that they were like dogs chasing their own tails. Afterwards, he walked back to his own tent, lit an oil lamp and squatted on the camp bed, staring out at the night. What would happen when he went back to Nebanum? If the commander refused to march any faster? Amerotke lay down on the bed, wrapping his cloak around him, closed his eyes and murmured a prayer to Ma'at.

In another part of the camp, well away from the royal enclosure, the Amemet leader was also making a prayer to his own dreadful god. All around him sprawled members of his gang, weapons piled beside them. The Amemet leader did not care about the Mitanni or the threatened prospect of battle. This was not the first time he had followed in an army's wake. Where armies went, plunder and easy pickings were always available. If it came to hard knocks or any real danger, he and his troop of killers would simply disappear into the night. True, he had accepted the small cask of gold and silver, the little leather sack of pearls and the commission which went with it. He was to follow the royal army and, at a given time, receive instructions on what to do.

The Amemet leader sighed. So far the journey had been uneventful and uncomfortable. His men had stolen from the villages, swindled the soldiers and lived on the fat of the land. If the rumours were true and the Mitanni were close? The Amemet leader looked at the stars then closed his eyes. Well, he'd wait no longer but disappear into the shadows. After all, he reasoned as he lay down, he was a craftsman and could only work with the materials given.

Anubis: god of the dead depicted as a jackal-headed man.

CHAPTER 13

'Amerotke! Amerotke! Wake up!'

Senenmut was shaking him by the shoulder.

'Quietly!' Senenmut ordered. 'Follow me!'

Amerotke grabbed his cloak, pushed his feet into sandals and followed Hatusu's confidant out of the tent. The night air was harsh and cold. The camp had settled for the night, the silence broken only by the cries of sentries and neighs of horses. Camp fires had dulled, giving way to the darkness. Amerotke followed Senenmut across to Omendap's tent where Hatusu and Sethos were standing by the palm-leaf bed. Omendap lay on his side, blankets pushed back; the cup on the small table beside the camp bed had been knocked over. A physician was trying to force a cup between Omendap's lips. The general groaned, rolling over on his back, his face pallid and sweat-soaked.

'What are you doing?' Hatusu hissed.

'My lady, I'm giving him mandrake, fleabane and sulphur with a dash of opium. His stomach must be cleansed.'

The physician pressed on. Omendap rolled back and vomited violently into the bowl the physician held to his lips. Time and again the general was made to drink, time and again he vomited. Occasionally, the physician gave the ailing general a sip from a water gourd. Senenmut picked up a small wine flask and passed it to Amerotke.

'It's Charou,' Senenmut said.

Amerotke read the inscription around the neck. It came from Omendap's own cellars and, according to the date stamp, had been sealed some five years previously. He sniffed and caught the acrid smell.

'He's been poisoned!' Hatusu whispered. 'He took that jar from his own cellar. We're examined others. Some are good, others tainted.'

183

She walked up and down playing with the ring on her fingers. Hatusu was dressed in a plain white nightshift, the sandals on her feet unbuckled and loose. She looked to Amerotke like a frightened young girl.

'Was it done here?' Amerotke asked.

'Here or Thebes,' Senenmut replied. 'The general drew from his own cellars. It would be easy to slip in flasks of tainted wine. The inscription's probably false, the seal forged. Omendap was weary, he wouldn't even bother to look. This could have happened tonight, tomorrow or a week ago. It all depended on which flask Omendap picked.'

'Will he live?' Hatusu demanded.

'I cannot tell you, my lady,' the physician replied, opening Omendap's mouth. 'The general is strong, of good physique.'

'How did you discover it?' Amerotke asked.

'Our spies brought in the survivor of a Mitanni patrol. They still have him beyond the horse lines. I didn't want the camp roused. I came to tell Omendap and found him in agony, slipping in and out of consciousness. I woke the lady Hatusu, my lord Sethos and called the physician.'

'We've done all we can,' Hatusu said firmly. She grasped the physician by the shoulder. 'This is to be kept secret, you understand?' She squeezed harder. 'Or, I swear, your head will leave your shoulders!'

The physician, a narrow-faced old man, glared back.

'I understand you, my lady. If Omendap's sickness is known to the camp . . .'

'Senenmut!' Hatusu clicked her fingers. 'Order some of your strong-arm boys to guard the tent. Everyone, and I mean everyone, is to be turned away. Physician, if Omendap dies, you die. If he lives, I'll cram the cup you are using full of pure gold.'

They followed her out, across into her own tent. Amerotke was surprised at its sparseness: a simple cot bed, some costly chests, a small table with wine cups and a jug of water. Clothes lay tossed on the ground. On a stand was her body armour, the blue war crown of Egypt and at its foot a rounded shield and a war belt with curving sword and dagger. Hatusu sat down on a stool and put her face in her hands. The rest, without a word, crouched cross-legged on the ground around her.

'This was meant to happen,' she hissed, lifting her face. 'Omendap had to die. When I get back to Thebes, I'll take Rahimere's balls, stuff them into his mouth, then take his head!' She wiped the spittle from the corner of her mouth; her face was white and drawn, her eyes large. 'I'll take each and every one of them. I'll crucify them against the walls of Thebes! Rahimere and his gang wanted this: Hatusu and her army to die in the sands!'

'My lady, we do not know if Rahimere was responsible for the attempt on Omendap's life,' Amerotke warned.

'We do not know,' she mimicked, shaking her head. 'We do not know. What are you going to do now, Amerotke? Summon the court? Listen to all the evidence?'

Amerotke would have risen to his feet but Senenmut grabbed him by the wrist.

'My lady, Amerotke is simply giving a warning. The killer could be someone else. Now is not the time to be pointing fingers. The god Amun-Ra knows the truth. Justice will be done.'

'We have no gods,' Hatusu said. 'Nothing but the sand, the wind and the burning heat.'

She spoke so passionately, so fiercely, Amerotke flinched at the hate in her voice. Did she believe in anything? Had Hatusu changed so her only god was burning ambition? Her desire to rule?

She sat up and took a deep breath.

'Senenmut, have the Mitanni brought in!'

Her adviser disappeared. A short while later the guards brought in a bloodied, bruised man, his black leather body armour torn and cut, his beard and moustache caked in blood. One eye was closed, and his captors had ripped the rings from his earlobes. The prisoner was flung at Hatusu's feet. This was the first time Amerotke had seen a Mitanni warrior: he was short, thickset, his head shaven at the front, his long black hair, thick and oiled, falling down to his shoulders. He gasped for water. Senenmut, crouching beside him, forced a cup between his lips. The man drank greedily.

'You are going to die,' Senenmut told him. 'What you have to decide is whether you wish to die quickly or pegged out in the heat for the hyenas and jackals to gnaw at.'

The man gasped and sat back on his heels.

'Does he understand our tongue?' Sethos asked.

Senenmut spoke again, his language harsh and guttural. The Mitanni turned, lip curling, his thickened tongue licking at the bruises on the corner of his mouth. Senenmut spoke again then glanced at Hatusu.

'I've offered him his life.'

'Offer him the throne of Thebes for all I care!' she replied.

The questioning continued. Senenmut's face became grey. He kept swallowing hard; the Mitanni sensed his nervousness and chuckled until Senenmut slapped the prisoner viciously across the face. Senenmut looked at the guards.

'Take him out beyond the camp! Cut his head off!'

The Mitanni was dragged to his feet and hustled out. Senenmut went to close the flap. He joined the semi-circle before Hatusu.

'The Mitanni have taken over an oasis and one of our fortresses to the northeast. Their chariot squadrons are a short way off. They have plundered the mines and used the wealth to bribe the sand-dwellers and desert-wanderers, which is why our scouts have not returned. The information we have learned is false. Tushratta is only a day's march away. His army is at least twice ours. It's well provisioned, well armed, with at least six thousand heavy war chariots. If these break out, my lady, they could roll into our camp.' He spread his hands.

'And will they attack?' Hatusu placed her hands on her knees. She reminded Amerotke of the goddess Ma'at: all emotion was gone, her face was translucent, calm. She looked above their heads.

'They can't hide for ever,' Senenmut declared. 'Provisions and water are running out. If they attack then it will be soon. They want to bring us to battle and utterly destroy us.'

Hatusu's head went down. She sat there silently. Amerotke heard the cries of the camp, the neighing of the horses.

'You promised that Mitanni his life.'

Senenmut shrugged. 'My lord Amerotke, I gave him his life, for a short while, and his death will be quick. If he lived he could tell his masters how vulnerable we are or worse, let it be known here how strong the Mitanni really are. We have camp followers, the usual rabble which follows any army. They always seem to find out what is going to happen. They'll desert first, then the Neferu will follow. Within days we'll have half our force.'

'They'll attack soon.' Hatusu spoke sharply. 'My lord Amerotke, you will take a small chariot squadron. Go back down the Nile. Order Nebanum to bring the Anubis regiment up by forced march. My lord Senenmut, I will take over from General Omendap. His sickness is to be kept secret. I want the camp strengthened. The chariot squadrons are to be taken a mile to the north, and only a small squadron should be left here.' She got to her feet, clapping her hands. 'It will be dawn in an hour. Amerotke.' She went across to a table and, picking up one of her personal seals, thrust it into his hand. 'If Nebanum won't obey my order, kill him!' She clapped her hands again. 'Come on! There is little time to waste!'

A short while later Amerotke, his charioteer standing beside him, led the small squadron out of the camp. They followed the dusty, winding road they'd followed the previous day, a strange sensation as the sky lightened and the sun's rays grew stronger. The Nile, with its lush green banks, shimmered in the morning heat; flocks of birds rose up alarmed by some animal, crocodile or hippopotamus, splashing in the shadows. To their left the desert turned gold-red as if welcoming the sun's rays. The morning chill disappeared. The dew quickly evaporated and the sun rose, a glorious ball of brilliant fire. Under Amerotke's direction the chariot squadron kept close, travelling three abreast, one out in front, and another on their left flank to ensure they were not surprised. By the time the sun had fully risen the horses had moved into a gallop, the chariots swaying and bouncing.

They stopped at noon, sheltering down near the river, resting under palm trees against the fierce heat. The horses were watered and fed, the men ate and drank. Like Amerotke they had changed for battle into bronze corselets, linen kilts covered with leather straps, tightly fitting sandals. The drivers wore protective neck-plates and bronze collars with a linen loin guard. Their lightweight chariots were armed with quiver, bow and throwing spears.

The men did not question his orders. They were from Amerotke's squadron and, if necessary, would ride back to Thebes if he wished. Nevertheless, he could sense their unease. On one side flowed the quiet Nile, now sluggish, on the other lay the silent watchful desert. Amerotke wondered if rumour had begun to spread. Did the men sense that a huge Mitanni army was moving to meet them? They were travelling back to urge the Anubis to march on, so they must suspect something was wrong. Amerotke got up and clambered up the bank. He stood, hands on hips, staring out across the desert, flinching at the blast of heat. The air shimmered, disfiguring and twisting the distant rocks, the dips in the ground: a whole army could march there, he thought, yet keep its presence hidden. He urged the men to their feet.

'We must move on!'

The horses were re-harnessed. Amerotke himself felt an uneasy disquiet as if they were being watched. The horses, refreshed, broke into a quick canter, the silence shattered by their snorting, their galloping hooves, the rattle of the wheels, the cries of their drivers.

They reached the Anubis camp shortly before nightfall. Amerotke told his squadron to stay outside, to eat and drink the little food they had brought. Accompanied by an officer, he went into the camp. The Anubis was well organised, the palisade and ditch dug according to regulations. A shrine for the god had been set up in the centre of the camp but there was none of the sense of frenetic activity Amerotke expected. Nebanum, heavy-eyed with sleep, came out, a linen robe thrown over his shoulders. Sharp-featured and hooded-eyed, Nebanum scratched his balding head and yawned as Amerotke introduced himself then, turning, ordered the priest beside him to fill his beer jug. Nebanum took a gulp, washed his mouth out and spat, barely missing Amerotke's feet.

'So, Omendap sent you.' He glanced over Amerotke's shoulder at the standard planted before the shrine. 'I suppose you've brought orders for me to hurry up. But I can only march with due regard for myself and my horse.' He yawned.

'My lord.' Amerotke smiled and stepped closer. He produced the cartouche Hatusu had given him. 'General Omendap has not sent me but her highness.'

Nebanum forced a smile and, following protocol, bowed and brushed the cartouche with his lips.

'My orders are quite simple,' Amerotke continued. 'I am here to re-emphasise Pharaoh and Pharaoh's power.'

'Life, health and prosperity,' Nebanum cynically murmured.

'You are to force-march within the hour,' Amerotke ordered. He drew his sword and his officer did likewise. 'Or I'm to execute you now and take over your command! That is Pharaoh's divine will!'

The change in Nebanum was startling. Amerotke realised Hatusu and Senenmut had made a mistake. They had treated this troublesome commander softly and he had grown insolent in his disobedience, but like any officer he had to obey without question Pharaoh's authority.

Within the hour the camp was roused, baggage wagons hastily stacked, chariots hitched and, before the sun had fully risen, the Anubis regiment was force-marching along the road. Columns of sweating men, fully armed, moved rapidly to the north, signal trumpets brayed, drums beat.

Amerotke ordered his squadron to hang back in the rear. As the morning wore on little could be seen to left or right, because the tramping feet and the chariots alongside raised thick clouds of dust.

At first the regiment had been startled; the men grumbling at the meagre rations and the discomfort of the urgent march. Eventually they settled down. Priests led battle hymns which were taken up. The morning drew on and the heat, the dull pain of aching limbs and the all-enveloping dust imposed a harsh silence, broken only by the rattle of the chariot wheels and the rhythmic pounding of thousands of marching feet.

Now and again a short break was ordered. Water was quickly distributed, then the march continued.

By late afternoon Amerotke realised they were close to Hatusu's camp. The dusty plain gave way to more luxuriant bushes, shrubs and trees. The dry heat of the day subsided; suddenly Amerotke heard shouts and yells. Scouts in lone chariots were now racing back to the column. Amerotke urged his driver on. As he did so an ominous rumble, like thunder, rose from his right. He reached the front of the column where Nebanum and the other officers were clustered. They, too, had heard the rumble and observed the growing cloud of dust from the east; scout chariots were racing back. One of them reached the column and reined in. The driver was wounded, an arrow in his shoulder. When his companion jumped down, they saw his helmet was discarded, his bow broken. He threw this on the ground and knelt before Nebanum.

'The Mitanni, my lord! A screen of chariots!'

But Nebanum was not listening. He stood like a man transfixed, staring out across the desert.

'In the name of all that's holy!' Amerotke shouted. 'Order your men to deploy!'

He stared down the ranks where confusion was breaking out. Some of the veterans were unslinging their shields, trying to bring the different corps into some sort of formation, but the recruits were beginning to panic, fearful of the growing dust, the rumbling noise, the loss of their own chariots. They were pressing forward, breaking ranks, ignoring the screams of their officers. The ripples rose to waves as men surged forward. Amerotke looked round in horror at the line of chariots which broke out of the dust. Row upon row of Mitanni, horses galloping like the wind, chariots bouncing. They charged in closed, massed ranks, standards displayed. Chaos broke out in the Anubis regiment. Egyptian chariots charged forward to meet the enemy. Some of the foot formed a shield wall. A few other quick-thinking officers went back to their posts. Nebanum, however, jumped into his chariot, screaming at his driver who lashed the horses into a gallop, away from the sea of bronzed might heading towards them.

Amerotke cursed. Hatusu's camp could only be a few leagues away. If the Anubis broke and fled, the Mitanni would simply follow them back into camp. He signalled to his own squadron, shouting and yelling. A few of the chariots joined him, but of the rest there was no sign. The Mitanni were now closer, horses' heads straining forward, war plumes nodding, the sun shimmering on the bronze-work of the chariots. Amerotke could make out the black-scaled armour, the grotesque war helmets. The air sang with the hum of arrows. Men began to fall and then, like a wave racing into the shore, the Mitanni struck the disintegrating ranks of the Anubis regiment. The front of the column was spared but Amerotke saw rank after rank of them go down, cast aside by the charging horses, crushed and beaten by the spiked wheels. One or two brave souls tried to leap for the chariots, only to fall away, jabbed at by spear or sword or taking the full impact of the horn bow carried by the archer inside. The Mitanni chariots were heavier than the Egyptian, the wheels in the middle of the chariot, the axle strengthened to support a driver, spearman and archer. The charge was like a child's game, with the Egyptians going down like skittles before a ball. The right flank of the Anubis column collapsed as spears flashed out, left and right, in an orgy of killing. The Mitanni whipped their horses to a lather as they ploughed like a sword into the crumbling Egyptian ranks. Discipline collapsed. Shields, bows and swords were cast aside. Panic destroyed all order. Behind the Mitanni came hordes of foot soldiers. Now and again a Mitanni chariot would overturn, spilling out its three-man crew. The Egyptians would close, clubbing and hacking, but others came to their rescue. More and more of the Egyptian foot pressed to the top of the column. The first wave of the Mitanni chariots was now turning, sweeping back into the fight. The dust rose blocking out the sky, vultures glided in attracted by the noise and the horror, the iron tang of blood.

'My lord!' One of Amerotke's officers ran up and grasped the chariot rail. 'My lord, we must warn the army!'

Amerotke nodded. He closed his eyes and thought of the long, rectangular Egyptian camp. At the far end stood the royal enclosure. He would avoid the main gate and ride along its eastern flank where he could warn Hatusu and Senenmut about what was happening. He signalled to his driver. The man heaved a sigh of relief and snapped the reins. Amerotke's chariot shot forward; the horses, restless and frightened by the noise and clamour, were only too eager to escape this place of slaughter. In a short while the chariot was at full gallop. Amerotke screamed out what directions the driver could take, repeating the order over the rumble of the wheels and the drumming hooves.

He looked behind him. The Anubis regiment was now enveloped in thick clouds of dust. Some men had broken free. Other chariots were following them. The Mitanni had noticed this and detached forces in pursuit. When Amerotke's driver screamed a warning, Amerotke looked to his right to see that Mitanni chariots were now heading in his direction, either to cut off their escape or simply ride them down. Amerotke unslung his bow. He notched one of the long arrows, leaning against the side of the chariot, feet apart. He quietly prayed that the wheels wouldn't buckle or the horses falter. A fall would injure or stun and Amerotke knew the Mitanni would not take any prisoners. The driver was now screaming at the horses. The Egyptian chariots were lighter, the horses faster but Amerotke's horses had also taken part in the hasty journey the previous day, not to mention the full rigours of the forced march. The one on the right began to falter. The chariot swayed precariously. Amerotke looked to his right. They were breaking free of the Mitanni line. However, one enemy chariot, its driver more skilful, had turned in an arc, hoping to block Amerotke's flight. The world had now come down to this: pounding horses, the rumble of chariots, the rocky ground speeding beneath them, the hot dust and that war chariot, its colours of black and gold, horses straining at the leashes.

Amerotke noticed one of his squadron was now coming up on his right to shield him. The driver had seen what was happening and Amerotke thanked the gods for the bravery of this officer. As the Mitanni drew closer the Egyptian officer brought his bow to bear. Amerotke heard his driver bellowing to shoot at the horses. The officer did and then the chariot pulled back, allowing Amerotke to shoot. He found it hard to keep his balance, standing slightly behind his charioteer. He breathed in; shooting at the men would be futile, two carried shields. He released his arrow. He thought he had missed, then one of the Mitanni horses stumbled. The chariot swayed and, tilting over, crashed and bounced along the rocky ground. Amerotke was free. His horses seemed to find fresh strength and, in the distance, through the dust, Amertoke made out the palisades of Hatusu's camp.

In the camp itself Hatusu stood on a parapet. Like her officers, she had been summoned by the tell-tale clouds of dust. Jabbing fingers directed her attention to the flashes and glints of bronze which could be seen as the dust clouds moved.

'Chariots at speed!' Senenmut whispered into her ear. 'Massed squadrons!'

Hatusu stood, heart in her throat. Would it all end here? Out in the northern desert? Would her body, once soaked in the most precious perfumes and oils, be left out for the jackals and hyenas to fight over? Would she never know the rites of embalming, the ritual which would allow her Ka to go forward? Was Amun-Ra dealing out judgement and punishment? She felt her stomach churn, her legs grow weak as the sweat broke out over her body. Around her officers were shouting. Chariots were now breaking free of the dust clouds. The keen-eyed among them declared they were Egyptian, but in full flight.

'Come down,' Senenmut urged her hoarsely. 'You are not a god, my lady.'

Hatusu felt a wave of panic from the officers and men clustered about her. She grasped Senenmut's wrist.

'What is happening? What is happening?'

Senenmut pulled her down. She had no choice but to follow him back through the camp.

'Go to your tent!' Senenmut said urgently, pushing her forward. 'Arm yourself!'

And, before she could object, Senenmut was marching away shouting for officers. All around her, in a mad scramble, Egyptians were grabbing weapons which lay at hand. Chariot crews hastened to hitch up their teams. Trumpets bellowed. Officers lashed out with their white wands of office. Senenmut realised he could do little here. In the royal enclosure the strong-arm boys were already manning the palisade. Mercenaries in their horn helmets massed at the gate. Senenmut pushed his way through. In her tent Hatusu was arming herself. She had thrown her robe to the ground, pulling the armour over her head, a long sheath of protection from neck to calf. Her face was pale. Senenmut helped her put on her sandals. The war belt she hitched over her shoulder and, before he could stop her, Hatusu snatched up the blue war helm of the Egyptian Pharaohs, which she fastened on her head. From the far end of the camp they heard a roar as the first Mitanni chariots tried to break through. An officer came running up to report what was happening.

'The Anubis regiment,' he gasped, 'have been ambushed! The Mitanni army have now rolled them up and are pursuing them into the camp!'

Hatusu closed her eyes. Senenmut was offering advice but she couldn't understand what he was saying. She was back as a girl with her father out in the royal gardens. He had a stick, drawing symbols in the earth, describing his victories.

'My lady!'

Hatusu's eyes flew open. Amerotke, his face and body armour covered in dust, cuts to his cheeks and shoulders, was standing in the entrance to the tent. Behind him were other men from his squadron. Hatusu waved him forward. Without thinking she picked up a wine goblet and thrust it into his hands.

'I know what has happened!' she said. She pointed to the writing table littered with scraps of papyrus.

'Show me clearly, Amerotke, what hope do we have?'

Amerotke gulped at the wine then, taking a stylus, dipped it into a pot of red ink. He found he couldn't stop trembling. Tears came into his eyes, his stomach was clenching as if he had drunk too much and wanted to be sick. Senenmut noticed his shaking hand.

'It will pass,' he reassured him. 'It will pass, Amerotke.'

The judge rubbed his eyes. He had reached a side gate of the camp, screaming at the guards to let him through the palisade and into the royal enclosure. He wished Shufoy was here, shouting good-natured abuse.

'Show me!' Hatusu's voice was harsh.

Amerotke drew a rectangle.

'This is the camp,' he explained as he drew a line across the bottom of the rectangle. 'This is the royal enclosure.' He then scored the top of the rectangle. 'The main gate, yes? The Anubis regiment has broken, badly led, badly prepared. They panicked and are now trying to break into the camp.' He curved an arrow from the left, down towards the front gate. 'Here are the Mitanni, not a patrol or a few squadrons but massed chariots supported by phalanx after phalanx of infantry. They are trying to break into the camp.'

'If they do,' Hatusu said, 'like water, they'll find the easiest route. Not through the parapet but the main gate. They'll force their way in. Their ranks will break among the tents and carts.' She pointed to the bottom of the rectangle. 'This is where our principal chariot squadrons mass!' Her finger moved a little to the right, indicating the edge of an oasis. 'Here the rest of our chariot force. My lord Senenmut, you will leave immediately and take over these squadrons.'

'And you, my lady?'

Hatusu grabbed Amerotke's stylus and drew an arrow from the royal enclosure along the rectangle to the front gate.

'The Mitanni chariots are heavy. Their horses will be tired. The crews will disengage to search for plunder.' She summoned an officer.

'You are Harmosie, commander of the Isis regiment?'

'Yes, my lady.'

Hatusu could hear the cries and shouts, the crash of weapons from the camps, but she kept her voice steady.

'You are now camp commander.'

'My lord Omendap?'

'He's still feverish. Now, listen, man, you have one order, to organise your force into a phalanx, a wall somewhere just beyond the royal enclosure. You are to hold the Mitanni back. Do not advance, I repeat, do not advance until our chariots have struck!'

The council broke up, Senenmut hurrying away. Hatusu, now determined, rapped out more orders and playfully slapped Amerotke on the shoulder.

'Come, my lord judge. Let us now mete out judgement to the enemy!'

Amerotke stared wearily at her. 'It's the killing time?'

'Yes, Amerotke,' she replied quietly. 'To seize power you must kill! To hold power you must kill! To strengthen it you must kill! If you are divine-born, that is your lot: you have no choice!'

Re or Ra : the self-engendered eternal spirit.

CHAPTER 14

Hatusu, Amerotke and her group of officers joined the chariot squadrons where, under the direction of commanders, they were now massing on the far side of the camp. A long line of chariots stretched out, horses prancing and rearing, war plumes dancing, drivers checking reins and harnesses while their warrior companions ensured bow, quiver and throwing spears were ready. The late afternoon sun caught the bronze and gilt work, the edge of spears, in flashes of shimmering light. Wheels creaked as the chariots swayed forwards and backwards. The officers moved along, repeating the same instructions. They were to ignore the chaos in the camp. They were to advance behind the divine Hatusu. Those on the far right were to swing in an arc and they would smash into the flank and rear of the Mitanni. Lord Senenmut would bring a relief force around the other side to close the trap. The foot soldiers and strong-arm boys in the camp would hold the enemy. They would clasp the Mitanni into a tightening circle and so defeat them. The order was simple, the directions repeated time and again.

Amerotke climbed into his chariot. The driver had changed the horses. He smiled.

'This time, my lord, it will be our surprise!'

Amerotke was about to reply when a swelling murmur of acclamation rose from the ranks. Hatusu in her chariot, her principal bodyguard around her, now swept along the front of the chariot squadrons. She was dressed in the blue war helm, her bronze armour glinting in the sun. In one hand she carried a spear, the other held the rail of the chariot. She did not speak but studied the lines of men as if impressing upon them, by her very presence, what was about to happen. Despite the urgency of the situation she reached the end of the line and turned back. Amerotke smiled. Hatusu was a born actress; standing in the chariot immobile, spear held up, she looked like the female incarnation of the war god Montu. The chariot stopped and turned. Hatusu lowered her spear. Her chariot moved slowly forwards. Amerotke and the squadron leaders followed. Behind, like some great hymn to death, rose the creak and rattle of the massed squadrons. All eyes watched that small figure standing next to the standard of Amun-Ra fixed in the front of her chariot. The driver was one of Senenmut's lieutenants. He turned, one fist raised.

'Life, health and prosperity to the divine Hatusu!'

A roar greeted his words. Hatusu's chariot moved a little faster. Somewhere among the squadrons, a priest chanted a hymn of war.

'Hatusu, destroyer like Sekhmet!'

'Hatusu!' came the roar back.

'Hatusu! Sword of Anubis!'

'Hatusu!' This time the roar was deafening.

'Hatusu, spear of Osiris!'

'Hatusu!'

The litany was now taken up by thousands of voices.

'Hatusu! Conqueror!'

'Hatusu! Daughter of Montu!'

'Hatusu! God's golden flesh!'

The chariots were now moving faster. Amerotke wondered if the divine litany was spontaneous or arranged but now he had little time to think. Hatusu's chariot was moving fast like a bird skimming across the ground. Behind her rumbled hundreds of other chariots. The entire earth echoed with the drumming of hooves, the creak of harness, the clatter of metal. Behind Hatusu the principal officers gave directions. The line slowed down as it turned, the far right moving faster in its arc. The sound of the battle from the gateway of the camp wafted on the cool evening breeze though all they could see ahead of them was a great cloud of white dust. Amerotke unslung his bow, squaring his feet. The chariots had now picked up speed. The horses, urged on by their drivers, headed like the devourers towards the unsuspecting Mitanni. The roar of battle, the sheer delight of killing, drew them on. They were approaching the white cloud of dust, then they were in it, smashing like arrows into the ranks of the Mitanni.

The chaos was indescribable. Men and horses lay strewn on the ground. Here and there Egyptian foot soldiers stood in phalanx but some of the Mitanni had swept by these into the camp. The arrival of Egyptian chariots took them completely by surprise. The Mitanni had been interested in plunder while their horses were exhausted, their heavy chariots difficult to turn in the chaos and confusion of massed ranks of men.

Amerotke was aware of faces screaming up at him. He loosened arrow after arrow and then drew sword and club. Faces, hands, chests appeared before him only to fall away in great red spouting wounds, the blood splashing him and his driver, drenching the floor of their chariot. All around him men became locked in individual combat. It grew difficult to distinguish friend from foe as armour, standards, helmets and faces got coated in dust. Amerotke looked up. Hatusu was deep in the enemy, her spear rising and falling. A group of strong-arm boys had now surrounded her, finishing off the Mitanni soldiers and charioteers, protecting their Queen as she drove deeper and deeper into the enemy ranks.

At first it was just a fierce, bloody fight: men screaming and yelling; the enemy trying to turn their horses and bring their own chariots into play. Amerotke, however, sensed a change of mood. The Egyptian foot soldiers in the camp, who had heard of their arrival, were now pressing the Mitanni back. He heard the distant bray of trumpets, more shouts. Senenmut's few chariot squadrons had crashed into the Mitanni's far flank. The battle turned into a massacre. The Mitanni were trapped in a horseshoe formation. Some tried to break out and were successful but now Hatusu's officers threw some of their squadrons into pursuit. Amerotke's arms grew heavy, his eyes hurt, his mouth was so full of dust he thought he would choke. No mercy was being shown, nor pardon given. The strong-arm boys were now cutting the throats of any of the enemy who threw down their weapons. In some cases these rough, cruel fighters were sodomising their fallen foe. Amerotke grasped his charioteer's arm.

'It's finished!' he yelled. 'It's all over! This is no longer a battle but a slaughter yard!'

The driver gazed, round-eyed.

'Withdraw!' Amerotke roared. 'The battle is won!'

The driver reluctantly turned his horses, driving back through the wedge, seeking openings in the Egyptian ranks, pressing in on their fallen enemy.

Soon they were free of the slaughter. In the light of the setting sun the rocky desert ground seemed to shimmer in blood. In some cases the corpses lay two or three thick. Men groaned and moaned and horses struggled to break free from the ruined traces of their chariots. The camp followers had already swarmed in looking for plunder, stripping the corpses, cutting the throats of the enemy wounded.

Amerotke pointed towards the small, grassy oasis which lay just outside the camp. Already the Egyptian wounded had been taken there to be tended by physicians. In the shade, near the coolness of the pool, Amerotke climbed down from the chariot and walked like a sleep wanderer. Men groaned, begged for a drink, an opiate, anything to relieve the heat, dust and pain. Amerotke found he didn't care. He took off his body armour and lay down, pushing his face into the water, splashing his head, the back of his neck, lapping it like a dog. He found it hard to move; all he wanted to do was sleep, close his eyes and ears. He became aware of a man beside him: a long-haired mercenary in cheap leather body armour.

'A great victory, my lord Amerotke?'

The judge turned. The face was darker, disguised by a shaggy moustache and beard, yet Amerotke still recognised those eyes as he clasped the outstretched hand of Meneloto.

The following morning the camp palisades were taken down so the massed might of Egypt's army could stand in serried ranks. During the night a great dais had been constructed using wood and other materials from captured chariots. In the centre of the dais stood a huge tabernacle made of cloth looted from the Mitanni camp. Next to this stood Senenmut. He had been hailed as one of the great heroes of the battle and, like a true actor, he had not washed or changed but stood in his war kilt and bronzed cuirass, helmet in one hand, the other on the curved sword in his scabbard. He had been responsible for awarding the golden eagles for valour to different commanders and individual soldiers. Now and again he'd turn and glimpse Amerotke standing in the front ranks. He smiled with his eyes. The judge's withdrawal from the battle had not been commented on and, the previous evening, Hatusu had sent a gift of wine to Amerotke's tent. On either side of Amerotke stood squadron commanders and principal priests carrying the insignia and standards of the different gods and regiments of Egypt.

No one had slept the previous night. The Mitanni camp had been looted and the darkness given over to celebrating Hatusu's crushing victory. Tushratta had escaped but leading noblemen among the Mitanni detachment were now crowded into huge stockades hastily constructed outside the camp. The foot soldiers, charioteers, guardsmen, strong-arm boys and mercenaries now stood, all eyes on the great golden tabernacle placed so prominently on the dais. Amerotke suspected what was about to happen.

Senenmut raised his hand. The trumpets blared. Shrill blasts were taken up by other musicians stationed around the camp. The cluster of white-robed priests beside the dais now held up their incense burners, the fragrant smoke rising like prayers to the bright blue sky. Cymbals clashed and Senenmut turned, gesturing with his hand. Two priests ran forward, the golden curtains were slowly pulled back. On the throne of Horus, covered in precious cloths, her feet resting on a footstool, sat Hatusu. On her head she wore the blue war crown, the silver spitting cobra around its rim. Over her shoulder hung the Nenes, the beautiful coat of Pharaoh. The lower half of her body was hidden in white goffered linen. Her arms were crossed. In one hand she held the crook, in the other the flail of Egypt and in her lap rested the sacred sickle-shaped sword of Pharaohs. Fan-bearers moved on to the dais around her, the great ostrich plumes wafting perfume through the air. Amerotke regarded Hatusu's beautiful face which had, only a short time earlier, been contorted into the terrible rictus of battle. He gazed in wonderment at the false beard, used by Pharaohs, now fastened under her chin. The rest of the army stared, stunned by her majesty and the surprise of the occasion. Hatusu sat immobile as a statue, looking out over her soldiers' heads.

'Behold the perfect god!' Senenmut shouted, his powerful voice carrying through the camp. 'Behold the golden flesh of your god! The golden throne of the living one! Behold your Pharaoh, Hatusu, Makaat-Re: the truth of the soul of the holy one! Beloved daughter of Amun, conceived, by divine grace and Amun-Ra's favour, in the womb of Queen Ahmose!'

Senenmut paused to let his words sink in. He was not only proclaiming Hatusu as Pharaoh but of divine origin.

'Behold your Pharaoh, King of Upper and Lower Egypt!' he continued. 'Golden Horus, lord of the diadem, the vulture and the snake! King of abiding splendour, most beloved of Amun-Ra!'

He paused. The silence grew tense. Never before in the history of Egypt had a woman held the crook and the flail and been proclaimed as God's child, King, master of the nine bows.

'Hatusu!' The shout came from behind Amerotke and was immediately taken up by the whole army.

'Hatusu! Hatusu! Hatusu!'

Spears were clashed against shields. The roar grew. The acclamations rang out as if to ensure their salutation would go to the far ends of the earth, beyond the distant horizon into the palaces of the gods. The ranks shifted backwards and Amerotke knelt with the rest, all pressing their foreheads against the ground in total submission. Amerotke smiled to himself: Hatusu was now victor of both war and peace. The trumpets blared, the men rose. Senenmut had five of the leading prisoners brought before the throne, their hands bound behind them. They were forced to kneel.

Hatusu rose, grasping the ceremonial club one of the priests handed to her. She seized the hair of each captive, now held fast between two soldiers, and brought the club down. Amerotke closed his eyes. He heard the groans and moans of the prisoners, the awful death-bearing crunch and, when he looked again, the prisoners, clad only in their loin cloths, sprawled before the dais, great pools of blood spreading out around them.

Hatusu was again proclaimed and, through Senenmut, declared her favour for her 'beloved soldiers'. More rewards were offered. The plunder would be divided; a victory parade would pass through Thebes and the strengthening of the kingdom would take place. Nebanum was dragged before her. Senenmut was short and quick. The discredited commander was ordered to be taken out of the camp where men from each regiment would stone him to death. After that Hatusu took her seat. The golden curtains around the throne were closed like the doors of a tabernacle, hiding the god's golden flesh from the impure sight of men.

*   *   *

Amerotke looked up at the great pyramid, marvelling at this harmoniously shaped limestone staircase to the sky. Its burnished cap caught the rays of the rising sun like an oil wick catching a flame. Dark, impressive, the pyramid brought back memories of his father who had brought him here to show him the glories of ancient Egypt.

No one knew the real reason why these had been built by the ancient ones. Amerotke recalled his father's stories: that somehow these were linked to the gods of the first time, the period known as Zep Tepi, when the gods came down from the skies and walked among men. When the world was at peace. When the Nile was not a narrow green line but a lush valley which carpeted the face of the earth. Where the lion was man's friend and the panther a household pet. His father, a priest, had been full of such tales, of how the pyramids were an attempt to climb back to the gods.

Amerotke glanced back to the quayside where the imperial war fleet lay berthed. Hatusu and her council were now hastening back to Thebes ahead of their victorious army. She intended, in the words of Sethos, to deliver judgement on those rebels and opponents back in Thebes. The troops now saw her as a god, divinely touched, King and Pharaoh, and her word was law. Even Senenmut treated her more warily while Omendap, recovering from the murderous assault about which he could tell them nothing, deferred to her in every matter

Hatusu had not physically changed. Her eyes would still crinkle up in amusement. She could flirt with the men but these were weapons, devices. Even dressed in a sheath of linen she emanated a power. Her moods were fickle, as if she had studied the hearts and souls of men and knew how they worked. She could, in a matter of moments, turn from coy temptress to petulant girl. When her head went down, her lips tightened and she looked from under her eyebrows, a chill descended; Hatusu would brook no opposition. She carried the crook and the flail. All Egypt, all peoples of the nine bows should tremble before her. She had hardly talked to Amerotke except once, after the others had left the tent, when she'd risen and caught his wrist.

'You received no reward, Amerotke, for what you did.'

He looked back but didn't speak.

'But you want no reward?' she teased. Her hand went up to his shoulder.

'This is your reward, Amerotke. You are my friend. You are Pharaoh's beloved.'

Amerotke had bowed at the supreme tribute any Pharaoh could bestow: to be called 'friend of the King' was life-long protection, amnesty and pardon for what was in the past and what might happen in the future. His clumsy reply, however, was blurted out before he could stop it.

'Your majesty,' he declared. 'You have my soul, my heart; but both will always try to follow the truth.'

Hatusu smiled and, taking his hand, kissed the back of it.

'That's why you are my friend, Amerotke.'

Hatusu had also shown the troops her vengeance. Nebanum had died under a hail of rocks. More prisoners had been sacrificed. The Mitanni camp had been ransacked and chariot squadrons despatched into Sinai, to regain the mines, reorganise the garrison and launch raids of terror, fire and sword into the Land of Canaan.

'Teach those rebels a lesson!' she had proclaimed. 'Let my name go forth to the ends of the earth! Let them know there's a power in Egypt!'

The enemy dead had been collected. The death toll had risen to thousands; line after line of stinking cadavers stretched out in the sun. Hatusu had ordered the penis of every enemy soldier to be cut off and collected in baskets.

'Send them to Rahimere!' she demanded. 'Let him and the people of Thebes know the extent of our victories!'

No one had objected. It was customary for the right hand to be cut off but Hatusu's grisly gift was a reminder to all of them how she had struck at the world of men, turned everything on its head. The emasculation of her dead enemies served as a grim reminder to Rahimere and his gang of the horrors yet to come. The strong-arm boys had shown no qualms about their bloody task. If Hatusu had told them to climb to the sky and grasp the sun, they would have obeyed. Hatusu was not only their Pharaoh but their goddess, beautiful, terrible, blood-thirsty.

Amerotke sighed. The fleet had stopped at Sakkara where Hatusu was now holding court receiving officials, commanders from the local

Nomachs. She accepted their obeisance and gifts, proclaiming her power, confirming her authority.

This visit to the pyramids was Meneloto's idea. Four days had passed since they had left the battlefields, the skies still dark from the black smoke of the funeral pyres. Meneloto would always visit him by night. He would squat in the shadows and tell how he had escaped from the Amemets and travelled into the Red Lands where he had met a group of mercenaries. This group had joined the royal army as it marched north.

'I trust you, Amerotke,' Meneloto had said. 'Your judgement in the Hall of Two Truths was true and sound. However, while I have been out in the wilderness, I have reflected. All this began with Pharaoh's visit to the pyramid at Sakkara. With his entrance through the secret doors.'

'Secret doors!' Amerotke had exclaimed.

'At the time I thought nothing of it,' Meneloto confessed. 'The pyramids, we know, are riddled with galleries and secret passageways. I thought divine Pharaoh was visiting some shrine or had even stumbled on secret wealth. I am a soldier, Amerotke, I follow orders.'

'How often did he go?' Amerotke asked.

'Three, four times. Ipuwer and a small cohort took us to the Cheops pyramid. They waited outside. We went up the steps, in by a small door in the north face and then through a secret gate. I stood guard while divine Pharaoh and Amenhotep went further.'

'And now?'

'We must visit there. We must return! Discover what lies at the source of all this.'

'And me?'

'You carry the royal cartouche,' Meneloto said. 'You enjoy divine favour. No questions will be asked. You are the judge of my case. And there's something else?'

'What?' Amerotke asked.

'Among the camp followers hide the Amemets. I'm sure of it. Like the rest of the jackals which follow the army, they may have lost some of their pack in the battle but they have gained tremendous plunder.'

'They are probably here for that?'

'No. They must be here for something else.'

Amerotke walked away from the curtain wall which surrounded the pyramid, looking out across the rocky ground. He wished Shufoy was here. Ever since he had left the royal camp he had felt a prickle of fear. Was it his imagination or was he truly being followed? Or was it simply this holy place? These mysterious shapes, the pyramids, the mortuary temples, the mastabas, the causeways and, in the far distance, the luminous, brooding, sand-dusted Sphinx which stared sightlessly out over the desert. The whole place held an atmosphere of dark menace.

'Health and prosperity!'

Amerotke whirled round. Meneloto stood, a shadow in the poor light. He'd come along the wall, slinking like a cat. Amerotke grasped his outstretched hand. Meneloto stared back over his shoulder.

'What's the matter?'

'I am uneasy,' Meneloto admitted. He gestured with his head. 'The guardian priests are sleeping off their cheap beer. I feel as if we are being watched. Shadows . . .'

He drew closer. Amerotke smelt his wine-drenched breath, the tang of onions.

'Do you believe in ghosts, Amerotke? That the shadows of the dead survive and have an existence of their own?'

Amerotke tapped the side of his head. 'I have enough ghosts in here.' He made to turn but Meneloto caught his arm.

'Your wife, the lady Norfret?'

'She is well,' Amerotke said. He went to go on but Meneloto held him fast.

'I can read your heart, Amerotke, I am sure half of Thebes has. When you were hand-fast, betrothed to Norfret, I was a callow officer. I paid court to her.'

'And?' Amerotke asked coldly.

'She liked me,' Meneloto replied. 'She liked me very, very much but her heart and body are yours, Amerotke.' He walked on by. 'You worship the truth,' he said over his shoulder, 'so accept it for what it is!'

They entered the pyramid complex, winding their way through the narrow muddy lanes. A guardian priest was aroused. There were protests and objections which died on the old man's lips as he saw, in the flickering torchlight, the royal cartouche. A woman's voice called out but the old priest snapped back and muttering under his breath he led them out until they stood at the base of the towering pyramid.

'Why now?' the priest whined. 'It will be light soon!'

'Why not?' Amerotke jibed.

He grasped the torch from the priest's hand and began the long, hot climb up the crude steps to the entrance in the north face. The priest followed. The doorway had been hollowed out. Inside smelt musty, dark. More torches coated in pitch were lit. The priest crouched down at the entrance.

'I'll wait here,' he said fretfully.

Amerotke and Meneloto, carrying a torch in each hand, entered the pyramid. The air was hot and oppressive. The silence seemed to hold terrors of its own as if the dead were gathering, watching with unseen eyes. They walked along the main gallery until at the end they turned left and went down some steps.

'The place has been open for centuries,' Meneloto said, his voice echoing off the granite rocks. 'Robbers and thieves have looted it to their hearts' content.'

'How do we find our way out?' Amerotke asked.

'Divine Pharaoh worried about the same,' Meneloto replied. He led Amerotke to the wall and held up his torch. 'See the arrowhead marks.'

At first Amerotke couldn't but then he did. They were cut in the shape of a leaf or arrowhead and pointed back to where they had come. Meneloto moved further along.

'Look, here's another one. They cover the pyramid. Cheops, the builder, was not only Pharaoh but a wizard. The pyramid has a labyrinth of galleries and passageways. Some of them lead nowhere. Others simply take you round and round till you drop in exhaustion. So, look for the arrowhead. If a wall carries these, you are following the line back.'

They went on deeper into the pyramid. Amerotke found it difficult to control his fear and panic. The walls seemed to close in; sometimes they crouched as the ceiling swept down. This was no longer an old mausoleum, a ransacked tomb but, in Amerotke's mind, a living thing, watching them, wondering whether to close in and crush the breath out of their bodies. Thankfully, Meneloto knew his way. Every so often he would stop to check the arrow points on the wall. Now and again they passed signs of others who had entered the pyramid. A crumbling skeleton lay in one corner, a knife broken at the hilt still grasped in skeletal fingers. They passed other grisly remains.

'Thieves still take their chances here,' Meneloto whispered. 'And pay the price.'

Amerotke was about to answer when he heard a sound, echoing through the corridors behind him.

'What was that?'

He turned. Meneloto drew his dagger.

'I am sure,' Amerotke insisted. 'Someone shouted.' He looked at Meneloto. 'Are we being followed?'

Meneloto pointed down at the sandy floor, at the trail of ash left from their torches.

'Perhaps the priest follows? But come, we cannot wait!'

They hurried on. At the end of one gallery Meneloto paused and sighed in relief. He approached the wall and pressed his hand against some of the stones. Amerotke lowered the torch and noticed scuff marks at the base of the wall. He heard a sound and looked up. The stones had moved. A hidden door had swung back on oily pins. A rush of cold air made the torchlight dance.

'Wood,' Meneloto explained. 'Wood dressed and painted so it looks like rock.' He doused one of the torches and stuck it very carefully beneath one of the hinges. 'It can be opened from the outside,' he said. 'But I am not too sure from within. This is where I stood on guard. Divine Pharaoh and Amenhotep went further.'

Amerotke followed him inside. The corridor abruptly dipped and they had to almost run to keep their balance. At the bottom there was nothing but a square chamber, rock floor and granite block walls.

'Nothing!' Amerotke remarked.

However, Meneloto was already busy, examining the wall, pressing it with his fingers. Amerotke noticed how the sand in one corner was piled high, slightly patted down. He went over and started digging. Meneloto joined him. They found an iron ring in one of the flagstones. Sweating and cursing they pulled this up and pushed the flagstone aside. Meneloto lowered a torch to reveal a flight of jagged stairs stretching into the darkness. They hurried down. At first the light made some impression but the darkness closed in.

'It's like a chamber from the Duat,' Meneloto remarked. 'One of those dreadful rooms in the underworld.'

He walked on, then cursed. Amerotke hastily joined him. They stretched out the torches; their eyes grew accustomed to the shifting shadows. Amerotke gasped as the torches flared. They revealed a long, vaulted chamber. Down both sides were great wooden pillars. Meneloto had walked into one of these. When Amerotke held his torch up he glimpsed cracks in the ceiling.

'It must have begun to crumble,' he said. 'And these beams were put in to reinforce it.'

'In the name of the lord of light!' Meneloto exclaimed.

He'd walked forward. Amerotke followed; at first glance, he thought countless pieces of rag hung from the ceiling but he could see they were strips of leather, each ending in a noose. From most of these hung decaying skeletons, sometimes only the skull, the chest cage and part of the spine. A few were empty, the bones fallen to the ground, mouldering into heaps of dust. They walked forward, past these grim tokens of the dead Pharaoh. The hall seemed to stretch for ever, full of these leather straps and their grisly burdens. As they walked grains of dust fell from the ceiling, smatterings of gravel.

'Cheops must have built this,' Amerotke mused. 'He laid out a secret maze beneath his pyramid. He dug too deep and his engineers put these pillars in. Afterwards, to ensure no one knew what had happened, he hanged the slaves: deathly guardians of his secrets.'

His words echoed hollow through the darkness. Amerotke found it hard to control his fear. He felt the dead close in around him. This army of the hanged. Were they now demons guarding this secret place? And what was Cheops so eager to hide? What was so special it had to be dug deep into the bowels of the earth and then sealed with murder? All around him lay the remains of those who had toiled here: shards of cloths and pottery, tools, broken dishes.

They went further along. On each side rose the great wooden pillars and from the roof hung those dreadful leather straps. Underfoot they crunched bones, their sandals kicking away human dust. At last they reached the far wall. Amerotke gazed at the great inscription carved there. He held his torch up. The hieroglyphics were of the old period but he had studied them in the House of Life. He made out a few phrases: 'Cheops, beloved of the lord of light, Pharaoh, King, wizard, he has placed behind this wall the secrets of time: the records when god and man lived in peace and harmony.'

Amerotke mouthed the words for Meneloto to hear him.

'The time of the first time,' Amerotke continued his translation. 'The Zep Tepi, when the being of light, the creator in the godhead, sent his emissaries from the heavens.'

Amerotke paused. A sound came ringing through the chamber as if a weapon had been dropped, clanging through this place of death like the shrill of a trumpet.

'Stay there,' Meneloto whispered. 'See what you can find.'

Amerotke read on hurriedly, ignoring those hieroglyphics he could not understand or decode. Now he realised why Tuthmosis had changed. Beyond this wall were archives, manuscripts which talked not of gods but of one god, a being of light, all-powerful, all-creative. God had once walked with man; he had sent his messengers from the stars, from beyond the far horizon. That had been a time of plenty, when all creation was in harmony until man had risen and murdered these envoys from the stars, to whom they now gave names such as Osiris and Horus. Amerotke moved to see if he could discover the hidden door. His foot struck something which he picked up. It was a piece of metal, jagged and blackened but harder than Amerotke had ever felt. Not bronze, yet still a metal made by human hands. He struck it against the rock. The metal was unmarked but the rock was scarred. The sudden movement brought clouds of dust from the ceiling. He heard a sound. Meneloto came hurrying back.

'We've been followed,' he whispered.

'Who?' Amerotke urged.

Meneloto grabbed him by the arm. 'Only the gods of light know. We must hurry!'

Amerotke recalled the Amemets. He took one last look at the inscription and, grasping the torch in one hand and the piece of metal in the other, followed Meneloto back along the chamber of death. Meneloto pushed him past the steps deep into the shadows. They tossed the torches into the dust just as the Amemets slipped like wraiths down into the chamber.

Amerotke closed his eyes. He thanked Ma'at that Meneloto had left one of the torches fastened in a niche on the far wall as this glow of light lured the Amemets on. There were eight or nine in number, dressed like sand-wanderers in black from head to toe. They each carried a torch and a naked sword. They, too, stopped in horror, astounded by the sight before them. There were hurried whispers. Some were reluctant to proceed but the Amemet leader urged them on, pointing with his sword to the distant glow of torchlight.

'Now,' Meneloto whispered. 'Let them go!'

'But we must see beyond that wall!' Amerotke hissed back.

Meneloto shook his head.

The Amemets were now moving deeper into the darkness. Amerotke realised that they had no choice but to flee. In the gloom he followed the former captain of the guard back up the steps. They were halfway up when a figure in black, torch in one hand, sword in the other, appeared at the top of the steps. He gave a cry and lunged at them with his sword. Meneloto tried to avoid it but the sword tip took him deep in the chest. He stumbled back, dragging the assassin with him, crashing into Amerotke. All three tumbled down. The Amemet was first on his feet but, in the darkness, he dropped his torch. Amerotke threw the jagged piece of metal, sending the assassin crashing back into one of the pillars. There was a creak, a snap. The Amemet clung to the column of wood; there was a crack, and the pillar slid away followed by a cascade of crashing masonry and rocks. At the far end the Amemets came hurrying back but the collapse of the pillar had caused a ripple. Other parts of the roof fell away, raining down rock and sand.

Amerotke picked up the fallen torch and hurried back to Meneloto, who lay at the foot of the steps. He turned his companion over. The sword had taken him in the heart, and a deep cut where the jagged edge of the step had caught his head seeped blood. Amerotke searched for the life pulse but could feel nothing. A cloud of dust made him cough. From further down the chamber came the yells and screams of the Amemets. Amerotke put his hand on Meneloto's face, whispered a quick prayer and raced up the steps. The chamber above was empty. Only a torch glowed where it had been placed in a wall-crevice. Amerotke took the flagstone, grasping it by the ring, pushing and shoving, coughing at the dust which now swirled up the steps. At last he had it in place, shutting off the terrible sounds from the pit below. He then grasped the torch and sped down the gallery, following the life-giving arrows to the door in the north face of the pyramid.

Atum: 'the complete one', creator of God: one of the oldest gods of Egypt.

CHAPTER 15

Amerotke pushed back the headrest of his bed and lay flat down. He gently freed his other arm. Norfret stirred. Her beautiful kohl-ringed eyes fluttered, her perfume-drenched body turned, as she murmured something and smiled in her sleep. Amerotke lay listening to her breathing. He stared at the frieze painted so cleverly along the far bedroom wall: two leopards playing a ball game like children did in the marketplace while a hare acted as umpire.

Amerotke closed his eyes. It had been two weeks since he had escaped from that terrible pit in the pyramids at Sakkara. Once he had reached the imperial fleet, washing off the dust and bathing the scratches, he'd quickly changed. Sethos, sharp as ever, had recognised something was wrong. During the morning meal, held in the stern of the royal galley, he had gazed quizzically at him. Amerotke had just shaken his head and refused to talk. He decided not to tell anyone about what had happened.

The royal fleet had reached Thebes and been greeted by a frenzy of celebration. The quayside was thronged, the Avenue of the Sphinxes packed with citizens and visitors from elsewhere.

'Life, prosperity and health!' the crowd had roared as Hatusu, garbed in Pharaoh's robes, had been borne on a palanquin into the city.

'She has stretched out her hands!
She has shattered the enemy!'

the priests sang.

'The earth in its length and breadth,

217

westerners and easterners are subject to you!
You have trampled all countries, your heart is glad!
The beauty of Amun is in your face!
The glory of Horus in your golden flesh!
Heart of the fire! Light of light!
Glory of Amun-Ra!'

Hatusu had stared implacably before her as auxiliaries, coal-black Negroes, helped the royal bodyguard to keep back the crowds. Huge ostrich plumes had wafted costly perfumes round the divine presence. Hatusu had sat immobile, her gold-sandalled feet resting on the helmeted crown of the King of Mitanni.

The procession had coiled its way through the decorated streets of Thebes. Amerotke had walked before her; behind Hatusu moved his own squadron of chariots, a long, glittering line with burnished harness; horses, adorned with victory plumes, pulled carts full of booty. After these trudged columns of bedraggled, dusty prisoners of war.

The great bronze door of the temple had been opened. The priestesses, shaking their sistra, came down to greet their new Pharaoh. Incense, holy water, garlands of beautiful flowers were scattered all around the palanquin. Hatusu had swept up the steps, burned incense to Amun-Ra and then sacrificed more of the prisoners.

Amerotke had been pleased to get away. Norfret, his sons, Asural, Prenhoe and Shufoy had been waiting for him in his small chapel near the Hall of Two Truths. An ecstatic homecoming! Nights of celebrations, parties and feasting had followed. Amerotke's stomach found this hard to digest after the harsh rations of the camp. Norfret had been ecstatic, exhausting him night after night, her beautiful, golden body twisting beneath him. Amerotke had found it all a dream. His body still ached from the rigours of the campaign. His dreams were plagued by that terrible charge of the Mitanni, the carnage of battle, that chamber of the hanged beneath the pyramid; the severed head of the chapel priest whom he had found near the entrance to the pyramid.

Amerotke turned over. He had felt guilty at Meneloto's death and his own escape. But what could he have done?

Shufoy had told him all that had happened during his absence. Amerotke had half-listened. He didn't really care. He was home. The horrors were behind him. All of Thebes was talking about Hatusu's accession to the throne. The boy Pharaoh, never truly crowned, had been gently moved sideways, relegated to the rank of a prince, left to play in the royal nursery. Amerotke had stayed clear of the intrigue. His mind kept going back to that inscription in that awful chamber beneath the pyramid. He now knew what Tuthmosis had discovered, why Amenhotep had lost his faith. If it was true, there were no gods. The priests of Egypt had led their people down narrow alleyways away from the truth. Amerotke hadn't found the message so shocking. Hadn't he always been a heretic, cynical about the elaborate temple ritual of Thebes? He'd always been suspicious of the worship of a crocodile or a cat. His veneration of Ma'at was different. Statue and temple ritual aside, the truth did exist; it had to be served and closely followed.

Amerotke wondered if he should go back but he recalled that falling masonry. He closed his eyes. The chamber was a fitting resting place for the Amemets. Let their spirits guard it. He would pay sacrifice for Meneloto. But to whom? The stone gods of Egypt?

He heard a sound in the corridor outside and pushed back the sheets. He slipped on a robe and sandals, washed his hands and face in the scented water and went downstairs. The servants had not yet risen. The sun was only beginning to come up and he caught the distant notes of the sun heralds drifting in from the city. He went out into the garden, where the breeze was still cool. Shufoy sat a short distance away under a sycamore tree. Amerotke slipped his sandals off and walked quietly over. The dwarf heard him and turned hastily, his hand going to cover the precious objects laid out on the blanket. Amerotke crouched down.

'Where are these from, Shufoy?'

'I bought them,' came the quick reply. 'A man has to trade from dawn to dusk to earn a crust of bread.'

'I am sure he has,' Amerotke replied drily.

Shufoy shuffled closer, his quick, bright eyes studying his master.

'You've changed, lord, since your return.'

'I saw things: horrors!'

Shufoy nodded. 'They will go, master. In the end all things die.'

Amerotke sifted among the precious objects.

219

'You're becoming a wealthy man.'

'When the army left Thebes, master, all panic broke out. People were selling as fast as they could.'

Amerotke noticed a small gold cup. He picked it up. Around the rim was a scene depicting Osiris weighing a soul, Ma'at kneeling beside him. Beneath this was inscribed the regnal year of Hatusu's father, Pharaoh Tuthmosis I; beside the divine seal, the name of its long-dead owner, a scribe from the House of Silver.

'Where did you get this?' Amerotke asked, his interest quickened.

Shufoy looked guarded. 'I was taking it back to the city to sell, master.'

'This is a funeral cup,' Amerotke insisted. 'Especially made for this scribe, small enough to contain a little wine to be placed in a tomb.' His hand shot out and he grabbed Shufoy's shoulder.

'Master, I swear on your children's lives, I bought it from a merchant in Thebes! A seller of cups and precious dishes. The price could not be resisted.'

'It's stolen!' Amerotke declared. 'And you know it is, Shufoy. This has been taken from a tomb!' He took the four corners of the blanket and wrapped them up, ignoring Shufoy's pleas and groans. 'Go into the city,' he ordered. 'To the Hall of Two Truths. Collect Asural and some of his burly lads. Then, visit the stall-holders, I don't care what it takes, I just want the name of the man they bought these from. Shufoy, this cup could have come from my father's grave. What is yours is yours, but what happens if the news leaked out that Shufoy, the great scorpionman, was involved in tomb robbing?'

A short while later Shufoy left the house armed with sword and sack, grumbling under his breath and muttering every proverb he knew. Amerotke was pleased at his discovery. He felt more alert. He washed and changed, ate some fruit and was in the garden when his visitor arrived just before noon.

Lord Sethos came striding across the grass: he seemed unchanged by the campaign along the Nile. He had taken part in the fighting and been confirmed by Hatusu in his place of honour though his resentment at Senenmut was growing. He sat down on a garden seat.

'Life, health and prosperity!' he wished Amerotke.

Amerotke poured a small mug of beer and brought it over. Sethos sipped at this and studied the ornamental lake as if fascinated by the ibis perched daintily on its edge.

'Turbulent days, my lord Amerotke?' He took the lotus flower out of his sash and twirled it. 'Her majesty gave this to me this morning. A mark of favour.' He sniffed at the flower and put it on the bench beside him. 'You did not attend the meeting of the royal circle?' Sethos looked across at the garden where the vine dressers were moving down the trellises inspecting the stems.

'I am still exhausted,' Amerotke replied.

'Rahimere, Bayletos and the others have been arrested,' Sethos announced. 'Members of my police seized them last night just as they left the royal palace.'

'On what charge?'

'High treason.'

'There's no proof of that.'

Sethos smirked, his clever, smooth-shaven face creasing into a smile as if savouring some secret joke.

'They will go on trial before you in the Hall of Two Truths.'

'Then I'll dismiss the charges for lack of evidence.'

'You are bull-headed, Amerotke!'

'Is that the same as not being corrupt? My lady Hatusu knows that there is no evidence of treason against Rahimere. How many have been arrested?'

'About ten in all. Divine Pharaoh,' Sethos emphasised the word. 'Divine Pharaoh believes that, if they are not guilty of treason, they are certainly responsible for the deaths of Tuthmosis II, Ipuwer and the chapel priest Amenhotep. She waits for you, my lord Amerotke, to sift the evidence.'

'What do we have?' Amerotke replied. 'True, her husband died by snake bite but how or when?' Amerotke shrugged. 'I cannot tell. True, someone put a snake into Ipuwer's writing bag but that could have been anyone in the royal circle. And, as for Amenhotep, he certainly met someone from the royal circle just before he died.' He paused. 'How is General Omendap?'

'He's recovering fast. He says the poisoned flask of wine could have been arranged in Thebes or by someone in the camp. He, too, believes it was Rahimere. If he died the royal army would have become confused and been forced to retreat.'

'But it didn't, did it?'

Amerotke rose and filled his own beer cup. He offered a plate of bread and cheese to Sethos, who shook his head.

'What happens, my lord judge,' Sethos leaned closer, 'if Hatusu or her Vizier Senenmut, either singly or together, plotted these deaths? You've seen how ruthless she is. The troops adore her. They see her as a combination of Sekhmet and Montu.'

'My lord Sethos, you are a priest of Amun-Ra: a chaplain to the divine household as well as royal prosecutor. You are ruthless but does that make you a murderer? There's something else. Something we've missed. Something the divine lady has not told us. I understand Tuthmosis' mood when he returned to Thebes.'

'What do you mean?' Sethos asked sharply.

'I'm beginning to see a shadowy outline. However, if the assassin is to be caught, the divine lady is to be more truthful and direct. Simply sending me, like a messenger boy, to dig among the rubbish will not unearth the truth. Ah!'

Amerotke glimpsed Shufoy waddling across the garden. Behind him followed Asural, Prenhoe and a small cohort of temple police. Shufoy bowed to Sethos.

'You have the name?' Amerotke asked.

Shufoy pushed a fragment of papyrus into his master's hand. Amerotke unrolled it and smiled.

'My lord Sethos.' He got to his feet. 'I think you should come with me. You'll find this most interesting. Peay,' he murmured. He recalled the pompous little physician stamping through the lanes of the Necropolis, carrying his pet monkey. A thought occurred to him.

'My lord!'

'What is it?'

Prenhoe came forward with a scroll.

'I had a dream last night, my lord. I think you should . . .'

'Not now!' Amerotke snapped. 'Asural, your men are ready?'

The chief of temple police nodded.

'Good, then let's make our physician's visit.'

Peay was resting in the small garden of his lavish house, which bordered one of the irrigation canals that ran into the Nile.

Asural did not stand on idle ceremony but kicked the gate open, thrust aside the porter and marched up to the porticoed entrance, Amerotke, Sethos and the others behind him. The physician, all a-tremble, led them inside his sumptuous hallway. The floor leading into Peay's private chamber was of fragrant cedarwood. Peay waved them to couches and sat on his high-backed chair, rearranging his robes.

'I am greatly honoured,' he blustered.

As if summoned, the vervin popped nimbly through the window of the garden carrying the silver-encrusted cup Peay must have been using.

'Ah!' Amerotke said. 'Here comes your accomplice.'

Peay's face paled. 'What do you mean?' he gabbled.

The monkey jumped into his lap and thrust the cup into the physician's podgy, trembling fingers.

'You are a tomb-robber, aren't you?' Amerotke continued. 'And, being a physician, you know about all the wealthy, the powerful who die in Thebes. You are even invited to the funerals, to join the mourners when they congregate in the tomb. A few weeks later you return with your little friend. You put him into the air vents, and along he'll go. He's trained to pick up small, precious objects: a cup, a ring, a porcelain pot, a vase, a necklace, then out he'll scamper and give them to you.'

Peay's mouth sagged. He stared horror-struck.

'Now, I've seen you in the Necropolis where you are well known,' Amerotke continued remorselessly. 'Your robberies supplement your income. But, how can I put it, in the recent crisis, you realised you might have to flee Thebes so you sold your plunder in the marketplace where my servant bought some of it.'

Peay went to rise but Amerotke poked him back into the chair.

'What do we do with a grave-robber, eh, my lord Sethos? Crucify him? Hang him? Bury him alive out in the Red Lands? Or perhaps just allow him to take poison in the House of Death?'

Peay sank to his knees, his hands clasped together, his fat cheeks soaked with tears.

'Please!' he begged. 'Mercy, my lords!'

Amerotke glanced at Sethos who stared back, eyebrows raised.

'Yes, you can beg for mercy,' Amerotke replied. 'Because you know it's available. That nimble brain is already asking, why should the lord Amerotke come to arrest me personally? Why not just send Asural to arrest you in the dead of night? Right, you have one chance of mercy. You may leave Thebes with a horse and cart and whatever that can carry. This house and all its possessions are confiscated, forfeit, its revenues will go to the House of Life in the temple of Amun-Ra.'

'Oh, great kindness!' Peay observed ruefully.

'On one condition!' Amerotke snapped. 'You attended the divine Tuthmosis. Had he been bitten by a snake?'

'Yes, my lord.'

Amerotke's heart sank. He leaned forward and grasped the man's shoulder. 'Is that the truth?'

'Yes and no. My lord, he had the marks above his heel. But . . .'

'But what?'

'The leg was puffy, I suspect . . .' Peay's voice trailed off. 'I'm frightened!' he whimpered.

'It's even more frightening being buried alive in the hot sands of the Red Lands,' Amerotke reminded him.

'The snake bite was there,' Peay declared, rubbing his fat cheeks. 'But the poison hadn't moved. Divine Pharaoh showed all the symptoms of dying from the falling sickness.'

'What are you saying?'

Peay raised his head. 'My lord, and this is the truth. It looked as if divine Pharaoh was bitten by the snake *after* he had died.'

Sethos and Amerotke walked up the steps leading into the House of a Million Years, which Hatusu had taken for herself, near the great mooring place on the Nile. Artists were decorating the pylons, the great walls on either side of the gateway, with dramatic scenes from Hatusu's famous victory in the north. Slaves, under the directions of master masons, were bringing in, on rollers, huge blocks of granite.

'Divine Pharaoh,' Sethos observed, 'is going to ensure that we do not forget her victory or her glory! Two obelisks will be put on either side of the doorway. Every inch will proclaim her divine birth and great victories.

They will be capped with gold, so the people know that Amun-Ra's favour rests upon her.'

Amerotke covered his mouth against the cloud of dust and ran his thumbnail round his lip. He had instructed Asural and Prenhoe to ensure that Peay was out of Thebes before nightfall. Yet he was still angry. If Tuthmosis had been dead when the snake struck, the divine lady must have known this yet how could he raise such a matter with this magnificent Pharaoh? This warrior Queen intent on glory? He grasped Sethos' arm.

'I will go alone.'

Sethos made to object.

'I go alone,' Amerotke repeated.

The captain of the royal bodyguard immediately recognised Amerotke, to whom he gave the most reverential bow before leading him through marble corridors into the small pleasure garden Hatusu had now taken for her own use. It was a beautiful green paradise of lush grass, sweet-smelling flowers, shady trees, flower-covered arbours and, in the centre, an ornamental pool of polished marble, the water so clear Amerotke could see every detail of the brilliantly coloured fish. Garishly plumaged birds pecked for seed on the lawns. Gold and silver cages hung from the branches, in which songbirds trilled sweetly in this most opulent of paradises.

Senenmut and Hatusu were squatting like children by the side of the lake trying to catch the fish, heads together, laughing and giggling. Hatusu looked up and smiled. She was clothed simply in a transparent linen gown. A short, oil-drenched wig covered her head, a little paint enhanced her eyes, her feet were bare. Senenmut was dressed in a small white kilt, his upper torso gleaming with water where Hatusu had been splashing him.

'Amerotke!' Hatusu scrambled to her feet. She ran round the lake and grasped the judge's hand. 'Have you been sulking? Why didn't you come to the royal circle?' She stood on tiptoe, staring impishly into his eyes. 'Don't you love me any more?'

'I've been to see Peay,' Amerotke replied. 'Divine Pharaoh, your husband and half-brother was already dead, wasn't he, when the snake bit him?'

Hatusu let go of his hands and stepped back.

'Do you like coloured fish, Amerotke? Come! Take off your sandals.'

'My feet are dirty.' Amerotke was confused by Hatusu's response. He glanced over her shoulder at Senenmut, who was staring grimly at him.

'Oh, don't worry about him,' Hatusu whispered. She joined her hands together. 'We are one flesh, one soul, one heart, one mind.'

Amerotke saw the passion in her eyes.

'You want me to find the truth,' he replied. 'But I cannot find it, your highness, if you do not trust me.'

Hatusu crouched down and undid the clasp on his sandals.

'Come, bathe your feet.'

Amerotke felt slightly ridiculous. He sat on the edge of the lake, his feet in the cool water, Hatusu on his right, Senenmut on his left. She splashed her feet. Amerotke found it unreal. She was the lioness, the woman who had dealt out judgement to her enemies, both at home and abroad. Now she sat like a young girl waiting to tell a story.

'I loved Tuthmosis,' she began. 'He was kind, weak and sickly but his heart was good. He had the falling sickness and claimed to see visions. He found it difficult sometimes, Amerotke, to believe in all the strange gods of Egypt, to worship a crocodile, and he wondered why should the lord Amun-Ra have the head of a stupid ram? He would question the wise men. He wasn't an atheist but he was searching for something else.' She sighed. 'He marched north against the sea people. At the same time he received a letter from Neroupe, the keeper of the pyramids near Sakkara. Tuthmosis apparently went there on his return. Neroupe had died but he'd left secret instructions with Tuthmosis on how to enter certain tunnels which would take him to the lost library of Cheops, the great Pharaoh who had lived hundreds of years ago.'

Hatusu paused, dabbing at the sweat on her neck.

'He wrote to me after he had visited the pyramid. I destroyed the letter but it contained a few lines. How he would return to Thebes and issue judgements on behalf of the one God against the false idols in our temples.' She shrugged. 'I paid little attention to Tuthmosis the mystic.' She took a deep breath, splashing her toes in the water. 'I just looked forward to his return. The rest of his officials arrived back in Thebes to prepare for Tuthmosis' grand entrance.' She paused.

'Tell him all,' Senenmut urged. 'Tell him about the blackmailing letters.'

'While waiting,' Hatusu continued quickly, 'I began to receive messages, small scrolls of papyrus written in a clerkly hand.' She shook her head. 'They were blackmail.'

'Blackmail!' Amerotke exclaimed.

Hatusu turned and pressed her finger against his lip; her nail, painted a crimson red, dug deeply into the skin.

'What I tell you must never be told to anyone, Amerotke. When I was a child, my mother Ahmose took me aside and told me I was divinely conceived by the god Amun-Ra, who visited her chamber.' She touched the side of her wig, pressing a strand, squeezing the perfumed oil out. 'I was a child, my mother was so wrapped up in the gods and their doings, I thought it was a fable. These blackmail letters took up the story. They claimed how my mother had been unfaithful to my father and had lain with a priest from the temple of Amun-Ra. I was not of Pharaoh's bloodline but a bastard, illegitimate, a blasphemy. I was instructed to do everything I was ordered to or face the consequences. I had no choice. The blackmailer claimed to have evidence to prove his story.'

Amerotke looked across the lake. A black-tipped hoopoe had frightened away a gold-feathered songbird and was greedily pecking at the ground. He recalled Senenmut's declarations before the soldiers after the great victory over the Mitanni.

'You know all this?'

'Yes,' Senenmut replied. 'I decided to turn it on its head. If the divine Hatusu was divinely conceived then why hide it in the dark? Why not proclaim it to the world?' He smiled. 'It apparently worked. Since our return to Thebes, the divine lady has received no further letters.'

'I want vengeance!' Hatusu broke in. Her face had changed, eyes grown larger, the skin drawn tight over her high cheekbones. 'I want to see that blackmailer hang by his hands from a cross! His body given to the dogs so that his Ka never reaches the far horizon.' Her nails dug into Amerotke's leg.

'And the divine Tuthmosis?' he asked.

'He died of a seizure. A terrible fit before the statue of Amun-Ra. The excitement had proved too much for him. He fell to the ground. All he said was: "Hatusu, it's only a mask!" He died a short while later. I moved his body to the royal mourning chamber. I stayed with the corpse. Others

227

came in, members of the royal circle, I don't know how or who but I became hungry. When I turned for some food on a tray inside the door, I found a small black bag. Inside was a note. The threats were explicit. I was to follow the order carefully.' She sighed. 'The bag contained a fork, the ivory prongs tipped with poison.'

'Like a snake's mouth?' Amerotke asked.

Hatusu nodded. 'I was to dig the prong into my dead husband's leg, just above the heel. I did so. To all intents and purposes it looked like a snake bite. The skin was discoloured, the poison seeped deep. I then burned this weapon and the note that came with it.' She flailed her hands. 'Even then I knew something could go wrong. My husband's blood had stopped flowing, the poison did not move, but what could I do? Before my husband returned to Thebes, I was terrified the blackmailer would whisper in his ear, destroy my position. After all I had not given him a son. Once Tuthmosis died, I was even more vulnerable. I had to face the opposition of Rahimere and the others. If the blackmailer began to publicise such rumours throughout Thebes, how long would I have lasted?'

'And Meneloto?' Amerotke asked.

'Two days after my husband died I received another letter. By then I had heard about his tomb being desecrated and the portents seen on his return to Thebes. I had no choice. A viper had been found on board the royal barque: I was to press charges against Meneloto and mention nothing about Sakkara.'

'And the deaths of the others?'

'We know nothing of these,' Senenmut intervened.

'What could I do?' Hatusu asked. 'I was being taunted about my parentage. I had to face the opposition of Rahimere. I was sent north to lose a battle yet the gods have vindicated me.' She lifted her head. 'My mother was correct. I am divinely conceived. I am the beloved of Amun-Ra!'

'And the perpetrators?' Amerotke asked.

'Rahimere. Sethos has some evidence, a little. He may have been responsible for Amenhotep's death and that of Ipuwer.' She turned and smiled. 'But we don't need that any more.' She pushed her face closer, her breath fragrant. 'We have been through the seized records of the Mitanni. Rahimere was in secret communication with King Tushratta. So, go tell him that, Amerotke! Let him confess. Die he will, though he can still choose the way he travels to the fields of the blessed!'

Ma'at: the goddess of truth.

CHAPTER 16

Amerotke entered the dark passageways of the House of Death beneath the temple of Ma'at. Guards, their faces masked, stood beneath spluttering pitch torches. A gaoler lifted the wooden bars and kicked the door open. Rahimere's cell was small, a hole at the top of the whitewashed wall providing some light and air. The former Vizier was almost unrecognisable. He had bruises high on his cheeks, his sallow face was grey and unshaven though his eyes still gleamed with malice. He did not bother to rise from the green matting bed but squatted there, hitching up the dirty loin cloth around his waist.

'You've come to mock?'

'I've come to question.'

'About what?'

'The deaths of Ipuwer, Amenhotep, the murderous assault on General Omendap and the blackmailing of the Queen.' Amerotke could have bitten his tongue.

Rahimere curled his legs. 'Blackmail! Of our divine Pharaoh?'

'And the murders,' Amerotke stammered. He still felt slightly shaken, disconcerted after his meeting with Hatusu and Senenmut.

'I'm guilty of no murder. Ipuwer's death?' Rahimere moved his hands. 'Why should I kill Ipuwer?' He leaned forward. 'Ipuwer liked young girls. I promised him a room full of them but this blackmail?'

Amerotke realised he was wasting his time. He turned back towards the door.

'You'll get no evidence on me!' Rahimere screamed. 'If that bitch is going to kill me, she'll have to send her dogs down!'

'She won't have to.' Amerotke paused at the door. 'They found your letters to the Mitanni King. You know the sentence for treason!'

Slamming the door behind him, Amerotke stormed up the corridor, brushing by the masked guards. The place stank of death! He wanted to get out, to think, to prepare a speech to the divine Hatusu, urging that these deaths, these murders, this blackmail would remain a mystery. He walked into the Hall of Two Truths. The place was deserted. The court would not sit for at least another five days and Amerotke knew that the number of cases awaiting trial would have been swollen by the recent troubles. He leaned against one of the pillars, looking down at the judgement chair, the small polished table and cushions of the scribes: the rolls of judgement. From the courtyard outside came the murmur of conversation, the chatter of scribes, the shouts and cries of the children.

Amerotke walked slowly across and studied one of the frescoes on the wall. The goddess Ma'at, an ostrich plume in her hair, leaned back on her heels before the lord Osiris who held the scales. What judgement would he give here? Amerotke thought. How would he resolve it? He walked back, into his small chapel. Inside the tabernacle stood the statue of Ma'at. The floor had been freshly sanded, the holy water stoups brimmed and someone, probably Prenhoe, had filled the incense burners. Small pots of cassia and frankincense had also been placed about. The chapel looked clean, smelt fragrant; new cushions had been placed before the shrine.

Amerotke knelt and tried to pray for guidance, then realised he hadn't purified his mouth or hands. Was he becoming like Amenhotep? Images bright as any painting teemed in his mind. The bloody carnage outside the camp; men screaming and writhing; the blood lapping around chariot wheels; the horses pounding, mangling the corpses of the fallen. The screams for mercy. The strong-arm boys sodomising young Mitanni noblemen before smashing their faces into the ground. Hatusu brilliant in her glory; Meneloto at the bottom of those steps, the Amemets, like shadows, around him. And that dread stela of Cheops? Amerotke gazed at the open tabernacle. Was it all false? Was there no one to listen? A shadow came in and knelt behind him. Amerotke looked over his shoulder.

'I had a dream last night, my lord. I dreamed that I was sitting in a palm tree and then it changed into a sycamore. Beneath its branches you were destroying your clothes.'

Prenhoe's face looked so intense, he clutched the papyrus scroll so tightly, Amerotke bit back his angry reply.

'And what does that mean, kinsman?'

'It means that I will do good. And that you will be released from all evil. Master, I am a good clerk.'

'Preferment will come.'

'Master, I am a good clerk,' Prenhoe repeated. 'And I copy down faithfully what is said in court. And, while you were away,' he continued hurriedly, glimpsing the anger in Amerotke's eyes, 'I consulted with my colleagues.'

Amerotke sighed. 'Prenhoe, my mind is . . .' He gestured with his hand.

'Shufoy told me,' Prenhoe gabbled on. 'Shufoy told me about your visit to the old snake priest, the one who gave evidence. How he rescued you.'

'Do not tell the lady Norfret!' Amerotke interrupted.

'No, my lord, but I thought you should read this.' Prenhoe scurried round and undid the papyrus roll. 'This is what the old priest said. Isn't it strange?'

Amerotke, crouching down, peered closely because of the poor light.

'No, no, there.' Prenhoe jabbed with his finger.

Amerotke read the statement. He blinked and, forgetting all protocol, crouched closer again.

'I . . . I . . .' He stammered and looked up. 'What does it mean, kinsman?'

Prenhoe swallowed hard with excitement. 'I went out to the tombs, to the Necropolis. I went round the Houses of Eternity until I visited those of his parents. His mother was a priestess in the service of the goddess Meretseger.'

'The snake goddess!' Amerotke breathed.

Is that how truth worked, he thought? Was there some invisible fire to kindle the mind and soul? He turned and grasped Prenhoe's face between his hands and kissed him firmly on the forehead. The young scribe coloured with embarrassment.

'You are my kinsman, Prenhoe, and you are my friend. What you have discovered, I overlooked. What you found, I ignored and, next time I sit in judgement, you shall be my eyes and ears. As far as I am concerned, you can dream to your heart's content. Now, this is what you must do.'

Amerotke spent most of the day near the Hall of Two Truths. He went out to the lake and purified himself, washing his body and his face in the waters where the ibis had drunk. He dressed in fresh robes which he kept in a small room behind the chapel. He purified his mouth with salt and sprinkled more incense before the goddess. Then he knelt, forehead touching the ground.

'I have sinned!' he confessed. 'I have doubted! Yet, my heart is pure and I wish to look on your face. Let me walk in the truth, let me keep the truth!'

He felt so excited he forgot to eat but, as the sun began to set, he walked out into the temple precincts and bought some strips of goose being cooked by one of the younger priests over a bed of charcoal. He squatted on the ground to eat, and drank a little wine. Across the courtyard Asural had gathered some of the temple police. Prenhoe was there and, just before he left, Shufoy also arrived. He told them to stay there and not to disturb him though he took a knife from Asural which he concealed beneath his robes, and walked back into the shrine. He sat with his back to the wall. The doors of the Naos were closed. He lit the alabaster oil jars so all was ready when Sethos walked in. Amerotke gestured at the cushion opposite.

'My lord Sethos, I am glad you could come.'

The royal prosecutor squatted down, his lean, sharp face a mask of concern, his eyes watchful. He placed a small writing bag beside him.

'What did the divine lady have to say?'

'That Rahimere will go on trial for treason.'

'But not for murder?'

'No, my lord Sethos. You will stand trial for that!'

Sethos sat up, his face creased into a smile.

'Amerotke, Amerotke, has the sun fuddled your wits? Has the heat of battle . . . ?'

Amerotke pointed to the shrine. 'She watches you, Sethos. She who is truth knows the darkness in your heart. Sethos, royal prosecutor, eyes and ears of the King. Close friend of divine Pharaoh Tuthmosis who revealed to him all that he had learned in those dark, cavernous chambers beneath the pyramid at Sakkara.'

Sethos did not flinch.

'Sethos,' Amerotke continued. 'High-ranking priest in the Order of Amun-Ra, royal chaplain, formerly a confessor to Queen Ahmose, divine Hatusu's mother. What happened, Sethos? Were you chilled by what Tuthmosis told you? How the gods of Egypt were nothing but stone idols, eh? How you were to come back to Thebes and deal out judgement, destroy the shrines, create a new order, dedicated to the One who once walked with men, in the first time, before war broke out? Before the mirror of truth was shattered and all we were left were shards?' Amerotke leaned forward. 'You do not object?'

'A good story is a good story,' Sethos commented.

'Tuthmosis told you all. You, Sethos, were sent back to Thebes to prepare for Pharaoh's arrival, to lay plans for his dealing out of judgement. But your soul was in turmoil. It would be an end to the temple worship, the dispossession of priests, the seizure of treasures. How you must have seethed, frantic at what to do! Perhaps you pretended to listen, to agree, but deep down you plotted revenge. You cast about.' Amerotke paused. 'You are the royal prosecutor. You know the dirty depths beneath the city of Thebes. You hired the guild of murderers, the Amemets. You wanted to cause confusion and chaos. You paid them to go across to the Necropolis and desecrate Pharaoh's tomb but that was more anger than malice. Your mind teemed and turned. You could not control Tuthmosis, his stubbornness was legendary. Ever since a boy he had a cynicism about the priests and the temple worshippers of Thebes. Hatusu was different. She was young, she was vulnerable. She had not produced a living male heir for her husband.'

Sethos breathed in deeply, nostrils flared.

'If you could not control Tuthmosis then you would control Hatusu and she, uncertain and anxious, rose to the bait.'

'And what are you going to say next?' Sethos broke in. 'That I murdered the divine Tuthmosis in the temple of Amun-Ra?'

'Oh no, you weren't in the temple,' Amerotke replied. 'You were down at the quayside.'

'What, putting a viper aboard the royal barge?'

'Oh no, that came later. You are a priest of Amun-Ra. You took some of the white doves which nest in the temple to some lonely spot. You then cut their bodies and released them. Doves, of course, wounded or not, fly back to their dovecotes. How many, Sethos? Six or seven? Some would die on the way, others fall from the sky, a few smatter the crowd with blood. A bad omen for the Pharaoh's return! What were you planning to do? Increase such portents? Frighten Tuthmosis or arouse opposition against him?' Amerotke stretched out his hands, studying his fingers. 'You wanted to control Pharaoh. To destroy the notions and ideas he had conceived at Sakkara. Frighten him with portents and signs then control him through the lady Hatusu.'

'Tuthmosis died!' Sethos replied sharply.

'Oh, you must have seen that as a sign from the gods,' Amerotke replied. 'An answer to a prayer. Tuthmosis, tired, his mind teeming with plans, collapsed and died before the statue of Amun-Ra. Now you had no need for wounded doves or desecrated tombs. Tuthmosis was gone, so you had to tighten your control over the lady Hatusu. You must also depict Pharaoh's death as divine judgement: stung by a snake, a symbol of the Duat, the darkness of the underworld.'

Sethos raised his eyebrows. 'How?'

'You are a high-ranking priest of Amun-Ra. The royal eyes and ears of the King. You can travel hither and thither and no one will question you. You left the poisoned fork in the mourning chamber, forcing Hatusu to stab her husband's corpse with it. Meanwhile you had placed that viper in the royal barque. You had other plans, hadn't you? You had to create confusion, chaos, dissension, so that any notion of Tuthmosis' plans was forgotten. Certain people also had to be taken care of, those who had escorted Pharaoh to the pyramids at Sakkara: Meneloto, Ipuwer, Amenhotep. If Pharaoh had opened his heart to you perhaps he'd opened it to others? They had to be silenced. You ordered Hatusu, through your mysterious letters, to bring charges against Meneloto. Ipuwer you killed in the council chamber while poor Amenhotep, he would answer an invitation from my lord Sethos. He would go down to some lonely plot on the banks of the Nile. Did you kill him personally? Or were the Amemets waiting? Did you give them clear instructions to kill him, remove his head and send it as a gift to cause further dissension when the royal circle met at that fateful banquet?'

'A good story,' Sethos said. 'But why should I do all this?'

'To defend the temple worship. To create such confusion and chaos that Tuthmosis' dreams and anyone involved in them would be forgotten. You must have thought you were chosen by the gods. The rivalry between Hatusu and Rahimere was fertile ground for your sowing.'

'With snakes?' Sethos jibed.

'Ah! Do you remember the trial of poor Meneloto? He summoned in his defence the old snake priest Labda. He was talking about snakes, vipers, but he also made a startling reference to you. In describing the poisonous nature of vipers, he said, "My lord Sethos himself will also know this"! At the time no one paid any attention but you did. Labda was referring to the fact that, although your father was a priest in the service of Amun-Ra, your mother was a priestess in the service of the snake goddess Meretseger. She would have knowledge of vipers, those snakes which thrive in the desert or along the lush banks of the Nile. Her tomb in the Necropolis attests to this. My kinsman, Prenhoe, went to investigate. He was the one who brought my attention to the old priest's words. Prenhoe may be a dreamer but he is a sharp, keen observer. He found your parents' tombs. On the outside is a picture of your mother.'

Sethos blinked and looked away.

'You remember it well, don't you? She's garbed in priestly robes, holding a snake while teaching a young boy, with a lock of hair falling down the side of his face, how to hold it. You are that boy, skilled in the handling of snakes.' Amerotke made himself more comfortable. 'You took a viper and put it on board the royal barque, while the fork you gave divine Hatusu is often used by snake priests!'

Sethos was now breathing quickly, head going back, eyes half-closed.

'If you know how to handle snakes,' Amerotke continued, 'they are not dangerous. You brought one into the council chamber concealed in a scribe's writing satchel. Fed and quiescent, lulled by the dark bag, the viper would rest there. When the council meeting adjourned you exchanged writing satchels. Poor Ipuwer thrust his hand in and the snake struck immediately. As for Omendap, did the wine contain some sort of snake venom? Did you put the poisoned flasks among his personal belongings before we left Thebes or during the march north?'

'Proof!' Sethos grated. 'You still have to offer proof.'

'You thought everything would be lost in the confusion,' Amerotke answered. 'But then you suspected that I was stumbling towards the truth. You also realised how dangerous old Labda was. He remembered your family, your training. He had to be silenced. You went out to his shrine, murdered him and lured me there. You took away those planks. It might have been months before what the hyenas left of me was found. Another mystery to fuddle the minds and feed the rumours in Thebes.' Amerotke paused. 'I would have disappeared as Meneloto was intended to. The Amemets were to take him out into the Red Lands, murder him and hide his corpse. All Thebes would have considered him an escaped criminal. Confusion upon confusion! Did the Amemet leader deliver those wax dolls, the harbingers of death? Oh, and did he tell you Meneloto had escaped?'

Sethos' lips curled in a snarl.

'As a royal prosecutor,' Amerotke continued, 'you'd certainly know how to communicate with that guild of assassins. You must have paid them well to follow the army, to wait for their moment, to strike at me, Omendap or Hatusu.' Amerotke joined his hands together. 'I know the great secret,' he said quietly. 'I have read the stela at Sakkara.' He paused, his eyes on Sethos. 'They followed Meneloto and me in. They provided all the evidence I need. One of them was captured.'

'They are all dead!' Sethos snapped. He closed his eyes at the terrible mistake he had made.

'Did you go there yourself?' Amerotke asked. 'Did you follow the secret passageway?'

Sethos squatted, head down.

'Look at the evidence, my lord,' Amerotke urged. 'As royal prosecutor you would have knowledge of the Amemets. You were a close confidant of the divine Tuthmosis. You were, as a novice priest, chaplain to the Queen Mother Ahmose. You would know about her fanciful ideas regarding Hatusu's conception. You were down at the quayside on the day Pharaoh returned to Thebes. You were present in court when the old priest made his revelation about your antecedents. You know about snakes. You were present when Ipuwer was killed. Amenhotep would trust you and certainly obey your summons, even though he was depressed and withdrawn. You would be able to approach General Omendap. Your presence near his personal baggage would go unnoticed. I do not sit in judgement on you now but, if I was in the Hall of Two Truths, I'd certainly rule you have a case to answer.'

Sethos rubbed his face, smiling slightly.

'In the end,' he began slowly, 'in the end, Amerotke, I was victorious. I achieved what the gods wanted me to achieve. Tuthmosis told me all that he had discovered at Sakkara.' He spread his hands. 'What could I do? Allow that daydreamer to return to Thebes? Destroy the temple worship which had existed for hundreds of years? Ransack the treasury? Turn out the priests? He was like a boy with a new toy! Confessing all to me as if I would leap and dance in triumph!' He shook his head. 'I hurried back to Thebes. I prayed for guidance. Oh, the desecration of his tomb, the wounded doves, they were just panic, but when Tuthmosis collapsed and died, I realised the gods had answered my prayer. Hatusu I could control, or thought I could. She has proved us all wrong, hasn't she, Amerotke? She's more man than her husband and father together. But, yes, I wanted to create confusion. I wanted to wipe away all memory of Tuthmosis' ideas and revelations. I thought Meneloto's trial would cause more dissension, more uncertainty. I also wondered how much he knew, how much he might confess in open court. But, of course, the lord Amerotke sat in judgement. I knew I had made a mistake. Meneloto had to be killed but he escaped. And the others?' He shrugged. 'Amenhotep had to be silenced and I wonder how much the divine Tuthmosis had told Ipuwer or even General Omendap. I thought if I exploited the rivalry between Hatusu and Rahimere, any madcap plans of the dead Pharaoh would be forgotten.' He stretched out his hands. 'Tuthmosis might be dead but who else knew? Hatusu? Rahimere? Omendap? Meneloto? Amenhotep? If the succession was peaceful, smooth, who knows what fanciful ideas might have been put forward? Can't you see, I had no choice! Tuthmosis, or those he'd convinced, would have struck at the very heart of Egypt's religion. I am sorry about the Amemets and the Valley of the Kings, but again, I had no choice.' His head came forward, eyes staring. 'The gods were leading me, Amerotke! Seth ruled my soul. What is the meddling of men compared to the wishes of Amun-Ra?'

'You will die,' Amerotke replied.

'We all do, Amerotke. Every day the shadows grow longer and draw closer. I beg one favour. I do not wish to be buried out in the Red Lands, or have my naked body hang from the pylons. I don't want the mob mocking me. I don't want others to know the reason why I acted. Let the sands blow over Sakkara and Cheops' pyramid keep its secrets.' He licked his lips. 'I would like some wine, just a little.'

Amerotke walked over to where the priest had placed the food and drink for the goddess. He half-filled an earthenware cup. He heard a movement and turned to see Sethos with his head back, shaking the last drops of whatever was in the small jar he had taken from his writing satchel into his mouth. He let this fall to the ground.

'Venom,' he said. 'Poison that will stop the heart and cake the blood.'

He lay down like a child going to sleep, resting his head against the satchel. He stretched out a hand.

'Not alone, Amerotke.'

The judge knelt beside him. He grasped Sethos' hand, already turning cold and clammy though the grip was still strong.

'Say the prayer for me,' Sethos whispered. 'Let my corpse be buried properly. Let my Ka go into the hall of Osiris where I will account for what I did.'

He lay for a while then his body convulsed, specks of foam appearing at the corner of his mouth. His eyelids fluttered and his head fell slack. Amerotke let go of his hand. He recited a short prayer then looked at the closed door of the shrine, the incense bowls, the sacred cups and plates. He bowed his head.

'In the end,' he prayed, 'only the truth remains!'

AUTHOR'S NOTE

This novel reflects the political scene of 1479 BC when Hatusu swept to power. Her husband died in mysterious circumstances and his wife only emerged as ruler after a bitter power struggle. In this she was assisted by the wily Senenmut, who had come from nothing to share power with her. His tomb is still extant, now known as Number 353, and it even contains a sketch portrait of Hatusu's favourite minister! There is no doubt that Hatusu and Senenmut were lovers. Indeed, we have ancient graffiti which describe, in a very graphic way, their intimate personal relationship.

Hatusu was a strong ruler. She is often depicted in wall paintings as a warrior and we know from inscriptions that she did lead troops into battle.

The possibility that the pyramids and the Sphinx are built over secret passageways, caverns, temples and libraries has been a constant rumour amongst Egyptologists. The scene described in the novel of the Hall of the Hanged is recounted in Otto Neubet's interesting study of Tutankhamun. Indeed, the theory of lost knowledge, both scientific and religious, has been brought to the fore by skilled Egyptologists such as Bauvey and Hancock. In August 1997 the *Sunday Times* also reported that the lost libraries of Cheops might still be accessible.

Egyptian theology, by the time of Christ, had degenerated into the worship of animals and insects, so much so that it was bitterly satirised by the Roman poet Juvenal. However, in the beginning, the Egyptians searched for a theological unity. The idea of a single God, a loving Mother-Father figure, plays a major role in Egyptian history. We must remember that Egypt was the home of the great Jewish leader Moses and that, only a hundred and thirty years after the period in which this

243

novel is set, Pharaoh Akhenaton brought Egypt to the brink of civil war over his revolutionary religious policy to set aside the temple worship of Thebes in favour of the worship of 'The One'.

In all other matters I have tried to be faithful to this exciting, brilliant and intriguing civilisation. The fascination of Ancient Egypt is understandable: it is exotic and mysterious. True, this civilisation existed over three and a half thousand years ago yet there are times, when you read their letters and poems, you feel a deep kinship with them as they speak to you across the centuries.

Paul Doherty